Too Many Cousins

BY

DOUGLAS G. BROWNE

Dover Publications, Inc.
New York

To

GEOFFREY EDWARDS

WITHOUT WHOSE CONNIVANCE
THIS BOOK COULD NOT HAVE
BEEN WRITTEN WHEN IT WAS

This Dover edition, first published in 1985, is an unabridged and slightly corrected republication of the work first
published by MacDonald & Co., London, 1946.

Manufactured in the United States of America
Dover Publications, Inc., 31 East 2nd Street, Mineola, N.Y.
11501

Library of Congress Cataloging in Publication Data

Browne, Douglas G. (Douglas Gordon), 1884–
    Too many cousins.

    Reprint. Originally published: London : MacDonald,
1946.
    I. Title.
PR6003.R49T6 1985   823'.914   84-18864
ISBN 0-486-24774-0 (pbk.)

CONTENTS

RUTLAND SHEARSBY

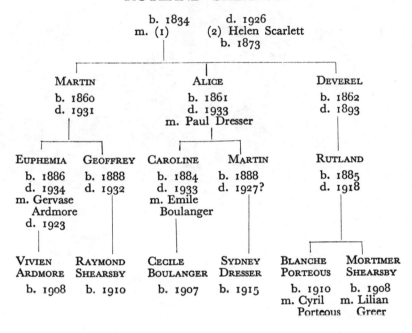

b. 1834　　　d. 1926
m. (1)　　　(2) Helen Scarlett
b. 1873

MARTIN
b. 1860
d. 1931

ALICE
b. 1861
d. 1933
m. Paul Dresser

DEVEREL
b. 1862
d. 1893

EUPHEMIA
b. 1886
d. 1934
m. Gervase
Ardmore
d. 1923

GEOFFREY
b. 1888
d. 1932

CAROLINE
b. 1884
d. 1933
m. Emile
Boulanger

MARTIN
b. 1888
d. 1927?

RUTLAND
b. 1885
d. 1918

VIVIEN
ARDMORE
b. 1908

RAYMOND
SHEARSBY
b. 1910

CECILE
BOULANGER
b. 1907

SYDNEY
DRESSER
b. 1915

BLANCHE
PORTEOUS
b. 1910
m. Cyril
Porteous

MORTIMER
SHEARSBY
b. 1908
m. Lilian
Greer

PART ONE:

SIMPLE ARITHMETIC

CHAPTER I

HARVEY TUKE'S opponent accomplished a neat follow-through cannon and grounded his cue.

"That takes me out, I think," he said.

"It has been a good game," Mr. Tuke said, glancing at the scoreboard, which showed less than a dozen points between winner and loser. "We'll drink to it in that Amontillado, if they have any left. I haven't been here for a month."

"No, we don't often see you," his companion rejoined, as he slid his cue into its case.

"I'm a domesticated man," said Mr. Tuke, who affirmed with some truth that he only visited his clubs from a sense of duty. At the Sheridan he was at least able to combine business with pleasure, for here he met the entertaining and unorthodox—painters, writers, musicians, actors, creators all of one sort or another. Harvey himself qualified for election to a society which required of its members some proof of intelligence because in a small way he too was a creator. His rather odd hobby (for a lawyer) was the campaigns of Napoleon, and by-products of the book he hoped to complete one day on the penultimate campaign of 1814 appeared from time to time in that hardy monthly *The Midlothian Magazine*.

He understood that his present companion, whose name was Parmiter, had something to do with the press. Beyond this he knew nothing about him. A common passion for billiards—almost the only game which Mr. Tuke recognised —had brought them together. Parmiter was a very tall man, an inch or two taller than Harvey himself, so that he stooped a little to talk to the latter as they walked together down the wide corridor from the Sheridan's billiard-room to the lounge. He was considerably the older of the two, a man probably approaching sixty, with a lined, cynical face, touched with melancholy in repose, heavy-lidded sunken eyes, and an untidy thatch of grey hair. A straggling grey moustache failed to hide a mouth that could be sour or humorous according to his rapid changes of mood.

In the lounge, when the loser had ordered drinks—the Amontillado was still to be had—Parmiter took up the topic interrupted by their departure from the billiard-room.

"Unlike you," he remarked, "I am here every day. Most of the day, sometimes. Grist to my mill, you know—in a prospective sense."

"What exactly does your mill grind?" Harvey inquired.

"I am an obituarist."

Mr. Tuke's black brows went up a trifle. "Indeed? I don't think I have met one before. That is what I like about this club. One is always encountering something new. Do you find your rather macabre occupation interesting?"

Parmiter's lined face became animated. "Absorbing," he said. "There is endless fascination in the study of humanity from the angle of the epitaph. The contrast between the apparent and the real. I watch some pompous old humbug, for instance, and reflect that in a few years I may be dismissing him in a subtly contemptuous paragraph."

Mr. Tuke looked at him with sardonic amusement.

"I always thought," he remarked, "that this post mortem publicity was hedged about with conventions."

"There can be art even in an obituary notice," Parmiter replied with one of his cynical smiles.

Mr. Tuke shook his head. "You fill me with misgivings. Here you sit, among your prospective victims, waiting your opportunity to damn us with faint praise when we can no longer retaliate."

"Oh, not all of you," Parmiter said. "I try to be fair. I may say, indeed, that I have done something to establish or restore a number of reputations. And others can stand on their own legs. Yours for example."

"I breathe again."

"You might be surprised, Tuke, to learn how much I know about you. Of course, since I am much the older, I shall, I hope, never be in a position to employ my knowledge in your case. And I can hardly pass my material on to a successor. After my death, my files will be destroyed."

"Files?" Mr. Tuke commented. "Of course, I suppose you will have acquired a good deal of data. But I thought the newspapers themselves collected that sort of thing."

Parmiter shrugged contemptuously. He seemed to be studying his companion.

"Every newspaper has its morgue," he said. "But I am the expert they call in to fill in the gaps. But besides that, I have built up for myself a unique position. I supply the press with information about persons of whom it has never heard, or has overlooked, or has not considered of sufficient importance to merit a niche in the morgue."

"How have you yourself acquired this mass of miscellaneous knowledge?" Harvey inquired.

"By assiduous study of the newspapers themselves. I subscribe to almost every sheet published in this country, and, in normal times, to many from abroad. I have filing cabinets full of cuttings, and a system of cross references by which I can turn up any name I want in a few minutes. My memory, I may say, as the result of years of practice, is quite remarkable—if I have ever filed a name I never forget it. Then I have correspondents all over the country, who do any necessary research work, and I undertake quite a lot myself when I am really interested."

"Not only a system, but an organisation as well. And you talk as though you often were interested."

The obituarist uncrossed his long legs and leaned forward, the light of enthusiasm in his rather lacklustre eyes.

"My dear fellow," he said, "it is an absorbing pursuit, as I told you. I do it now for the love of it. Only a hundredth part of the information I unearth can ever be used. But it is often a romance in itself. You read of some death, it reminds you of another, you search back in the files, you add item to item—a bit about this, a bit about that, an advertisement, a will, perhaps—and gradually the whole history of a family is built up like a mosaic over several generations. And very queer reading such histories can be, I assure you, when put together in this way . . ." Parmiter paused, his eyes under their heavy lids again studying Mr. Tuke's saturnine features. "I am often tempted," he went on, "to follow up some of my clues. But I am not an inquiry agent, in the accepted sense. On the other hand, you know, Tuke, you could do with someone like me at the P.P's office. Or at Scotland Yard. Not that I am for hire. It is merely my hobby, as well as my work. But I am convinced of this—there are crimes and plots that have never been suspected concealed in obituary columns."

"The idea has not altogether escaped us," Mr. Tuke said. "There is a branch of C.I. which studies the newspapers."

The other made an impatient gesture. "Oh, I know, I know. But not even Scotland Yard has my system or my memory." He looked with an abstracted air at the pipe he had been holding for some time. It had long since gone out. Laying it on a table beside him, he gave Harvey one of his half-veiled looks. "I'll give you an example of the sort of case I have in mind," he said. "It was only two days ago that a new development caused me to consider it in earnest, and it may, after all, have a perfectly innocent construction. But it will illustrate my argument."

"I should like to hear it," Harvey said. "Have a cigar."

Parmiter accepted a Larranaga rather absently, and lighted it with a carelessness that made its donor wince. He appeared to be thoroughly in the grip of his hobby. The pair were sitting in a quiet corner of the lounge, which at seven o'clock in the evening was sparsely occupied. Behind them the August sunshine of double summer time poured slantingly through the tall windows overlooking the Mall.

"Two days ago," said Parmiter, "I read in a Surrey paper, published weekly in Guildford, the announcement of the death, 'accidentally', of Blanche Porteous, who was described as the widow of Cyril Porteous and the daughter of Rutland Shearsby. In the body of the paper was a brief account of the inquest held three days after the fatality. This occurred, by the way, on Bank Holiday Sunday. Mrs. Porteous, who was a teacher of elementary chemistry at a girls' school—Guildford is full of schools—had somehow swallowed a dose of sodium nitrite at her home, where she had some chemicals. The verdict at the inquiry was 'accidental death'."

The obituarist remembered his cigar, drew on it violently, and had a fit of coughing. Mr. Tuke decided that never again would he offer good tobacco to a man so obviously unfitted. to appreciate it.

"No effort of memory," Parmiter went on when he had recovered, "was required to make me take notice here. Only a week ago I filed the report of an inquest on another Shearsby."

"Not Raymond Shearsby, by any chance?" Harvey inquired.

Parmiter gave him a quick glance. His brows drew together.

"You knew him?"

"No. But I know his short stories, and very good they are. I am sorry to hear you refer to him in the past tense."

Parmiter blew a gusty cloud of smoke. "Yes, it was Raymond Shearsby who died just over a week ago. On the 28th of July. I know his work too. Indeed, when I read of his death I wrote a short appreciation which appeared in one or two London papers."

"I must have missed it," Harvey said. "Was he an old man?"

"Only thirty-four."

"What did he die of?"

"Another accident. It was reported in a Hertfordshire paper. He fell into a stream and was drowned. Apparently he stunned himself in falling. At least, that was the theory advanced at the inquest."

"You think he was a relative of this Mrs. Porteous?"

"He was not her brother," Parmiter said. "*The Authors'*

Year Book gives his father's name as Geoffrey. But Shearsby is an uncommon name. There is not one in the current London Telephone Directory. It would seem likely that the two were related. Now it is not remarkable," Parmiter went on, "to learn of the deaths, even the accidental deaths, of two persons bearing the same name within a week. One is constantly meeting coincidences of that kind. But the ratio of improbability is compound. When I find *three* people, sharing the same name, all in the prime of life, dying of accidents inside a few months, I begin to wonder."

"Being inveterately and by training suspicious," Mr. Tuke agreed, "I should do likewise. I take it you have another dead Shearsby up your sleeve?"

"Not a Shearsby patronymically, but I think one may presume one of the family. At least the odds must be greatly in favour of it. As soon as I read of Raymond Shearsby's death, I recalled this previous case. Again, it was no feat of memory, for it occurred as recently as March. A Captain Dresser, whose Christian names were Sydney Shearsby, was killed in a traffic accident in the black-out, here in London."

"You are too modest," Mr. Tuke commented. "I suppose you deal with several hundred surnames alone every week, but you remember Christian names as well, and associate them with their appropriate patronymics."

"Oh, it is a matter of practice making perfect," Parmiter said again. "My cross-reference system does the rest."

"You say these three people were in the prime of life?"

"Raymond, as I said, was thirty-four. Mrs. Porteous was the same age, and Captain Dresser a year younger."

"It certainly suggests that they were cousins."

"That is what I think," Parmiter said.

He paused, and looked at his fellow member. There was something of expectancy in his look. Mr. Tuke returned it with one of faintly amused curiosity.

"From what you tell me of your methods," he remarked, "I presume you will follow this up, for your private satisfaction?"

The obituarist shrugged. "A visit to Somerset House would settle the question of relationship. If it should turn out that these unfortunate people are in fact cousins, further inquiries as to other relatives, and any Shearsby wills, might prove instructive." He shrugged again, watching Mr. Tuke with the same look of expectancy. "I am very busy just now," he said.

"Oh, come," said Harvey. "You disappoint me. After all you have said, I could have betted you would want to wring the last drop out of an affair like this."

Parmiter drew in his violent way on his cigar. He took it from his mouth and frowned at it, as though wondering what it was. He seemed to be trying to make up his mind about something. Then he looked up with a little smile, and said abruptly:

"Well, as a matter of fact, Tuke, this accident of meeting you here, with this puzzle fresh in my mind, has put an idea into my head. You will agree that these three deaths suggest some curious speculations?"

Mr. Tuke considered this. "Yes," he said, "I would go as far as that. I think I implied as much before."

"Do you feel sufficiently interested to take the matter further yourself?"

"I? This sort of thing is not my business. If there is anything in it, it is a police matter."

Parmiter's smile broadened. "Oh, I know your reputation."

"If you mean what I suppose you mean," Harvey said a trifle stiffly, "you exaggerate. Anyway, the discovery— if it is a discovery—is yours. As a law-abiding citizen, it is for you to take it further."

"Which I am doing," Parmiter rejoined lightly. "You are not merely an officer of the court, you are an official of a department concerned with crime. For all I care, let sleeping dogs lie. Or," he added, "let the dead bury their dead. Well, think it over, Tuke."

CHAPTER II

IF Mr. Tuke had not happened to meet Cecile Boulanger so soon after that game of billiards at the Sheridan, his reactions to the tale of fatalities in the Shearsby family would perhaps have been limited (in Parmiter's own phrase) to a few curious speculations. And if that talk with the obituarist had not happened to take place shortly before Harvey met Mlle Boulanger, her own story would scarcely have influenced him as it did. For while, in his capacity of the most senior of the Senior Legal Assistants to the Director of Public Prosecutions, he might emit blasting criticisms of the police, no one knew better than he how painstaking and reliable were their routine methods—though he drew a distinction here between the Metropolitan force and certain of the provincial constabularies. But on the whole, if, after investigation, the police decided that an accident was an accident, and nothing more, then an accident it most probably was. Two, or even three, such mishaps in one family within a short space of time did not affect the argument. Coincidences, in police work, called for stringent inquiry; but genuine ones cropped up almost every day, as they crop up almost every day in everyday life, of which, after all, if regrettably, police work is no more or less than a part.

It was a coincidence, for that matter, that Mr. Tuke should have had that talk with Parmiter not long before his meeting with Mlle Boulanger; or, conversely, that he should meet her when he did. Cecile herself might be classed as the most striking coincidence of all. For Harvey had known of her for some time. She was a very confidential clerk at the headquarters in London of the Fighting French Navy, soon to become once more the navy of a liberated France. Mrs. Tuke, who was French, and who held high rank in the *Service Feminin de la Flotte*, the equivalent of the W.R.N.S., often mentioned her valuable assistant. Mr. Tuke, however, had never met Mlle Boulanger until the Sunday immediately following his lesson in the methods of an obituarist.

Yvette Tuke had just returned from France. Apart from her rank in the *Service Feminin,* one is not a Garay of the famous Clos Garay for nothing. To oblige a daughter of one of the greater Burgundies, strings had been pulled and urgent duties discovered, and Yvette had got herself conveyed by air to a newly freed Paris, and from Paris to Dijon, where after four anxious years she was able to spend four hours with her parents. She had used this mission to learn all she could about the relatives of exiles who would have to wait some time longer before they could even revisit France. Mlle Boulanger had an aunt and some cousins in the Côte d'Or, and it was for news of them that she called that Sunday afternoon—it was the 20th of August—at the Tukes' flat in Westminster, Mrs. Tuke having flown back only the evening before.

It might be described as yet another coincidence that Mr. Tuke was just beginning his holiday. However, since the day was Sunday, and his wife had been away in that France which was almost as much his country as hers, he would no doubt have been at home in any case when the visitor was announced.

There was at a first glance nothing particularly French about Cecile Boulangér, except her navy blue uniform with its cross of Lorraine and the letters F.N.F.L. in gold on her round cap. As was to appear, she was half English, and she spoke that language idiomatically and with scarcely a trace of accent. At a second glance, her dark good looks, if one excepted a short nose, showed her Latin strain. Her hair was almost black, her brown eyes large and liquid. Her mouth was a little pinched and fretful, and Harvey put her down as capable and conscientious, rather fussy, and without much sense of humour. He estimated her age, correctly enough, at the middle or late thirties. He had then no reason, however, to feel any special interest in Mlle Boulanger; and, having been introduced, he left her with his wife and retired to his study.

It was a quarter of an hour later that his wife came in to him.

"Tea is in," she said. "And Cecile wants your advice."

"What about?" Harvey asked suspiciously.

"She will tell you. The police know about it, and they say it was an accident. But I *think* Cecile is frightened."

When Harvey re-entered the drawing-room, Mlle Boulanger was sitting bolt upright, her eyes on the door. With her little round sailor's cap removed from her severely waved hair, she appeared older. Her look seemed to search Mr. Tuke's dark and devilish face rather anxiously. Being neither vain nor self-conscious, he did not always realise how formidable his satanic features sometimes appeared to strangers. Cecile Boulanger was perhaps already regretting her impulse to confide in this somewhat terrifying personage.

Mrs. Tuke, reading her thoughts, rested a hand lightly on her shoulder as she passed on her way to the table where a silver spirit-stove heated a gleaming kettle, which was singing briskly. Harvey sank into a chair beside the guest. "What is the trouble, Mlle Boulanger?" he asked.

Cecile was still eyeing him warily.

"It seems rather silly now," she said.

"Perhaps we can make it seem sillier, and then it will altogether cease to trouble."

The kettle emitted a jet of steam. Mrs. Tuke, her charming face set in a little frown of concentration, ladled tea from a rosewood caddy. Then she looked up.

"Cecile thinks somebody tried to kill her," she announced in her direct way.

"Dear me," said Harvey. "Why?"

Mlle Boulanger twisted her hands together. "It was perhaps only an accident after all," she said.

"I meant, why should anybody wish to kill you?"

"Oh, that is such a long story."

"All the same, let us have it."

She still hesitated in a way which seemed rather odd in one who had the air of being normally very self-sufficient. Then, encouraged by a little nod from Mrs. Tuke, she took the plunge.

"Well, to begin with, Mr. Tuke, a few months ago a cousin of mine was killed in the blackout. He was run over. Everybody said it was an accident. He was an Englishman—I am half English—and an officer in the army. I didn't know him very well, but I had dinner with him sometimes, and I liked him. He was always kind——"

"We may as well have his name," Mr. Tuke said.

"Yes, of course. It was Dresser. Sydney Dresser."

Yvette looked sharply at her husband. Mlle Boulanger, though she was watching him closely, detected no change in his enigmatic face; but his wife knew that the name meant something to him."

"Go on," he said.

"Sydney was killed in March," Cecile continued, more at her ease now the plunge was taken. "The next thing that happened was what Mrs. Tuke spoke of. *My* accident. . . . It was on the 10th of April. I live in Pimlico, and I'd been to one of the cinemas near Victoria Station. When I came out it was after nine, and quite dark. I walked down Wilton Road. At the crossing at Warwick Way a convoy of lorries was going by—heavy traffic uses Warwick Way to get to Vauxhall Bridge—and I had to wait on the pavement. There was a little crowd there. Suddenly someone gave me a terrific push in the back. I was knocked right out into the road, and almost fell under one of the lorries. I don't know how I saved myself."

She shuddered at the recollection. Harvey rose to hand her a cup of tea.

"I take it you didn't know who pushed you?"

"No. And it was so dark—there was no moon, and it was before double summer-time began—the people there were just blurs."

"You referred to the affair as an accident. Did you think it was one at the time?"

Mlle Boulanger sipped her tea. "Yes, of course," she said. "Well, I thought it must be, naturally. I thought somebody must have stumbled against me. Though none of the people who were there, beside me, apologised. A

man said, quite crossly, 'You oughtn't to have tried that
on, miss. Gave me a turn, it did'—as if it was *my* fault.
Of course, it happened very quickly, and then the last of
the lorries went by, and we all crossed the road. I was
feeling very angry," Cecile added, with a tight little smile.
"I suppose because I'd been frightened."

"And very naturally," Harvey said. "Have one of these
things with jam on them. What, by the way, has made you
alter your mind about the accidental nature of the episode?"

Mlle Boulanger took a jam tart abstractedly, her eyes
on his face. Mrs. Tuke was watching him too, having an
idea that he suspected what had caused Cecile to alter her
mind. But the latter appeared to have no inkling of this.

"Something that happened a fortnight ago," she said.
"Another cousin of mine has been killed—by accident."

"Your family is having a run of bad luck. Who was this
other cousin?"

"A Mrs. Porteous. Blanche Porteous. She was a schoolteacher, and she took poison by mistake. Or they say so."

"But you are not so sure?"

Cecile Boulanger's rather thick dark eyebrows contracted
in a frown of worry and perplexity.

"Oh, I don't know what to think!" she exclaimed fret-
fully. "It would never have occurred to me that it was
anything but an accident if it hadn't been for what happened to me. And to Sydney. That was how he was killed.
By a lorry, or a van. Of course, I don't really mean that
he was *pushed*. I just don't know. But now. . . . I mean,
three of us, in a few months, killed or nearly killed, by accidents. . . ." She shrugged, and went on more quietly:
"Well, Mr. Tuke, one half of me, the English half, I suppose, tells me not to be a fool. Accidents *are* happening
every day. But then the other half, the French half, says
I ought to think clearly and logically about it, and not be
casual and woolly. And when I do think it out like that,
it seems very queer. . . ."

Mlle Boulanger's French half, Harvey reflected, would
think it queerer still if it knew that not two, but three other

members of her family had met with fatal accidents in those few months. But apparently Cecile had not yet learnt of the death of Raymond Shearsby. The possibility that he was not her relation occurred to Mr. Tuke, and was dismissed. There was a limit to one's acceptance of coincidences. Altogether it seemed that the thorough-going methods of his club acquaintance, Parmiter, had in this instance unearthed a story which at least called for inquiry.

"So we come back," was all Harvey said, "to the question I asked in the beginning. Why should anyone want to kill you and your cousins, Mlle Boulanger?"

"We are heirs to a large sum of money," Cecile replied.

CHAPTER III

PERHAPS it was the French half of Cecile Boulanger that animated her dark eyes and tightened her rather thin lips as she uttered the words, "a large sum of money". But even among the casual and woolly English, money is at the root of ninety-nine per cent. of crime, and, with such a motive declared at the outset, this sequence of fatalities in her family took on an even more suggestive aspect. Mr. Tuke, who had been lying back in his chair, sat up, crossed his legs, and put the tips of his fingers together, a sort of forensic attitude which meant that his interest was aroused.

"As you speak of cousins in the present tense," he remarked, "I take it that there are more of you."

"There *were* six," Cecile said.

"Of whom, to your knowledge, two have recently died?"

She nodded, giving him a curious look, as though her undoubtedly sharp wits were slightly puzzled by the qualifying clause.

"What is the exact relationship between you?" Harvey went on. "And how do you come to be heirs to a large sum of money? In fact, tell me all about your family."

"Give Cecile some more tea, Harvey, and something to

eat, before she begins," Yvette put in. "These *procès* of
yours are rather exhausting."

The guest's cup and plate were replenished, and Harvey
resumed his attentive attitude. Fortified by a bite into a
tomato sandwich, Cecile took up her tale.

"I had better give you a sort of family tree," she said.
"It will explain how the money comes into it."

"By all means make it clear. May I smoke a cigar?"

"Please do. I used to wish my father smoked them, but
he could not smoke at all, because of his profession." Mlle
Boulanger finished her sandwich, and continued: "It all
begins with my great-grandfather on my mother's side. His
name was Rutland Shearsby."

Again Yvette noted an all but imperceptible shade of
expression on her husband's face which implied that this
name held some meaning for him. He was lighting a Larranaga
with his usual care, rotating it between his lips so that the
flame of the match was evenly applied. Cecile Boulanger was
drinking tea. She put down her cup and resumed her tale.

She used to think of her maternal great-grandfather, she
said rather surprisingly, as a sort of Mr. Dombey. Rutland
Shearsby had been, in fact, an importer of oriental goods,
and Cecile remembered an old daguerrotype of him in
which he was shown with a bald head and whiskers, wearing
a low waistcoat and a stiff white shirt with two immense
black studs in it. She had known him in his later days,
when she was a schoolgirl and he was an octogenarian.
When he died in 1926 he was ninety-two. He lived in an
immense house in Lancaster Gate—a dreadful house, said
Cecile, like a prison. It was gone now, *ecrasé* by a bomb.
It had become an emergency water tank.

The oriental importer had three children—Martin, Alice
(Mlle Boulanger's grandmother), and Deverel. His wife
died before Cecile herself was born. And it was after Mrs.
Rutland Shearsby's death that the trouble began. In 1902,
at the age of sixty-eight, the widower married again.

He knew quite well what he was doing, Cecile said in
reply to a question by Mr. Tuke. He had only retired from

business three years before, and was still very active and full of interests. There was nothing the matter with his mind for another ten or twelve years. "Though you might say," Mlle Boulanger remarked acidly, "that his mind must have been failing, because the woman was only twenty-nine. But that sort of weakness seems to be rather common. Old men and young women, I mean." It was not, how-ever, the disparity in years, or even a second marriage as such, that perturbed the family. It was the lady herself. She had been the importer's housekeeper. And, as Cecile said, one did not have lady housekeepers in those days.

"Was there any addition to the family as a result of this second marriage?" Harvey asked at this point.

"No, thank goodness," said Cecile.

"Did you know the lady?"

"Oh, of course. I saw her several times while great-grandfather was still alive. She is not dead yet, you know."

Harvey's eyebrows lifted. "Indeed? Though of course, she will still be relatively young."

"She is seventy-one."

"A mere child. And I suppose your great-grandfather, having married her, drew up a new will which is bearing rather hardly on his descendants of your generation?"

Cecile gave him a sharp look, and smiled unmirthfully.

"You would think of that, naturally. You are a lawyer."

"The story also seems to be developing along familiar fictional lines. The unjust will is an essential feature of the step-relation theme. Though a step-great-grandmother is in every sense a novel variation to me."

"We are finding it rather hackneyed," Cecile said bitterly. "But you are right about the will, of course. I'll try to explain it. The lawyers made it sound difficult——"

She stopped, a little confused. Mrs. Tuke smiled.

"What are we for?" said Harvey. "Go on."

When Rutland Shearsby married again, his youngest child, Deverel, was dead. Deverel travelled for the firm, and he died in India in 1893. He was married, and the importer settled some money on the widow. The eldest son, Martin, was also in the business, and he became the head of it when his father retired. Alice, the daughter, married Paul Dresser, of Dresser's Bank at Chelmsford, one of the old private banks. This pair, born respectively in 1860 and 1861, were some dozen years older than their stepmother; and as Mr. Tuke remarked, such a situation called for great tact and forbearance on both sides. Mlle Boulanger seemed about to make some comment on this, but contented herself with an expressive shrug and passed on to the terms of her great-grandfather's will.

This, it seemed, was not drawn up at the time of the second marriage. According to Alice Dresser, though the new wife got round her father in some ways, he regarded the marriage as a kind of experiment, so far as the bulk of his fortune was concerned. He needed somebody, and he was used to her, but she was on trial, so to speak. For her part, she was well aware that she might lose everything if she played her cards badly. She was clever, and she waited; nothing was said about a will. She had plenty of time, and she was alone with the old man in that great house in Lancaster Gate. Nobody knew, said Cecile, how she worked on him all those years, being humble and grateful and making herself indispensable, and gradually turning him against his own children and grandchildren. . . .

"Because," said Cecile through tight lips, "that is what it came to. All his children, and now another whole generation, have died without getting one penny of the money that ought to have been theirs. . . ."

Old Rutland Shearsby, in fact, waited until he was nearly eighty before he made his last will. By the terms of it, after legacies and certain sums to be paid outright to his two surviving children had been deducted, a trust fund was to be created out of the residue of the estate, and of this fund the second Mrs. Shearsby was to draw the income as long as she lived, or until she married again.

"Which, of course," said Cecile, with a short laugh, "she was not such an imbecile as to do. After her death, the fund was to be shared equally between the children, or

if they died before her, between *their* children, and so on.
I am not explaining it very well, perhaps. It was all wrapped
up in words like residuary and increment and *per* something. . . ."

"*Per stirpes?*" Harvey suggested.

"Yes, that is it."

"It means that the capital in trust will, after the death
of your step-great-grandmother, flow down in three equal
shares through the descendants of the testator's children,
assuming that the latter are already deceased. I gather
from what you say that the next generation is also extinct,
leaving yourself and your surviving cousins to share the
residuary estate in the proportion of one third to each branch.
How much does the trust fund amount to, by the way?"

"It will be worth over £200,000," Cecile said.

"After payment of death duties?"

"Yes. I know, because my father made inquiries."

Harvey carefully removed the ash from his cigar. Yvette,
by a gesture, invited her guest's attention to the sandwiches
and cakes, but Cecile shook her head. The family fortunes
had her in their grip. Her brown eyes searched Harvey's
mephistophelian features, without learning much from them.

"Now let's go back," he said. "Tell me what has happened to the intervening generations."

It was, said Cecile, like a fatality. Before old Rutland
Shearsby died in 1926, the family business was in difficulties. It had something to do with Japanese competition,
and the post-war slump, and then perhaps her great-uncle
Martin was not so clever as his father. The latter knew
nothing about the trouble. It was kept from him at first,
and by the time the firm was in a really bad way his mind
had begun to fail. He was nearly ninety. So his money
could not be touched; and when he died, and Martin went
to his stepmother for help, she refused to give up a penny
of her life interest. And as by the terms of the will the
interests of the beneficiaries under the trust were inalienable,
they could neither sell their shares nor raise money on them.

And so in the end, a year or two after the old importer's

death, the business was closed down. Martin Shearsby, a ruined man, died a few years later. And in the meantime disaster had also overtaken his sister and her husband. Dresser's Bank had long since been absorbed by one of the big joint stock concerns, and Paul Dresser had retired on an ample pension. But he commuted this, and speculated, and lost everything. Alice Dresser applied to her step-mother for aid, as Martin had done, and with the same result. Then she and her husband died, early in the 1930's; and Martin's widow following him to the grave soon after, while Mrs. Deverel Shearsby had been dead for years, here was the end of all Rutland Shearsby's children and their wives.

Mlle Boulanger, with an expressive movement of her broad-tipped, capable fingers—as she warmed to her tale she grew more French—extinguished a whole generation. Refusing more tea, she accepted a cigarette, and Harvey, having risen to light it, crossed to his wife's bureau and provided himself with a writing-pad.

"Now we come to the second generation," he remarked. "The grandchildren—the parents, I presume, of yourself and your cousins."

"I told you it was like a fatality," Cecile said somberly. "All that generation is gone, too. I will try to put it clearly. You have got down the first generation, Mr. Tuke?"

"Yes. Martin. Alice. Deverel."

It appeared that two children had been born to the Martin Shearsbys—Euphemia and Geoffrey. Euphemia married a doctor named Ardmore. In the army during World War No. 1, he was taken prisoner by the Turks. His health was ruined, and he died in 1923. His wife died eleven years later. They left a daughter, Vivien.

Harvey was making entries on his pad. "Vivien, then, is another second cousin. Is she married?"

Cecile shook her head. "No. She is engaged."

"How old is she?"

"Thirty-four."

"Now we move on to Geoffrey Shearsby and his off-spring."

Geoffrey had gone into the business. When it failed, he obtained a post with another firm of importers. He died in 1933—the 1930's seemed fatal to the family—leaving a son, Cecile's second cousin, Raymond.

Harvey wrote this down. "And Raymond?" he queried, watching Mlle Boulanger through a cloud of cigar-smoke.

She returned his look with apparent candour. "He is a writer. I haven't seen him for some time. He was living in France before the war, and now he is somewhere in Hertfordshire. He isn't married, as far as I know, and he must be about the same age as Vivien. His mother, Aunt Juliet —I always called her that—was killed here in London in an air raid in 1940. The last time I saw Raymond was at her funeral."

"Two of the six cousins are now accounted for," Harvey said. "What about the descendants of Alice—Mrs. Dresser?"

The Paul Dressers had also had two children—Caroline, Cecile's mother, and another Martin. Caroline married Emil Boulanger, the London manager of Courtois et Cie., the Paris *parfumiers*. Cecile herself had been born in Paris, but she had spent most of her life in London. Her mother died during the lethal 1930's, and her father in 1941. After the fall of France, said Cecile, he had no work, no money, and no wish to live. "They were bad times, those." The perfumier's daughter shrugged away the bad times, and added, in her practical manner: "I worked in my father's office till 1940, when it was closed. I am thirty-seven."

"And your uncle Martin?" Harvey queried.

There was the faintest hesitation before Cecile replied briefly that Martin Dresser, like his father, had been in a bank in Chelmsford. He died abroad in 1927. It was his son, Sydney, who had been run over and killed the previous March. Sydney was with a firm of house agents in Birmingham until the war broke out. Being in the Territorials he was called up at once. He had not been married.

Harvey made another notation. "Leaving us," he said, "with a residue of two cousins, the grandchildren of Deverel Shearsby, I presume?"

Deverel Shearsby, Cecile went on, had one son, Rutland, who became manager of a firm of paint manufacturers and was killed in the last war. His widow died just before this one began. There were two children—Mortimer, the elder, and Blanche, who became Mrs. Cyril Porteous. Mortimer was now thirty-six: Blanche had been two years younger. The chemistry *motif*, which ran through her short life, was repeated in her brother's, for Mortimer was a research worker at the Bedford laboratories of Imperial Sansil, Ltd., whose name is known wherever artificial silk clothing is worn.

Harvey had written six names in a row at the bottom of his genealogical tree. Screening the pad from Mlle Boulanger's interested eye, he ran his pencil through three of the names, and put a query mark against her own.

"And now," he said, "tell me something about the root of the trouble—your step-great-grandmother."

Cecile's brooding air became definitely sultry. Her dark eyes glowed, and her mouth turned down in a bitter line.

"It has been like a poison running through the family. She and the money. *Our* money. We have always been thinking of it. All of us. It's natural, isn't it? All of us cousins, and our fathers and mothers, and *their* fathers and mothers, all feeling that this money ought to be ours, and wondering when this woman was going to die. . . ."

Cecile ground out her cigarette as though she were grinding the face of her step-great-grandmother. Then she went on more quietly. No doubt, she said, the first generation, her great-uncle Martin and her grandmother, Alice Dresser, scarcely expected to benefit by the trust fund, their stepmother being so much the younger. And in the beginning they were very comfortably off themselves. But when things went wrong, both died poor because she would not help them. Of the next generation, it seemed that Euphemia Ardmore and her brother Geoffrey in their turn asked her to do something for their children, and were similarly rebuffed. Finally, Euphemia's daughter, Vivien, when ill and out of work, and later Cecile herself, on her father's behalf—his salary had been paid from Paris, and the fall of France left him almost penniless—put their pride in their pockets and wrote to the ex-housekeeper, now in her sixties. All they got for humiliating themselves were two abominable letters. "She said things about France. Horrible things! She said we betrayed our friends . . ." Cecile's sallow cheeks were flushed: words began to pour out. "You can't wonder we hate her. A housekeeper! Treating us like that! Refusing us a share of money that is in trust for us. She's no better than a thief!"

She caught Mrs. Tuke's eye, and checked herself, biting her lip, breathing fast, the angry colour flaming in her face. Mr. Tuke looked at her with detached interest.

"No, I don't wonder that you hate her," he agreed. "But even housekeepers have been known to possess bowels of compassion. It looks as though she hates all of you. And if so, why? Have you and your cousins given her any cause, or is she visiting the sins of the fathers down to your generation?"

Cecile shrugged. "Oh, well, my grandmother and my great-uncle were not pleased when their father married again. And the way he left his money did not please them either. Do you wonder at that, Mr. Tuke?"

"No. Unwise of them to show their resentment, though."

She shrugged again. "Of course, they did show it. My mother told me. For example, when they met this woman, after the marriage, they went on treating her as if she was the housekeeper, and nothing more. Old Mr. Shearsby was angry. But that is what she was, after all. Many old men marry their housekeepers, so that they can be cared for. . . ."

"Possibly she did not look at it in that way. When her step-children, later on, came begging for help, it is not surprising that she enjoyed hitting back. The case of the later generations is different. I am not suggesting that the lady has a nice character, and antipathies are apt to grow on one with age. What else do you know about her?"

Cecile seemed to know very little. The lady's name had been Helen Scarlett. She was not a lady, in the social sense. Emile Boulanger had often told his daughter that old Rutland

Shearsby made three mistakes—he married beneath him, he never expected his second wife to outlive his grandchildren, and he thought the family business would go on making money for ever. After his death, his widow sold the big house in Lancaster Gate and for many years led a restless life at hotels in south coast watering places. For the past two decades, however, she had been settled with a companion in a flat in Chelsea. She had not now very long to live. She suffered from some incurable disease, and her mind was failing. Her doctor gave her another few months —perhaps until next year. These and other recent news Cecile had got from her cousin Blanche Porteous. It seemed that the wickedness of her step-great-grandmother had been even more of an *idée fixe* with Blanche than with the rest of the cousins. She had always been poor, and had resented it bitterly. She somehow scraped acquaintance with old Mrs. Shearsby's companion, and had some little piece of information about the Chelsea household every time Cecile met her.

"One or two stray questions," Harvey said at the end of this. "Apparently your great-grandfather's estate was not seriously affected by the failure of the business?"

"He lost a good deal of money," Cecile replied. "But the business was not bankrupt. Something was saved. And he had large investments outside it."

"Who were the executors and trustees of the will?"

"That woman"—Cecile seemed to shrink from naming her *bête noir*—"and great-grandfather's bank manager. When *he* died, she appointed her brother in his place. She had the power to do so, though it seems all wrong. Suppose——"

"You need not worry. They can't touch the trust fund."

Harvey looked down at the pad on his knee. Cecile, her nervousness and awe of him abated, was studying his marked and diabolic features—the dark hair coming to a point over his forehead, the dark eyebrows forming a flattened V, the other inverted V drawn by the deep-etched lines from his nostrils to the corners of his sardonic mouth. The resemblance to stage creations of Mephistopheles was striking.

He looked up at her again. "How did you hear of the death of Mrs. Porteous?"

"That was queer," said Cecile, recalling herself to current affairs. "Somebody sent me a copy of a Guildford paper, with an account of the inquest. It came the day before yesterday. I thought at first that Mortimer, Blanche's brother, had sent it, but it had a London postmark."

"Mortimer had not written to you about the death?"

"No. I haven't heard from Mortimer for a long time. We exchange Christmas cards, that is all—and his wife sends theirs. Mortimer is not like the others. Except for Blanche —and I think he patronised her, though she was his sister —he has always rather ignored us. He is too grand for us, I dare say. He is somebody—in Bedford."

"A little provincial, perhaps?"

"Yes. That is just what he is. Provincial. Bourgeois. *And* his wife. They both despise people who work in offices. All the same, Mortimer should have told me about poor Blanche. I wrote to him, yesterday, and said so."

"Did you mention your own misadventure last April?"

Cecile nodded. "I had been thinking about these accidents. I am curious to hear what Mortimer says."

"Does your cousin Vivien know about Mrs. Porteous?"

"I'm sure she doesn't, or I should have heard from her. I have telephoned to her twice, but she has been out. I am surprised," said Cecile, in the slightly acid tone she used when referring to her cousin at Bedford, "that Mortimer has not told her. He used to look down on Vivien too, but now she is secretary to a very important man at the Ministry of Supply. Imperial Sansil, you know, is practically a branch of the ministry. Or so Mortimer says."

Harvey put away his pencil. "You want some advice, I take it, Mlle Boulanger?"

She met his scrutiny with her look of candour. "I would like to know whether I am silly to take these accidents seriously."

"No, I don't think you are silly. Whether you are justified is another matter. My advice to you is not to think too much about them. At the same time, look about you before you cross roads in the dark. Don't stand too near the edge of railway platforms. By taking care, you will probably soon reassure yourself. You will feel safer. When you look round, you will see there is no one near you. After a time, you won't worry any more. You will put these accidents down to coincidence, and forget about them. And in a few months your step-great-grandmother will be dead, and your troubles ended."

On this somewhat specious note, which left the visitor looking a little dubious, she presently departed. When she had gone, Mr. Tuke met his wife's accusing glance with a thoughtful frown that made her raise her delicate eyebrows.

"What is it, Harvey? You have been keeping something back. And all that talk to Cecile about coincidence and forgetting after a time. . . . That was not like you. You are not usually what she calls woolly."

"What was I to say? She will take care of herself now."

"If you think she really is in some danger, you should have told her. It is a queer story, eh?"

"Queerer than you know. Or, apparently, than she knows. Could you get her out of this country, at once? Paris—anywhere. Even to some French naval base here, provided it is a good way from London."

His wife opened her dark blue eyes. "So you *do* think she is in danger?"

"Her family certainly seems to attract calamities. Her cousin Raymond has also recently died—by accident."

"Harvey! Why didn't you tell her?"

"*Ex abundantia cautelae*, my dear. In other words, you never know, do you?"

"You mean, Cecile herself? . . . Oh, that is ridiculous, Harvey! And horrible! . . ." Yvette brushed the idea aside. "But as for getting her away. . . . It will be difficult. Her work now is records. They are here, in London. There is no work for her at a base. And to get back to France at present is like getting into paradise. Besides,

Cecile has never even said she wishes to leave England. She is more English than French now."

"Well, suggest it to her," Mr. Tuke said. "See how she takes it."

CHAPTER IV

Sir Bruton Kames, the Director of Public Prosecutions, sat at his immense desk, looking very like a large comatose fish. It was the day after Mlle Boulanger's visit to the Tukes' flat—that is, it was Monday, a day when few office workers, however eminent and pampered, appear at their best.

The Director unhooked his horn-rimmed glasses, swung them violently, and glared malevolently at Mr. Tuke.

"What are you doing here? Thought you were on holiday. Aren't I to have *any* peace?"

"I forgot before I went," said Mr. Tuke, "to tell you about the two elderly Fellows of Oriel who craved an existence arboreal—

'They said 'We are bees,
But there aren't any trees',
So they swarmed on the Martyr's Memorial.''

Sir Bruton had a childish passion for limericks, and was compiling an anthology containing many of his own contrivance; and though he grunted in a disparaging way, he was making notations on a pad.

"I know a new one too," he said. "Old Lincolnshire folk song:

There was a young lady of Leadenham
Who said, 'Though I've ribbons to thread in 'em,
I'm in rather a fix,
For regarded as knicks,
Well, between you and me and the gatepost, I wouldn't
be seen dead in 'em.' ''

"You can be trusted to give a vulgar twist to the cleanest fun," Mr. Tuke commented. "But you might at least scan."

"Anyhow," retorted Sir Bruton, "you didn't come back to recite a bit of doggerel. What *do* you want?"

"Yvette sends her most distinguished compliments, and will you come to dinner to-night?"

"My compliments to your wife, with knobs on. I will. But you could have invited me over the 'phone—or she could, which I should have preferred," said Sir Bruton, returning to the charge. "What have you got up your sleeve, Tuke? When you go all bright and gladsome, it means you're up to mischief."

"I rather fancy someone else is," Mr. Tuke replied, taking out his cigar-case.

"Whaddayou mean?" The Director was regarding his assistant with a shrewd if fishy eye. "What have you stuck your nose into now?"

He was feeling in the cigar-box on his desk for a Trichinopoli, and Mr. Tuke withdrew ostentatiously to light his own cigar at a distance.

"It is the other way about," he said, when he had expelled a cloud of smoke. "Something has been stuck on my nose, so to speak."

Sir Bruton groaned, banged his glasses on his desk, and swore, for they were a new pair. He broke his spectacles, on an average, once a month, repairing them with wire, adhesive tape, or whatever came handy: in his days at the Bar he had been known to lead in a murder trial with pipe-cleaners hooked over his ears.

"Regular bit of fly-paper, aren't you?" he grunted. "What is it this time? Embezzlement, arson, barratry?——"

"It smells a bit of multiple murder."

The Director emitted a sort of howl. He threw up his hands, spectacles in one and cheroot in the other, and glared ferociously at his subordinate.

"I won't have it!" he roared. "You want to get your name in the cheap papers again, and I won't have it. D'you hear? Just because you've brought off a fluke or two, you want to meddle again. It lowers the department. How often have I got to remind you that the functions of this office are advisory and directive, not nosing about? Leave that to the police."

Mr. Tuke was adjusting himself on the small of his back in the only comfortable chair (the Director's own excepted) which the room contained. He stretched out his long legs and drew on his cigar.

"How you do go on," he said. "Now that the uproar has died down, perhaps I can finish. A rather queer business has been brought to my notice. Literally brought, and twice over—two complementary accounts from sources quite unrelated, to the best of my knowledge. As I say, it smells uncommonly like murder, in the plural, with possibly more to come. It may be nothing of the kind, but it wants looking into. Although I'm taking a well-earned holiday," Mr. Tuke added virtuously, "I've trotted along, like a good citizen, to tell you all about it. And you bellow at me before I can even start."

Sir Bruton remembered his cheroot, struck a match viciously, and blew a cloud of rank smoke in his assistant's direction.

"Why tell *me*, eh? Why come back here? If it's a police matter, go to the police. You're known to 'em—too well."

"I thought I would take your opinion on that."

"Damned modest all of a sudden, aren't you?"

"And then it is quite an interesting little story," Mr. Tuke went on. "It occurred to me that you might need entertaining. It is always dull here when I'm away."

Sir Bruton suddenly chuckled with a gobbling sound.

"Well, spit it out," he said. "Who's getting murdered now? More of your pals?"

"A friend of Yvette's seems to be in the danger zone."

"Same thing. I might have known it. You're becoming a regular Jonah, Tuke. But it's a bit tough on your wife's friends. You might leave them out of it."

"'*Quand messieurs les assassins commencent,*'" Mr. Tuke quoted, "I will with pleasure. Well, here's the story."

Since he had given it considerable thought, and was trained to a habit of clear exposition, the tale of Parmiter's confidences and the singular sequel contributed by Cecile Boulanger were related with precision and despatch. Sir Bruton, sunk in his chair, his protuberant eyes closed, the Trichinopoli reeking between his lips, seemed to be half asleep; but this was his normal attitude of attention. It disconcerted self-important persons, who expected their audience to hang on their words, and who were apt to be further thrown out of their stride by the somnolent listener opening his eyes to stare fixedly at the large kitchen clock which hung opposite his desk. These tactics had got even a too talkative Prime Minister out of the room in record time.

When Mr. Tuke finished there was a little silence. Sir Bruton breathed heavily. Then he stirred, shaking cigar-ash over his ample waistcoat. One eye opened.

"Looks a bit fishy," he rumbled. "But then so do lots of things. What the devil are you grinning at?" he demanded truculently, opening the other eye.

Mr. Tuke salvaged the elements of subordination and effaced his smile. The Director stared at him suspiciously. Seizing a penholder, he began to probe his ear vigorously with it as he went on:

"Well, what's your view, Tuke?"

"I told you. These three accidents should be inquired into."

"They have been, haven't they?"

"By three different police forces, you'll note. London, Hertfordshire and Surrey. In the case of the army captain, the chances are it was a genuine accident. The M.P. don't often slip up over that sort of thing. But the county constabularies aren't always so thorough, as we have cause to know. And, in any case, has anybody connected the three deaths? I doubt it. Different names, in different localities, and one case six months old. Parmiter wasn't so far out when he said that a man like himself would have his uses in a police force."

"Don't be so cocksure," said Sir Bruton, rapping the desk with his penholder. "The Central Office may have connected 'em, looked into it, and decided there was nothing doing. The Yard isn't fanciful, like you. And it does keep its eye on inquests and the papers. When was this last business, did you say?—the schoolmarm?"

"A fortnight ago. Bank Holiday Sunday. "

"Know anything about the inquest?"

"No. Parmiter referred to it, and Mlle Boulanger saw a report of it in the local paper rather mysteriously sent to her. It seems to have been quite slick. Too slick, perhaps."

"What do you think of this French gal?"

"Obviously," said Mr. Tuke, "anybody can say they've had a push in the back. If she is eliminating her cousins, it's the sort of story she would put out."

"Why draw attention to the thing at all?"

"Suppose she has another little accident in view. It might then seem good policy. Even as the case stands, sooner or later—when the second Mrs. Shearsby dies, for instance, and the trust fund is distributed—somebody may put two and two together, and ask questions. They are less likely to be asked of an apparent victim. Or again she may be planting evidence against one of the other survivors. I have no reason to suppose, of course, that she isn't telling the truth. I've asked Yvette to suggest packing her off to France, or well out of London. Her reactions may give us a line."

"She didn't appear to know about this writer chap being bumped off?"

"She talked about him, with a perfectly straight face, as though he were still alive. That's all I can say."

"Are you seriously suggesting another little accident?" Sir Bruton asked, reaching vaguely for an ashtray and hitting a bowl of paper-clips. "Damn it, if these *are* murders, whoever's doing 'em 'll collar a third of the cash now. Sixty or seventy thousand quid ought to be enough."

"You or I might think so," Mr. Tuke said. "We're

cautious blokes. We know when to stop. But the average mass murderer doesn't. It's like drink. Just one more quick one—nobody will spot it. You know that as well as I do."

"Better," Sir Bruton agreed with a sinister chuckle. "You needn't teach your old uncle to suck eggs. I've had some of these coves in the dock. Remember Scarsbrick, the solicitor, who did in three wives? If he'd stopped at two, he'd have got away with it. Excess of zeal. Armstrong was another, and Palmer, of course, though they only proved one murder in either case." The Director chuckled again. "Did you ever hear how the people of Rugeley petitioned the P.M. to have the name of the town changed after Palmer's trial? The P.M. was old Pam, and he wrote 'em a nice letter suggesting they might call the town after him—Palmers-town." Sir Bruton gobbled, banged his spectacles, and replaced them for safety on his nose. "Interesting thing about all these coves," he said, "is that they were educated men—not like Smith and his little tin baths. They ought to have had more sense." He wagged his head sadly at over-indulgence in murder by educated men. "But where would you and me be, my boy," he reflected more cheerfully, "if criminals had sense?"

"What an old ghoul you are," said Mr. Tuke. "Well, the Shearsby murderer, if there is one, is another educated man, or woman. It will be instructive to see whether he, or she, knows when to leave well alone."

"Ghoul to you," Sir Bruton retorted, hoisting himself up in his chair, into which he had slid so far that only his ample stomach prevented his slipping beneath the desk. He took off his glasses again to wave them at Mr. Tuke. "You and your busman's holiday! Now look here, Tuke. Whatever you're up to, you've got to turn the whole thing over to C.I. straight away. See Wray about it. No more of this gifted amachoor stuff."

"I'm going to see Wray about it in any case," Mr. Tuke said equably.

He got up and perched himself on the edge of the desk, where he reached for the telephone. Sir Bruton appeared

to have lost interest. His lips were moving silently, and
Mr. Tuke paused to inquire:

"What are you muttering about?"

The Director fixed him with a protuberant eye and began
to recite:

"The Mayor and Town Council of Rugeley
Disliked notoriety hugely.
They said: 'Well, we mean,
What with this 'ere strychnine,
It's a hell of a life for yours trugely.' "

Mr. Tuke made a face as he took up the telephone.

"Give me Scotland Yard, please," he said. "Mr. Wray."

CHAPTER V

MR. HUBERT ST. JOHN WRAY, the Assistant Commissioner
(Crime), was a small, dapper, reddish-haired man with a
marked general resemblance to a fox. Mr. Tuke and he
seldom met without bickering; and when, a little later on
that Monday morning, Harvey entered the large upper
room in Norman Shaw's lofty building on the Embankment,
Wray greeted him with a faintly malicious smile.

"Hello, Tuke."

"Hello to you."

"I thought you were on holiday."

"Why does everyone make that remark? Does a holiday
necessarily entail exile from all one's usual haunts?"

"It does, with rational people," Wray said, with his
neighing little laugh, which showed his gums. "We're only
too glad to forget our usual haunts. But I suppose you
must be different." He picked up a file from a tray on
his table. "Well, you're wasting your time now. Nice to
see you, and all that, but your little inquiry's a mare's nest.
It was a perfectly genuine accident. No doubt about it
at all. What made you think otherwise?"

Harvey had relapsed into a chair beside the Assistant Commissioner. "I didn't think otherwise," he said. "I know nothing about the case. I am merely curious."

"Why? Did you know the fellow?"

"Never heard of him till the other day. Tell me about the genuine accident."

Wray gave him a foxy look which was an example of Nature's thoroughness when she creates one of the higher animals in the image of a lower. Taking a Turkish cigarette from a silver box on his table, he lighted it and opened the file.

"This is all the Traffic Branch has on it. It's perfectly straightforward. Captain Sydney Dresser, R.A.S.C., was attached to the S. & T. Branch of London District. His office was in Curzon Street. He was a man of thirty-three, a bachelor, and lived in rooms in Bayswater. On the evening of the 14th of March he left his office just after seven. It was a filthy wet night, and pitch dark. Dresser always went home by bus, from the stop in Park Lane by Stanhope Gate. He'd just started to cross Park Lane when a van came down Deanery Street, by the Dorchester. The driver saw Dresser right under his lamps, stood on his brakes, skidded, and hit him sideways. Dresser's head was crushed in, and he was killed instantly. Our people say the man wasn't really to blame at all. There were a couple of quite sound witnesses, and they both state Dresser didn't look round. He could see the Lane was clear, and he forgot traffic coming down Deanery Street. That's all there is to it, Tuke. What put you on to it, and why?"

"I hadn't much doubt it was an accident," Harvey said. "You people don't often slip up over that sort of thing."

"Nice of you to say so," Wray said sarcastically.

"What do you know about the late captain's family?"

"His family? Why? He is described as having no parents living. The nearest relative they could find seems to have been a French cousin. Name given here as Mlle Boulanger."

Mr. Tuke took out a cigar. While he pierced and lighted it with care, Wray drummed impatiently on his table.

"Yes, cousins," Mr. Tuke went on. "The operative word. Captain Dresser's death has started a train of coincidences that are a little too odd for my simple faith."

"What coincidences? There's nothing more here."

"As I suspected. Apparently there is not always that close co-ordination between our police forces which would seem desirable."

Wray's sandy eyebrows drew together. "Indeed? What have we missed?"

"I am going to tell you. Dresser was one of six cousins. The six were, and the survivors are, joint heirs to an estate said to amount to over £200,000——"

"What exactly do you imply by survivors?"

"Ah, the implication has not escaped your nimble brain. It's like the old rhyme. Six little cousins were very much alive. One was run over, and then there were five. That was only six months ago. It may interest you to know that there are now only three. And apparently there were very nearly only two."

Wray stared for a moment. He laced his bony fingers together and made them crack in a startling manner.

"I presume you consider this some concern of ours, or you wouldn't have brought it up."

"Well, you can work it out for yourself, Wray. £200,000 divided by six. Now by three. And the deceased beneficiaries all died by accident."

Wray drew a pad towards him. "Come on, Tuke," he said. "How do you know all this? Give me the details."

For the second time that morning Harvey recited the story of the Shearsby family. Wray took notes, pausing only to light another cigarette from the stub of the first. At the end he picked up one of the telephones on his table and rapped out brisk instructions. He turned again to Harvey with a rather sour smile.

"I agree with you. Obviously this must be looked into. We shall hear in a moment if Records have anything on these other cases. I shall be surprised if they have. Your crack about co-ordination, Tuke, was beside the point. You

know perfectly well that inquests outside the metropolitan
area are not our concern, unless the locals have their doubts
and call us in. Hertfordshire and Surrey have not done
so. Presumably both are satisfied with the verdicts of accidental death."

"Presumably also they haven't linked the two cases, or
connected them with Dresser's. Neither have you."

"What do you expect?" Wray rejoined acidly. "The
name is different in each case. We haven't the time, if we
had the staff, to collate obituary notices from all over the
country, like your friend Parmiter, and then run round
asking the local people if they're satisfied. Damn it, what
are they for?"

"I have sometimes wondered."

"I often do," said Wray, rather unfairly. "But there
it is."

"Well, this time you have a *locus standi*," Harvey pointed
out. "Dresser was killed in your sacred metropolitan area.
Accident or not, his case gives you a lever with the country
bobbies."

The telephone buzzed, and Wray listened for a moment.
As he put the instrument back he shrugged at Harvey.

"Records have nothing on either of the cases. Which
means we were not asked to trace or notify any next-of-
kin. Both Hertfordshire and Surrey must have known of
one living outside the London area. Obviously the chemist
at Bedford. This Mrs. Porteous was his sister, and Beds
and Herts touch, so no doubt he saw something of the writer
chap. The Bedford police would be asked to notify him in
both cases."

Mr. Tuke, lying back in his chair, had closed his eyes.
Without opening them, he said:

"Ah, chemistry. What do you know about sodium nitrite?"

"Nothing. But I can find out." Wray picked up the
telephone again. "Inspector Tapp," he said.

During a brief colloquy with Inspector Tapp, he made
more notes. His gingery eyebrows rose a little.

"Dear me," he remarked. "Thank you, inspector." His

cigarette smouldering between his fingers, he looked meaningly at Harvey. "The formula is $NaNO_2$. One of the alkaline metal compounds. Extremely soluble in water. Has never been employed, to our knowledge, for criminal purposes. *But*, last September, a whole family in Bedford died of sodium nitrite poisoning because the stuff was mistaken for common salt and the potatoes were boiled with it. The man was employed by Imperial Sansil—sodium nitrite is used in dye-making—and he must have taken a dollop home. Probably as a fertiliser. It was the first known case of its kind, and was reported in the London press. If I saw it, I've forgotten about it. At the inquest, a witness from Imperial Sansil said the man handled the stuff in the course of his work. He could have got it elsewhere, and apparently it can be brewed by anyone with an elementary knowledge of chemistry."

"Which has been denied me," Harvey observed. "I was on the classical side. There is something to be said for a classical education. Catullus or Virgil can be safely boiled with the potatoes. I note by your expressive eyebrows, Wray, that the coincidence of the scene of the catastrophe has not escaped you."

"Bedford? And Imperial Sansil? Where the country cousin works? No, it sticks out."

"Fun for Cousin Mortimer. From what I hear of him, he won't enjoy police inquiries. Very *infra dig*." Mr. Tuke reached for his hat and sat up. "Well, good hunting, Wray. Having laid my little train, I will depart, leaving you to get on with it. I've done my duty, and I've done no more —so far."

"Are you going to meddle again?" Wray asked sharply.

"I'm on holiday. And I have a sort of proprietory interest in the case."

"If it is a case. I suppose you mean the Frenchwoman. Of course, though she's alive at the moment, it's no new thing for your friends to get murdered."

Mr. Tuke got to his feet. "If you mean Norman Sleight,[1]

[1]*Death Wears a Mask*. Douglas G. Browne, Hutchinson, 1940.

he was merely a member of one of my clubs. And you are still alive. I often wonder why."

Wray uttered his little neigh of a laugh. "Perhaps she is stringing you along, Tuke. If one of these cousins *is* liquidating the others, it may be Mlle Boulanger herself. She may be playing for the break. In the event of another death or two, she could say 'I told you so'."

"I had thought of that. But it would seem very rash of her to drag the matter into the light of day. So far as she is aware, no suspicions had been aroused. She can't know about Parmiter. If she hadn't confirmed his story, I doubt if I should have done anything about it. In which case, our conscientious but ill-co-ordinated police forces would never have begun to put two and two together."

Wray threw up his hands. "The conceit of the man! It was your pal Parmiter who put two and two together, not you. And you often forget, Tuke, that other people may not share your high opinion of yourself."

"Their mistake," said Mr. Tuke blandly. "Well, bye-bye, Wray. Get on with it. Co-ordinate. Stir up the county constabularies of Beds, Herts and Surrey. Set the mills of God, and the teeth of chief constables, slowly grinding."

Wray had picked up a telephone. "Oh, go to the devil!" he said.

With a grin that made him look more than ever like that personage, Mr. Tuke took his departure.

CHAPTER VI

MRS. TUKE, who had obtained a few days' *permission* to coincide with her husband's holiday, met him with a slightly worried expression on her charming face when he returned to St. Luke's Court to lunch.

"I told Cecile," she said.

"About Cousin Raymond?"

"Yes. I pretended you had just heard of it by chance."

"How did she take it?"

"I am sure she did not know about it. One could see what a shock it was to her. Harvey, she really *is* frightened now. I wish you had not asked me to tell her. You will have to do something to clear up this horror, for her sake."

"I have made a beginning. Wray's attention has been drawn to the sequence of fatal mishaps in the Shearsby family. Of course it was news to him. Not his department's fault, actually, but it would never do to say so. Discipline must be maintained. The police are always wrong. Did you suggest to your Cecile that she should leave London?"

"She does not wish to leave London."

"Oh, doesn't she?"

Yvette smiled. "You need not be suspicious, Harvey. It is only because there is a man in the background. Or so I have heard. And then there was Cecile's manner. She looked mulish and self-conscious."

"Try to find out something about the man, will you?"

Mrs. Tuke was looking curiously at her husband when the telephone rang in the hall. A minute later Chichester, the parlourmaid, announced that Mr. Tuke's office was calling.

"My office? I'm on holiday. I'm in the Kyles of Bute."

"It's Mr. Chaffinch, sir," Chichester said rather crushingly.

Mr. Tuke groaned, and went to the telephone. Chaffinch was his chief clerk, and would not telephone without good reason. When he rejoined his wife, several minutes later, he was smiling sardonically.

"Well, what do you know about that? The answer is, of course, nothing yet, but these Americanisms have a certain expressiveness. Another member of the persecuted Shearsby family is in my office. Mortimer, the chemist. With wife."

"What do they want?"

"To see me, urgently. He refuses to say why. Very hot and bothered, according to Chaffinch."

"But why *you*, Harvey? How does he know about you? I mean, it must be about these deaths."

"I hope so. Perhaps he has been in touch with Mlle Boulanger. She didn't mention him, I suppose?"

"No, but it was two hours ago when I saw her. I did not stay in the office. I am on leave, too."

"So you are. I'm sorry, my dear, if the Shearsby family are rather getting in our hair, to use another Americanism—I pick them up from Kames—but you began it."

"I was not complaining," Yvette said. "Only do not allow Cecile and her family *désagréments* to take up all of my holiday, to say nothing of yours. What are you going to do about this Mr. Shearsby?"

Mr. Tuke smiled affectionately at his wife. "You are becoming quite English in your habit of understatement. *Désagréments* is good. I told Chaffinch I could spare a quarter of an hour here at half-past two."

Lunch was over, and the Tukes were in the drawing-room with their coffee, when Chichester entered bearing two visiting cards on a tray.

"How formal they are in the provinces," Harvey said. "I didn't know anybody used cards in these days. Bless me, the fellow sticks his honours and awards on them, too. B.A., B.Sc. And his house is called 'Aylwynstowe'. I begin to see what Mlle Boulanger meant."

He finished his coffee and made his way to his study, where Mr. and Mrs. Mortimer Shearsby stood at the window, looking out over the chimney-stacks of Westminster. They turned about at Harvey's entry. Mortimer Shearsby was a tall man with a stoop and a vague and fussy air. According to his cousin Cecile he was only thirty-six, but his greying hair and lined face and spectacles made him appear considerably older. He had a long nose, unkindly reddened at the tip, washed-out grey eyes and a fretful mouth, and only a good forehead redeemed him from insignificance. A light overcoat, though the August weather was dry and warm, and a rolled umbrella beside the hat on Mr. Tuke's table, completed the picture of a man to whom life was obviously replete with difficulties and forebodings.

He came forward with his hand outstretched.

"Mr. Harvey Tuke? This is indeed kind of you, Mr. Tuke." His loose and rather moist hand enfolded Harvey's. "They told me at your office that you were on holiday. I would not have dreamt of troubling you, but—well, the fact is, Mr. Tuke, I am seriously perturbed. Very seriously. Mrs. Shearsby and I have made a special journey to London —I obtained permission, with some difficulty, to desert my post for the day—our branch of Imperial Sansil, as no doubt you know, is engaged on work of the greatest national importance—but I said to Mrs. Shearsby—yes, yes, my dear? What is it? *Eh?* . . . Yes, yes, of course. This is Mr. Harvey Tuke, my dear," said Mr. Shearsby, firmly underlining the obvious. "My wife, Mr. Tuke. . . ."

Mr. Tuke, having rubbed his hand on his trouser, was studying Mrs. Mortimer Shearsby as she joined her husband and nudged him with her elbow to remind him of her presence. Though the shorter of the two, it was only by a few inches, for she was a tall woman. Harvey's first impression of her was that she was also a handsome one. She had the good looks of well cut features—a short nose and upper lip, fine arched eyebrows, a pointed and determined chin. But her complexion, if left alone, would have been pasty, and her carefully waved hair was a nondescript brown. Art had been called in to enliven nature, and a lock over her forehead was bleached yellow. Behind rimless pince-nez pale grey eyes flitted about with quick little movements, like the eyes of a mouse or a bird. Unlike her husband, who wore a baggy tweed suit under his overcoat, Mrs. Shearsby was a thought overdressed. Her green coat and skirt, tailored to reveal a good figure, were set off by too many clips and bracelets, her little green hat was an exaggeration of a current mode, and her high-heeled shoes of patent leather were too smart for the costume and the occasion. Under her arm she carried an enormous green bag.

Her small gloved hand gripped Harvey's more firmly than the chemist's large one. Her quick eyes ran over him as he indicated chairs and offered a box of cigarettes. She took one with a little pouncing gesture and a faint giggle. Mortimer Shearsby shook his head.

"Thank you, I do not smoke. To return to the point, Mr. Tuke, we are inflicting ourselves upon you——"

"One moment," Harvey was holding a match for Mrs. Shearsby. "I can guess why you are here, Mr. Shearsby," he went on, returning to his chair, "so we can save a lot of talk. But why come to me?"

Mortimer Shearsby did not appear to relish this summary procedure. He coughed and blinked behind his spectacles.

"Of course, I know your reputation, Mr. Tuke. I followed with the greatest interest the case of those big insurance frauds a few years ago. A scandalous affair. It opened my eyes, I can assure you. Your name was mentioned——"

"Yes, yes," Mr. Tuke said impatiently. "I got into the wrong sort of papers in the wrong way, as my chief is always reminding me. But that sort of thing is not really my job, as you must know perfectly well. I am an official of a government department, not a detective. If you want help or advice about the recent events in which your family has been implicated, go to the police, or to a solicitor."

The chemist blinked again, and cast a harassed glance at his wife. Mrs. Shearsby made no effort to help him. She drew in a delicate manner at her cigarette, her eyes flitting between her husband and Mr. Tuke. They were shrewd eyes, the latter thought, though her pince-nez, flashing with every movement, baffled his scrutiny.

"But—but you gave my cousin advice," the chemist said. "Cecile Boulanger, I mean. It was Cecile who suggested that I should call on you."

"It was to see Mlle Boulanger that you came to London?"

"Yes, of course, Mr. Tuke. I had a letter from her yesterday which greatly perturbed me—I may say alarmed me. She told me of a deliberate attempt on her life."

"Well, that is one view of the incident. Anyway, I suppose it recalled to your mind other misfortunes among your cousins?"

Mortimer Shearsby nodded vehemently. "I trust I am

not a fanciful man, but Cecile's news opened my eyes to most disturbing possibilities." Mr. Shearsby, whose eyes seemed so often to be opened by the wickedness of the world, now wagged his head over this latest instance as vigorously as he had nodded it. "That was why I felt I must see Cecile. It was most desirable that we should have a consultation. Mrs. Shearsby counselled reflection, but I had made up my mind. Once I have made up my mind, I am——"

"Pig-headed," said his wife unexpectedly, with her little giggle. Her eyes met Mr. Tuke's through their baffling lenses, and flickered away again.

The chemist smiled dutifully. "Your phrase, my dear," he said. "Perhaps we mean the same thing. Anyhow, Mr. Tuke, I made the necessary arrangements—did I say I am engaged on work of the greatest national importance?——"

"You did. The sequence of deaths among your relatives had not perturbed you before?"

"No. No. I regarded them as sad and shocking coincidences. Nothing more."

"Then yesterday you heard of Mlle Boulanger's alarming experience. That has caused you to change your mind about these coincidences. Your eyes are opened. Well, I have told you what you should do. Go to your lawyer, anyway. Because the police will come to you."

"To *me?*" said the chemist in a horrified tone.

"Yes. Their attention has also been drawn to this halving of your cousinry in six months. Inquiries will naturally be first addressed to the survivors who benefit by these deaths."

"Good heavens!" said Mortimer Shearsby, blinking and looking rather wildly at his wife.

Mrs. Shearsby was sitting very upright in her chair. She ground out her cigarette in an ashtray. Her pale eyes for once were still behind her pince-nez as they met Mr. Tuke's.

"Well, *I* can tell the police a thing or two," she said. "*I* can tell them where to look. . . ."

His black brows raised a little, Harvey waited with interest for more, but the chemist turned on his wife with an unexpected exercise of authority.

"Be more careful what you say, Lilian! I warned you before. I will *not* have you making these random accusations. They may get about. Think of my position. If you are prepared to face an action for slander, I am not."

Lilian Shearsby met his frown mutinously. Patches of colour burnt beneath her make-up. Her hands, from which she had stripped her gloves, disclosing a number of rings, were clenched on her lap till the knuckles whitened. The pince-nez glittered as she glanced quickly at Harvey. Her emotions, whatever their cause, hardened and altered her features; and, like her husband, she seemed suddenly less commonplace. Mortimer Shearsby, his head thrust forward, his lower lip drawn in to show his teeth, looked indeed rather like an angry sheep, but his dominating tone was very different from his earlier fussy pomposities. There was a revealing quality in both these displays of temper which the cynically interested onlooker found most instructive.

"Oh, very well," Mrs. Shearsby said, rather sulkily.

"This is a serious matter," the chemist went on, more persuasively. "We must be discreet, my dear."

She shrugged. She was still ruffled and petulant. Mr. Tuke was glancing at his watch.

"Let us have a few facts," he said. "What do you know about your sister's death, Mr. Shearsby?"

"A most inexplicable affair," Mortimer Shearsby replied, resuming his normal style. "I was informed at once, on the Tuesday after the Bank Holiday. I attended the inquest, as next of kin. A painful ordeal." He blinked rapidly. "How such a calamity can have come about, I cannot imagine. My sister was forgetful and untidy, but to confuse chemicals with kitchen condiments. . . . However, somehow it happened. There was a woman who came daily, and it was natural to suspect some carelessness on her part, but she was very definite she never meddled with the chemicals, and the coroner——"

"There were other chemicals in the house, then?"

"It is a bungalow. Yes, my sister's husband had been

science master at a boys' preparatory school, and Blanche had a small science class."

"There was no suggestion of suicide?"

"The point was raised, Mr. Tuke. But why should Blanche do such a thing? She was in excellent health and spirits when I saw her last, only two months ago."

"And with your inheritance in view, she had every reason to live? Well, now tell me something about sodium nitrite, Mr. Shearsby. Don't you use it in your work?"

The chemist sat up as if slightly stung. He gave Mr. Tuke a pained look.

"It is used largely in the manufacture of dye-stuffs," he said. "But in justice to myself, Mr. Tuke, I should make it clear that the delicate and confidential work upon which I am now engaged—we are, as you will appreciate, practically a branch of the Ministry of Supply—this work has no connection with dye-stuffs as such, and for many months I have had no occasion to handle sodium nitrite."

"It appears to be highly poisonous."

Mr. Shearsby sniffed in a superior manner. "So are many of the alkaline metal compounds. Sodium nitrite is one of the most common in commercial use. It can be prepared, I may add, in any elementary laboratory. $NaNO_3 + SO_2 + CaSO_4$," he chanted, getting into his stride, "equals $NaNO_2 + CaSO_4$. In simple language, if you mix a concentrated solution of sodium nitrite with quicklime, insoluble calcium sulphate is formed, and sodium nitrite, the $NaNO_2$, remains in solution. Another method of preparation is to add lead to fused sodium nitrate—$NaNO_3 + Pb$,—add the fused mass to water——"

"H_2O," said Mr. Tuke. "I know that one. I am told, by the way, that there has been at least one previous case of fatal poisoning by sodium nitrite."

Again the chemist sat up with a startled jerk. He looked unhappily at Mr. Tuke, and then at his wife.

"I told you," Lilian Shearsby said, "that if you *would* drag all this into the daylight, that story was bound to come out. You had nothing to do with it, anyway."

Her husband brightened a little. "True, true. You are referring, no doubt, Mr. Tuke, to the fatality at Bedford last year. But though the man was employed by Imperial Sansil, he was not in my department. I did not even know him. But you will appreciate," said Mr. Shearsby, beginning to recover his aplomb, "that knowledge of this previous case confirmed my natural supposition that my sister's death was accidental."

"It must also have influenced the Guildford coroner."

The chemist coughed. "Ahem. The point was not raised."

Mr. Tuke's eyebrows were. "Not even by you?"

"No, Mr. Tuke." Having no doubt foreseen that this little awkwardness must arise sooner or later, Mortimer Shearsby dealt with it firmly. "I acted for the best. There was not the slightest connection between the two cases. But in the earlier one Imperial Sansil was indirectly involved. At the time there was some ill-natured talk in Bedford. Accusations of carelessness were flung about. As a senior and trusted servant of the firm, I am in a responsible position. We are engaged on confidential work of the highest priority, and I felt it would be most injudicious to revive this old story. It would be aiding the enemy. An act of moral sabotage," said Mr. Shearsby, rolling his words. "Had I been asked about it, I would have given all the information in my power. But I was not asked. As a man of the world, Mr. Tuke, you will appreciate my motives in letting sleeping dogs lie."

"The police ought to have known about the other case," Lilian Shearsby added. "There was enough about it in the papers, and Guildford isn't in Australia." Her tone grew more tart. "Anyway, if they come badgering us now, we can tell them of someone else who *did* know——"

Her husband turned on her again. "Lilian!"

She shrugged irritably, but subsided. Her pince-nez flashed as she shot her swift little glances between the two men. Harvey, after a moment, turned to the chemist.

"Now tell me something about your cousin Raymond. I know his stories."

"Ah, Raymond," said Mortimer Shearsby, with an air of relief. "Yes, yes. Poor fellow. I confess I have not read any of his writings. I have little time for reading. My work, my garden—I am in a small way a landscape gardener, Mr. Tuke, and my little plot is, I think, tastefully arranged, with a pool, and here and there a stone gnome or frog——"

"About Raymond Shearsby," Mr. Tuke reminded him, repressing a shudder at this libel on landscape gardening.

"Ah, Raymond," said the innocent offender again. "Well, really, we have seen very little of him, though he lived within twenty miles of us. He came to see us when he got back from France—before that, he and I had not met since we were children—but somehow the—the reunion never ripened. He never visited 'Aylwynstowe' again, but a few months ago Mrs. Shearsby and I made a Sunday jaunt to see him in his retreat. It was a pleasant outing, at any rate," said Mr. Shearsby, with the air of making the best of a poor business. He wagged his head. "Raymond was a queer fellow. Solitary, a little cynical, perhaps. How little I foresaw then——"

"Yes, let us get on to his accident."

A third start was made. Kept firmly to the point, the chemist described how he had been summoned to the earlier inquest at the Hertfordshire village of Stocking. It was only through finding an old postcard of his that the local police had known how to notify the family, for Raymond Shearsby had dropped out of the ken of his other cousins. The evidence at the inquiry showed that on the evening of the 28th of July the writer left the village inn at a quarter past seven. He was not seen again alive. His body was found next morning in a stream called the Cat Ditch, under a bridge which carried the lane leading to the cottage he occupied. He was very short-sighted, and it was supposed he had gone for a walk down the lane after dark—there was no moon, and July had ended with clouds and rain—and had blundered through a gap between the hedge and the parapet of the bridge. He had received a severe blow

on the head, presumably in falling against the stonework.
Stunned by this, he had fallen unconscious into the stream.

"A bad business, however you look at it," Harvey said
at the end of the story. "And now we have talked the whole
thing over, how *do* you look at it, Mr. Shearsby?"

The chemist took out a handkerchief and dabbed at his
high forehead.

"I don't know what to think. At the time—at the inquests
—everything seemed perfectly straightforward. No doubts
entered my mind. But now, after Cecile's story. . . . After
all, three of us. . . ." He peered hopefully through his
spectacles. "It was to glean *your* opinion, Mr. Tuke——"

"It may comfort you to know that the police still hold
the view that Captain Dresser's death was accidental."

The chemist brightened. "I am indeed glad to hear it."

"But of course it may have given somebody ideas."

Mr. Shearsby looked depressed again.

"Did you see much of him, by the way?"

"Sydney? Even less than I did of Raymond. He was
at Birmingham before the war, and then. . . . it was a little
difficult . . . there were reasons. . . ." Mortimer Shearsby
cleared his throat and went on rather hastily: "Yes, I fear
we cousins have drifted apart. Cecile saw more of Sydney
than any of us. It was she who wrote to tell me of his death."

"You did not reciprocate in the two recent instances?"

The chemist waved his hands in a vaguely apologetic
way.

"No, I have been very remiss. Cecile rightly reproached
me. I have been exceedingly busy——"

"I should have written," Lilian Shearsby said, though
in a rather perfunctory tone. "But with one thing and
another——"

"We are both busy bees," said her husband with heavy
humour. "Between us I think I may say we do our bit
towards the war effort. We pull our weight."

"It was not you, I take it," Harvey said, "who sent Mlle
Boulanger a Guildford paper with an account of the inquest
on your sister?"

"No, indeed. I should at least have written. Which reminds me. Cecile told me this morning that she had learnt of Raymond's death only an hour or so before. From Mrs. Tuke."

"Yes, I asked my wife to tell her."

The chemist obviously would have liked to know how Harvey obtained this news, but the latter went off on a fresh track.

"One of your cousins still remains shrouded in mystery. Miss Ardmore."

"Ah, yes, Vivien," said the chemist. "H'm. Yes. I am afraid I have put off writing to Vivien too. It must be done," said Mr. Shearsby firmly.

"She is in the Ministry of Supply, I believe?"

"She is personal secretary to Mr. McIvory." An unctuous note had crept into the chemist's voice. "A highly confidential post. Vivien is extremely fortunate. Especially as there was a time—well, well, that is better forgotten. We all have our ups and downs. Or some of us."

"We do indeed!" Lilian Shearsby put in with a touch of astringency.

"Now, my dear," said her husband uneasily.

"I am not going to kow-tow to that stuck-up madam just because she's secretary to some big-wig——"

"Never mind that now, Lilian."

The pair seemed to have forgotten Mr. Tuke. Mrs. Shearsby's pince-nez flashed. Words began to pour out.

"You know perfectly well, Mortimer, how she'll talk of us! Look how she behaved. Well, I suppose I oughtn't to be surprised now. As I said before, if anyone does come asking questions——"

"Lilian!"

In his agitation the chemist almost shouted. After a moment's stare of defiance, her lips parted, his wife closed them in a tight, angry line. Colour was flaring again in her cheeks. Harvey, who had watched this fresh display of temper with interest, turned to Mortimer Shearsby.

"I have your address, and my wife knows Mlle Boulanger's. Where does Miss Ardmore live?"

"In South Kensington," the chemist said, passing a harassed hand over his brow. " 10 Falcon Mews East is the address."

Harvey had again taken out his watch.

"I am sorry," he went on, "but I really have an engagement. You wanted advice, Mr. Shearsby. I have given it to you. This matter will have to be cleared up now, and after all, until it is the three of you cousins who are left will have no real peace of mind. You don't want to go about for the rest of your lives thinking that one or other of you may have engineered these tragedies. That is what it comes to, isn't it? It would give even your inheritance a nasty taste," he added sardonically as he rose to his feet.

The visitors rose with him. The angry flush had not left Lilian Shearsby's face. Her husband looked profoundly gloomy.

"There is another point," Mr. Tuke observed as he moved to the door. "I understand that your step-great-grandmother may live for some time yet. How unpleasant it would be if another fatal accident were to occur in her lifetime. A little police supervision should at least be a deterrent."

"You horrify me," said the chemist.

CHAPTER VII

AT half-past six that evening the incongruous red-brick building in Queensberry Place which is the home of the *Institut Français du Royaume Uni*, disgorged a chattering crowd into the desert of South Kensington. The crowd was preponderently French. Most of the men were in uniform. Mrs. Harvey Tuke, who seemed to know everybody, passed from group to group giving news of Paris, which she had so recently seen again. It was some minutes before the throng, which created the illusion that this desolate region was densely populated, began to disperse, allowing Mrs. Tuke to rejoin her husband, who was discussing wine with one of his own cronies, a very tough looking commandant of 73, himself not very long back in London from a little trip to organise the Maquis of the Jura.

When at length Harvey and his wife were alone, he remarked that he needed a walk.

"My legs want stretching. It was a good talk, but too long."

"You mean your legs are."

"Well, it comes to the same thing."

Very elegant in black, with a small black tricorne hat, Mrs. Tuke shrugged.

"And where shall we walk—in this?"

A wave of her gloved hand embraced the depressing scene. Queensberry Place, freakishly spared, much of its glass even intact, stood amid ruins that measurably resembled those of Caen or Aachen or Cologne, the result of four flying bombs exploding within a week in an area a few hundred yards square. Roads were still blocked; demolition gangs were noisily at work; debris cascaded upon debris, and dust clouds rose and hung in the air.

"I have seen London looking tidier," Mr. Tuke agreed. "But I thought we might stroll as far as Falcon Mews East— if it still exists, and if we can get there."

"That is where this other cousin of Cecile's, Miss Ardmore, lives. Why do you wish to see her mews, Harvey?"

"I really couldn't tell you. Local colour. Background. I'm interested in that family. And it's about time Mr. McIvory's secretary was returning from the office. She is the only surviving cousin we haven't seen."

Yvette shrugged philosophically. "Do you know the way?"

"It's just off the Old Brompton Road. Five minutes' walk."

Mr. Tuke's acquaintance with certain parts of London was extensive and peculiar. Well though his wife thought she knew South Kensington, where so many French and other exiles were living, and where the headquarters of the *Service Feminin* itself was situated, she was now led along a route

quite strange to her. A mews brought them into Queen's
Gate: across that wide thoroughfare they dived into another;
and a perfect labyrinth of these relics of Victorian carriage
days emerged presently in Gloucester Road. The southern
end of this being closed by more ruins, a fresh circuit was
taken to the Brompton Road; and a little way along this
Harvey turned into yet another mews, disguised under the
title of Brampton Street. Within a hundred yards it became
two more—Falcon Mews East and West. It was as they
approached the junction that Mrs. Tuke exclaimed in
surprise.

"Why, here is Cecile."

Mlle Boulanger, in her blue uniform, accompanied by a
tall man in the blacks and greys of business or the official
world, was in fact coming out of Falcon Mews West. She saw
the Tukes at the same moment, paused, and came to join them.

"Bon jour, madame."

"Bon jour, Cecile."

"I am calling on my cousin Vivien," Cecile added.

"And we, I am told, are in search of local colour."

Cecile effected introductions with a touch of self-con-
sciousness. Her companion, whose name was Mainward,
was probably a little the younger of the two. He was good
looking in a slightly florid way, with a high colour and large
brown eyes behind horn-rims with side-pieces so thick that
they resembled young hockey sticks. When he raised his
black felt hat, which had a rakish curl to its brim, he revealed wavy dark hair allowed to grow a trifle long. He carried
a pair of light tan gloves, and a heavy gold ring, suggesting
a nugget, gleamed on his left hand.

"Have you come to see Vivien too?" Cecile asked rather
curiously of Mr. Tuke. "I am tired of trying to get her on
the telephone. If she is not back, I shall leave a note. We
must have a talk. I told Mortimer he ought to see her.
Did he call on you?"

"He did."

"He is a little offended with Vivien just now. Or Lilian
is. What did he say, Mr. Tuke? What does he think?"

But before Harvey could reply, Cecile's attention was distracted. A young woman had turned into Brampton Street from Old Brompton Road.

"Here is Vivien," the Frenchwoman exclaimed.

Miss Ardmore strode towards them like Diana, hailing her cousin in a clear and pleasant voice.

"Hello, Cecile! I haven't seen you for months."

A pair of candid grey eyes roved curiously among Mlle Boulanger's companions. Vivien Ardmore had perhaps no claim to beauty; her features were irregular, her nose too long, her scarlet mouth too wide; but her fine eyes were widely set, and she obviously had intelligence. Her expression, a little hard in repose, was lightened and transformed when she smiled. An admirable figure was admirably set off by a tailor-made coat and skirt of light grey flannel. On her pale gold hair, elaborately waved, perched a tiny grey hat with white flowers. White gloves, a white handbag, and stockings and shoes which suggested neither economy nor utility completed an ensemble upon which Mrs. Tuke cast an approving eye. Miss Ardmore's glance at Yvette returned the compliment.

There were more introductions in Cecile's formal manner. Vivien Ardmore's left eyebrow rose as she said to Mrs. Tuke:

"Of course I've heard of you from Cecile. But I didn't realise your husband was Harvey Tuke."

"I am always discovering that he is famous," Yvette said. "Or do I mean notorious?"

Miss Ardmore waved a hand towards Falcon Mews East.

"Well, won't you all come in? I live in a queer little hovel, but at least there are some drinks. No, please"—as Mrs. Tuke seemed about to make excuses—"I'd love it if you'd come. I was feeling bored, and it will be a party."

Mr. Tuke said nothing in a masterly way, and Cecile added her plea to her commanding officer.

"Oh, if you would. . . . I *must* talk to Vivien, and you and Mr. Tuke know all about it. It's terribly important, Vivien."

Miss Ardmore's eyebrow rose again. Taking acceptance for granted, she began to lead the way with her long stride, and the impromptu party followed her into Falcon Mews East.

This, unlike Falcon Mews West, which had a double connection with the outer world, was a cul-de-sac. Two rows of stablings, six a side, having been converted into garages, had mostly been re-converted into residences for what would no doubt be described (in the new jargon invented to spare everybody's feelings) as the lower middle income group, for whom the chauffeurs of Mayfair, Knightsbridge and Kensington were already being driven forth, like the Acadians, to seek new homes long before war conditions in general and bombing in particular made large houses still more unpopular. In appearance, Falcon Mews East conformed to type: with its little dwellings painted white, its gaily coloured doors, its pots of flowers and window-boxes and dust-bins, and its cobbled roadway down the middle, it bore an odd resemblance to a Cornish fishing village. Only a few boats and lobster pots were lacking.

No. 10 was a flat above a garage. A stone stair with an iron handrail and worn treads about six inches wide led up to an apple green door. The party followed Miss Ardmore up the steps and through a narrow hall painted the same apple green into a pleasant low room distempered a soft honey colour and equipped with a divan, some comfortable chairs, and a few other pieces of good furniture. There was one big grey rug on the floor, and a large copy of a Provençal landscape by Van Gogh seemed to light up the rather shadowed wall facing the low window. Bookshelves, divided by a fireplace, ran the whole length of the end wall. It was an attractive room, and proof that Miss Ardmore's good taste was not limited to clothes.

"Charming. Charming," Mr. Mainward said as he entered, waving a plump hand to emphasise his admiration.

"Sit down, everybody," said Miss Ardmore. "Except you," she added, fixing Mr. Mainward with a compelling eye. "You can help me with the drinks. I've got gin and lime and a spot of whisky, and, believe me or not, the best part of a bottle of Pernod. A boy in the Air Force brought it. Oh, and there's some punch. I don't usually," she explained as she made for the door, "live with all this liquor about. It's left over from a party a fortnight ago."

"But, Vivien——" Cecile Boulanger said.

Miss Ardmore, however, had vanished, Mr. Mainward at her neat heels. Cecile stood frowning, the serious strain she inherited from her French father combining with her present anxieties to revive latent Gallic irritation at the carefree and informal habits of the English. Mrs. Tuke smiled at her, and her fretful face lightened a little.

"Of course, Vivien doesn't know yet," she said.

Harvey had turned to examine Miss Ardmore's books. They revealed a catholic taste. Fiction ranging from Jane Austen through Dickens and *Little Women* to G. B. Stern, Angela Thirkell and Dorothy Sayers, was mingled untidily with modern verse and plays, Macaulay, Shakespeare (the comedies), books on costume and furniture, some tattered Tauchnitz volumes and assorted literature of travel in Great Britain, France and Spain. The lighter touch seemed to appeal to Miss Ardmore. As his eye ran along the shelves, Mr. Tuke reflected on the immense apparent differences between these three surviving descendants of old Rutland Shearsby, the Victorian importer—Mortimer, a provincial prig, who had no time to read fiction because he was sticking frightful gnomes and frogs about his garden; Cecile, half French, canny, suspicious, without much humour, attracted by a poseur some years younger than herself; and Vivien, easy-mannered, sophisticated, at least interested in things of the mind—a very typical modern product. And then there were, or there had been, the other three: Raymond, the man of imagination, Blanche, who resented being poor, and the estate office clerk turned soldier, Sydney Dresser, who was a mere shade—just 'kind', as Cecile had said. Yet in all the six ran a strain of the same blood, and these dissimilarities might be more superficial than profound. Harvey Tuke, a convinced believer in the influence of heredity, felt he would

like to know more about the Victorian merchant and the
intermediate generations. For there was a plain possibility
that one of these three survivors, two of whom were women,
had deliberately set about the destruction of several cousins
and collateral heirs. No one, it was true, could look the
part less than the fussy chemist, or the perfumier's daughter,
or the smart secretary of that rising civil servant, Mr. McIvory;
but the experience of fifteen years in the Department of
Public Prosecutions had engrafted on Mr. Tuke's innately
cynical temperament a deep distrust of appearances. All
the world, in his view, was indeed a stage; and the more
compelling the motive, the better the actor.

Vivien Ardmore, returning with a tray of glasses, and
followed by Mr. Mainward bearing another crowded with
bottles, found Harvey still examining her books, Mrs. Tuke
reclining elegantly in an easy chair, and Cecile Boulanger,
her hands thrust in the pockets of her navy jacket, staring
out of the window at the mews below.

"A souvenir of France, Mrs. Tuke?" said Miss Ardmore.
"In other words, Pernod? Or gin and lime? Or will you put
your fate to the touch, and dare the punch?"

Mrs. Tuke declared for Pernod, and so did her husband.
Cecile Boulanger signified, by an impatient shrug, that what
she drank was all one to her, and had some punch foisted on
her. Mr. Mainward, with an air of gallantry, elected to try
this concoction, and sniffed it in a connoisseurish manner
before he drank.

"Remarkably good," he declared.

"So it ought to be," said Miss Ardmore innocently. Remarking that aniseed was wasted on her, she had taken punch
herself and was sipping it cautiously. "I remember now.
Someone brought some brandy—Courvoisier—and we shot
that in. The rest's practically pure Algerian and gin and sugar."

Holding the strong opinions he did on the proper treatment of wine and spirits, Mr. Tuke looked at her with pity.
Cecile Boulanger, who had set down her glass untasted,
evidently thought that her cousin had already taken enough
stimulant to fortify her against shocks, and said abruptly:

"Vivien. I suppose you haven't heard about Blanche?"

"What about her?"

"She's dead."

Vivien Ardmore stared. "Dead? *Blanche?* . . . I didn't even know she was ill."

"She wasn't ill. I mean, she took poison. By accident. Or that's what they say. And Raymond—he's dead too. I don't suppose you knew that either."

As a method of breaking bad news, this lacked finesse. Vivien Ardmore's grey eyes widened. She gulped down some more punch as though she hardly knew what she was doing.

"*Two* of us?" she said. "Good lord. Of course I didn't know. About either. Anyway, I haven't heard from Raymond for a couple of years, at least. What happened to *him?*"

"He was drowned, in a stream. Another—accident."

"When was all this?"

"Blanche died on Bank Holiday Sunday, and Raymond about a week before."

"Why on earth didn't you let me know, Cecile?"

"Because I didn't know myself, even about Blanche, till somebody sent me a newspaper the day before yesterday. I've been trying to telephone to you, but you're always out. And I only heard about Raymond this morning, from Mrs. Tuke. Mr. Tuke knew somehow. And then later on Mortimer came—I'd written to him——"

"Do you mean he didn't tell you about Blanche?"

"No. He said he'd been very overworked——"

Miss Ardmore made a contemptuous sound. She discovered the glass in her hand, and emptied it. Her look travelled from her cousin's tense face to Mr. Tuke, from him to his wife, from Mrs. Tuke to Mr. Mainward, and back to Cecile. Except for Yvette, they were all standing.

"Well," Vivien said. "Poor old Blanche. And Raymond wasn't a bad sort. At any rate, he could write. I say, it's a bit wholesale, Cecile. There was Sydney, too, you know."

"It isn't all," said Mlle Boulanger grimly. "Three months ago someone tried to push me under a lorry."

"Cecile, are you serious?"

"Of course I am serious. I tell you I was pushed. I am sure of it now. I was nearly killed too."

Again Vivien Ardmore's grey eyes travelled round the quartette. Her wide mouth smiled wryly.

"I could do with a cigarette. And some more punch. For heaven's sake, Cecile, drink yours up. You look pretty grim."

Mr. Mainward, with the air of *impressement* with which he did everything (for women, at any rate) leapt to refill her glass. Cecile, as though her own brusque announcements had indeed shaken her a little, emptied hers at a draught.

"I wish everyone would sit down," Vivien said irritably. "We look like a lot of stuck mutes." She sat down herself, her eyes on Harvey. "Mr. Tuke, where do you come in?"

"Mlle Boulanger came to see my wife and told us the story, as far as she knew it. I was able to carry it a stage further. I had heard of your cousin Raymond's death from another source. It was in some London paper, by the way."

"I didn't see it." Vivien Ardmore looked at Cecile. "I say, I can't get this. About your being pushed under a lorry."

"Nearly under," Cecile corrected her. "Well, it happened. *I* couldn't get it, as you say. But I can now."

"But *who* ? . . . Who, Cecile?"

Cecile's shoulders lifted in a very French shrug.

"You had better ask 'why'?" she said.

"Well, why?" For a moment her cousin appeared genuinely at a loss. Then the fine grey eyes dilated again. They seemed to darken. "Oh, my hat!" said Miss Ardmore in a small voice. "The money, I suppose you mean? . . . Oh, but that's nonsense, Cecile! Who *would* ? . . . I mean—— Oh, damn it all, it's impossible!" Her teeth bit into her red lip, and she looked almost wildly round the little company. "Why, there *are* only three of us now," she said.

Her clear, pleasant voice shook a little. There was a faint but perceptible air of tension in the room, as though the impact of brutal facts had tautened nerves and senses. Eyes, Mortimer Shearsby might have said, were opened. Vivien Ardmore's certainly seemed to be opened with a vengeance.

She was now staring at Cecile Boulanger as though there was nobody else in the room. Cecile stared back. For a moment the two cousins were in a world of their own, searching one another's face, probing, speculating, on guard and almost inimical.

Suddenly Vivien shook herself. With an exasperated gesture she pulled off her grey hat and flung it on the divan.

"Anyway," she said, "I don't know yet what *has* happened to Blanche and Raymond. For God's sake, tell me, somebody!"

She was looking at Mr. Tuke. "Passed to you, mademoiselle," he said. "I take it that Mr. Mainward knows all about this?"

"Oh, yes, Guy knows." Cecile's glance at that young man strangely altered her prim and guarded expression. She paused, frowning, her eyes now on her cousin. "Very well," she said.

She never took her gaze off Vivien Ardmore as she told the story of her experience in Warwick Way. Vivien's face was almost expressionless: only her left eyebrow rose as the other described the lorries thundering by and the sudden push in the darkness. Mr. Mainward reappeared at his hostess's side with a third glass of punch, which she accepted with an abstracted nod. Cecile was now running rapidly and briefly through what she knew of the deaths of Raymond Shearsby and Blanche Porteous—the facts about the writer's end being a repetition of Mortimer Shearsby's tale, told to her that morning. At the end, she sat still, breathing rather fast, watching her cousin, her brown eyes narrowed. Vivien, the stump of a forgotten cigarette smouldering in her fingers, was staring in front of her; and for some seconds after Cecile's voice, with its faint accent, had ceased, she remained motionless. Then, with another shake of her shoulders, she threw her cigarette into the grate and sat up. She looked at Mr. Tuke.

"Well," she said, with a wry twist of her lips, "I suppose *you* wouldn't be interested, Mr. Tuke, if there wasn't something pretty rum in all this. Pity Mortimer isn't here."

"He has been to see me."

"What ho!" Her brightness appeared a trifle forced.

"You *have* got the family round your neck, haven't you? What do you think of us? And what are you going to do?"

"It is not for me to do anything. I seem to have been co-opted as a consultant. In which capacity," said Harvey, knocking the ash off his cigar, "I have made inquiries in a quarter more likely to be interested—and active. As I told Mr. Mortimer Shearsby, the police are satisfied that your cousin Sydney's death was accidental. I think you may take that to be that. The other two cases are being reopened."

Vivien Ardmore's grey eyes were watching him closely.

"Oh, lord," she said, "what a mess! Well, Cecile, we're all in it together—you, and I, and Mortimer. Where were you on the fifteenth ult., or whatever it is." She gave a hard little laugh. Then suddenly her expressive eyebrow went up. "I say, there's still a dark horse. What about Cousin Martin?"

CHAPTER VIII

CECILE BOULANGER looked astonished. "Uncle Martin?" she exclaimed. "What do you mean, Vivien? He has been dead for years."

"That's the story," Miss Ardmore agreed. "But has he? You saw more of Sydney than the rest of us. What did *he* say about it?"

"He hardly ever mentioned Uncle Martin. And I did not drag in the subject—naturally." Cecile was still frowning at her cousin in a perplexed way. "I never even knew him. When Sydney did mention him, it was only *en passant*, perhaps when he was talking of something he did with his parents when he was a boy. That was all. He never spoke of the later time. And naturally, too. And then Sydney was always reticent. . . . Anyhow, Uncle Martin *must* be dead," his niece added with a touch of irritability. "I was always told so. He died in Belgium, when Sydney was quite young."

"Are you following this, Mr. Tuke?" Vivien asked. "I expect you are well up in our family tree by now."

"I know it like my own. Your cousin Martin—more correctly your first cousin once removed—was the late Captain Dresser's father. He was, therefore, Mlle Boulanger's uncle. She told me he was dead, with the rest of his generation. Have you any evidence to the contrary?"

"Not *evidence*," Vivien said. "But my mother, who knew him better than any of them, used to hint mysteriously that the report of his death had been greatly exaggerated. She said we only had Sydney's word for it."

"I don't believe it," Cecile exclaimed sharply. "It is the first time I have ever heard such a thing suggested. Why, Sydney sent mother an obituary notice from a Chelmsford newspaper. And I'm sure he would have told *me*."

Miss Ardmore shrugged. She reached for another cigarette, and Mr. Mainward was instantly at her elbow with a lighter.

"It's the one thing he wouldn't tell you," she remarked through a cloud of smoke. "Because if mother was right, there must have been some jolly strong reason for deceiving everybody. And anyway, it wasn't a story Sydney would want to dwell on." She turned to Mr. Tuke. "If you're acting as family adviser, you'd better hear it. It's the skeleton in our otherwise tolerably respectable family cupboard. Have you broken the news to Mr. Mainward, by the way, Cecile?"

"No," Cecile said shortly. "And I don't see——"

"Well, I think Mr. Tuke ought to know. Because mother didn't invent things. And if Martin *is* alive somewhere . . ."

She left the sentence, with its implications, unfinished. Mr. Mainward began to wrangle politely with Cecile, offering to depart, and being told rather pettishly that as Vivien had let the family skeleton half out of the cupboard he had better stay and hear the whole story. This he was easily persuaded to do, and Vivien took up the tale of Martin Dresser.

It was a very ordinary tale of human folly. When the cousins' great-uncle, Paul Dresser, of Dresser's Bank, retired with his ample pension, his son Martin was just entering his twenties. Brought up in comfortable circumstances, with a generous allowance from his father, the young man made no attempt to settle down to steady work. He hated office life, and wanted, said Miss Ardmore vaguely, to be a journalist or something. She believed he had actually tinkered at writing, among other pursuits. In the same amateur fashion, as she put it, he also got himself married. He could not have chosen a worse juncture, for his father, having cast overboard the provident habits of a lifetime, was rapidly losing in speculation the capital sum for which he had commuted his pension. In short, very soon, at the age of twenty-six, Martin had to find a job, and urgently, for he now had a son of his own to support as well as a wife. He was fortunate in obtaining employment in the local branch of the joint stock bank, which had absorbed the old private business.

This was in 1914, when the mental powers of his grandfather, old Rutland Shearsby, were beginning to fail, though he had another twelve years of life before him, and when Paul Dresser's health and spirits were breaking under financial disaster. It was in the following year that Paul's wife made her fruitless appeal for aid to her stepmother. Martin, in the meantime, was applying himself with unexpected industry to his career of banking. Family burdens and a weak chest enabled him to escape the army; and by the time he was in the middle thirties he had risen to be a cashier.

And then, in 1925, when he was thirty-seven, the erratic streak in his father's character blossomed suddenly to full growth in Martin, though in a different way. He went right off the rails. Some girl was involved, and he took the bank's money, and went to prison for twelve months.

His wife took the boy, Sydney, to her parents' home in Birmingham, and there, at fifteen, Sydney was already working in the office of a firm of house agents when Martin Dresser was released from prison and disappeared. A year later, ignoring his wife, who in fact was instituting proceedings for divorce on the ground of desertion, Martin somehow got in touch with his son. Having travelled abroad as a young man, and possessing a gift for languages, it was to Belgium that the ex-cashier had fled when he vanished. How he supported himself there, Miss Ardmore did not know. Her mother had a story that he had been a waiter.

With determination and self-possession remarkable in one of his years, Sydney defied his mother and went to Belgium during his next holiday. Later in that year, 1927, he went again, to find Martin Dresser on his death-bed. That, at least, was the story Sydney told on his return. With the exception of Euphemia Ardmore, Vivien's mother, none of the family, not even the exile's sister Caroline Boulanger, had shown much sympathy for Martin, and the news of his death was received with equanimity. The attitude seemed to be that a regrettable blot of the family record could now be forgotten. No attempt apparently was made to verify Sydney's story. After all, he ought to know. He had been there.

Euphemia Ardmore, however, was made of different stuff. She had always been fond of her cousin Martin, and attributed his downfall to his wife, whom she detested; and either because she made inquiries, or had other ground for doubts, to the end of her life she never referred to the death-bed scene at Bruges without a smile. Her daughter again was rather vague about all this; she was working out of London at the time, and never really discussed the family mystery (if such it was) with her mother, who herself died within a year or two. Vivien indeed confessed that she had thought so little about it that on the few later occasions when she met Sydney she had not mentioned his father. Anyway, she said, she was not greatly interested in her family: she always thought families were rather a curse, and what was now happening tended to confirm this view.

When Miss Ardmore had finished her narrative, Cecile Boulanger remarked in a curiously resentful tone that to produce this novel theory from up one's sleeve, as it were, made the present perplexing situation more perplexing still. Cecile, perhaps, resented the suggestion that her mother had not extended to Martin Dresser the affection he might have expected from his sister. She continued to ridicule the notion that he was alive. Mr. Mainward, however, who had listened to the story with becoming gravity, pointed its moral. If Martin were indeed alive, he would be no more than fifty-seven, and should the survivors of the younger generation come under any scrutiny on account of the recent fatalities in the family, it would be in their interests to divert that scrutiny in a fresh direction. Tactfully though this was put, in Mr. Mainward's most graceful style, the outright reference to the predicament in which the three remaining cousins might find themselves evoked another little interlude of tension. Vivien Ardmore and Cecile Boulanger looked at one another, and then away. Neither spoke. Mr. Mainward hastened to dissipate the slight awkwardness in the atmosphere by bustling about refilling glasses.

Mr. Tuke had made no comments. But when the glasses were full again he turned to his hostess.

"I seem to be getting a picture of most of your family. This Martin, for instance, appears to have been the odd man out in his generation."

Vivien nodded. "My mother said Martin was quite different from the rest. They were all so beastly smug. I bet some of them tripped up too, only they weren't found out. If you have seen Mortimer, you've seen a throwback to that era. I wonder, by the way," she added, with a little twist of her wide mouth, "what Mortimer said about me?"

"He seemed impressed by your connection with Mr. McIvory."

"Pharisaical snob," said Miss Ardmore roundly. "Anyway, I bet Lilian tried to say something." She looked shrewdly at Harvey. "Silence gives consent, Mr. Tuke. Well, I've no use for either of them." She sipped her drink, a brooding look in her grey eyes. "I'll tell you," she said. "A few years ago I'd been ill, and I couldn't get another decent job, and I wrote to Mortimer about it. I thought he might find me a hole with Imperial Sansil. I ought to have known better. He wrote back, saying nothing doing, but being Mortimer, that wasn't enough. He sent three sheets of sermon about improvident habits, with digs at my father, who was worth a hundred of him, though he couldn't keep money. That made me mad. Of course I'd asked for it, but it was the second slap I'd had from the family, and to get it from a little provincial pip-squeak of a cousin. . . ."

Her wide mouth was bitter as she paused to sip her drink. Then her hard look melted, and she smiled with genuine amusement.

"There's a sequel," she said. "My boss, McIvory, is a little tin god to Mortimer, and when he heard somehow I'd got this job he wrote off in a hurry, though we hadn't corresponded since the sermon. I didn't bother to answer, and he wrote again, practically imploring me to spend a week-end at Bedford. He went on writing, though I just ignored him. He has a hide like a rhinoceros. In the end, I suddenly thought I'd go. Vanity, Mr. Tuke, not to say common human vindictiveness. I sent a postcard, put on my smartest things, and crashed into Bedford in a very toplofty way. I don't know about Mortimer and Lilian, but I quite enjoyed my week-end. To be truthful, I know Lilian didn't. I saw to that. Very regrettable," said Miss Ardmore, with an impenitent grin, "but Lilian's behind a lot of Mortimer's futilities, and she wants taking down a peg. I took her down several. No doubt that's why I haven't heard from them since, even about Raymond and Blanche." Vivien's smile became apologetic. "Sorry to have talked so much about myself, but it may have helped you to fill in your picture of the family—including me."

"Were you referring to your step-great-grandmother when you spoke of a previous slap?" Harvey asked.

"Yes. I suppose Cecile told you? Because that particular slap has been distributed all round. I got a vile letter. . . ."

The clever irregular features had hardened again. Harvey, gently twirling his glass of Pernod in his fingers—it was some years since he had drunk Pernod—seemed to be savouring nostalgic memories evoked by the sharp tang of aniseed. He looked up over the smoky green liquid at Miss Ardmore.

"May we go back to Captain Dresser and his father? You think the former would connive at the fiction of Martin Dresser's death?"

"I think he'd have enjoyed it, in his quiet way," Vivien said. "Cecile won't agree with me, and she saw more of him than I did. But I always thought there were unsuspected depths in Sydney. And my mother said he was very fond of his father."

"Then where *is* Uncle Martin?" Cecile demanded. "Where has he been all this time?"

But nobody could answer that. Or before anybody could, there was an interruption. A voice was heard calling from the mews outside. With a small grimace at the company, Vivien got up from her chair.

"That's my young man." She went to the open window. "Hello, Charles! Oh, good afternoon, Mr. Payne. . . . Oh, yes, come up. . . . This is getting like a Rotary convention," she remarked as she turned back into the room, to find Mrs. Tuke also rising. "Oh, I say, don't go! We haven't decided anything, and Charles is practically one of the family, poor devil. And Rockley Payne looks a good sort. You may know his name, Mr. Tuke. He writes *romans policier*."

"I seldom read them. But I caught my chief the other day with one of Mr. Payne's books."

Two men came into the low, honey-coloured room. They were much of an age, in the middle thirties. One was tall, and extraordinarily thin: his office blacks and pinstripes seemed to hang upon him. His tie was carelessly knotted, and his felt hat had seen far better days. Very dark hair fell untidily over his forehead, and the almost inevitable horn-rims crowned a beak-like nose. The man's face was bony and intelligent, and he peered about him with the forward stoop of the shortsighted, contriving at the same time to convey a sort of disgust with what he saw, present company included.

His companion looked short beside this cadaverous figure. As carelessly dressed, but in tweeds, he was just a normal young man of medium colour and good looks. He had an ingenuous smile, and walked with a slight limp. The uninformed, seeking a writer of crime novels of the more scholarly brand, would have passed him by for his more striking companion. But the uninformed, as so often happens, would have been wrong. Miss Ardmore introduced him as Rockley Payne, while the disapproving skeleton was named as Charles Gartside—"Both," said Miss Ardmore, "of the Min. of Inf."

Mr. Gartside, ignoring everybody else, addressed his betrothed as though they were alone in the room.

"Payne has told me about your cousin, Vivien. Raymond Shearsby. A bad business."

"Worse than you wot of, Charles," said Miss Ardmore, a little grimly. "Did you know Raymond, Mr. Payne?"

"Slightly," the writer said. "The 'Ludgate' published a lot of his stories in the old days, and I've had one in every number since I took over."

"Oh, of course, you're the editor now."

"They have to put up with anything in wartime," said the editor, grinning. "I combine the job with far less arduous duties at the M.O.I. When I was asked to breathe life into the old hulk—it died, you know, and it's only a quarterly now, though we're hoping for better things—anyway, I thought at once of your cousin. We've had four of his stories —No, three, actually. There was a hitch over the last one——" Mr. Payne paused, adding rather hastily: "He was doing another, but now we shan't get that. Or any more. I'm sorry, for every reason. He was a good fellow, Shearsby."

Miss Ardmore's room now had the air of being rather congested. Mr. and Mrs. Tuke were edging towards the door. Cecile Boulanger, frowning at her thoughts, stood apart, Mr. Mainward hovering near. Charles Gartside had so far recognised the presence of other people as to turn his peering gaze on Mr. Tuke, rather (as Mrs. Tuke remarked later) as though he were something the cat had brought in. The editor of the 'Ludgate' also kept turning a curious eye in Harvey's direction. The name or the mephistophelian features were perhaps not unknown to him.

Mr. Tuke was explaining to his hostess that he and his wife must really be going, but that he was always at her service if there was anything he could do in the way of advice. When the Tukes were outside, Yvette remarked dryly:

"How polite you are becoming, Harvey. Of course, she is distinctly *chic*."

"It's the case," said Mr. Tuke with dignity. "I don't

want to lose touch with it. I want to hear more about this red herring dredged from the grave, to be trailed so conveniently across the original scents."

"Don't you believe Miss Ardmore?"

"My mind is quite open. But it is all extremely interesting, anyway."

"Your mind may be open," Mrs. Tuke said, "but I think it is rather a horrid one."

CHAPTER IX

MR. TUKE need have felt no anxiety about losing touch with the case of the Shearsby cousins. It continued to pursue him. More news was thrust upon him that same evening.

Sir Bruton Kames had come to dine at 28, St. Luke's Court. Dinner was over, and Mrs. Tuke had left the gentlemen to their port, a wine she considered fit only for the English and Portuguese. She had also remarked at an early stage of her acquaintance with the Director that though Trichinopoli had once been a French possession, the irridentist spirit should not be carried too far: and Sir Bruton was smoking one of his host's Larranagas.

Down the hall the telephone rang; and presently Chichester appeared at the dining-room door.

"Mr. Rockley Payne would like to speak to you, sir."

Harvey's eyebrows lifted as he glanced at his guest, for during dinner the day's developments in the case had been under review. Sir Bruton rose with him, and trundled away to the drawing-room, while Harvey went to the telephone extension in his study.

Over the line came the pleasant, eager voice of the editor of *The Ludgate Magazine*.

"Mr. Tuke?"

"Speaking."

"We met this afternoon, if you remember."

"Certainly I do."

"It's about Miss Ardmore's cousin, Raymond Shearsby. I've got a bit of information I think would interest you."

"Why me?"

"Well, I mean," said Mr. Payne, "I thought—oh, well, dash it, as a man and a brother, Mr. Tuke, you must *be* interested. I mean, they've all been at you, or so I gather. And it *is* a rum show."

"Have you passed on this information to those most concerned? To Miss Ardmore, for instance?"

"Well, no. I had a feeling I'd better keep my mouth shut. It was an effort," Mr. Payne admitted. "But I thought I'd get someone's advice first. Yours, for preference."

"Can you impart this item over the phone, or would you rather do it by word of mouth? Where are you now?"

"I'm at Victoria. I'd very much like to talk it over with you, Mr. Tuke, if I'm not being a frightful nuisance."

"Then come along, if you care to. I shall be glad to see you. You'll find one of your readers here."

"Which one?"

"The Director of Public Prosecutions."

"Moulting Manitous!" said Mr. Payne. "I'll just ring my wife, and hop over. I've got your address in front of me. Thanks most awfully. . . ."

And within five minutes—for by legerdemain or charm of manner he had secured a taxi—his voice was heard in the hall. Having been introduced to Sir Bruton, the latter at once tackled him on his latest book, and conversation proceeded along these lines until coffee and cognac were brought in. Harvey then caught the editor's eye.

"About this information of yours? . . ."

"Oh, yes, by Jove," said Mr. Payne. "Well, it's like this. After you and your wife left Miss Ardmore's place this evening, everything came out all over again. I thought the atmosphere was a trifle taut, you know, and I didn't wonder when I heard. You see, Charles Gartside had to be told the whole story—he didn't know about this Mrs. Porteous, or that French cousin's near miss with a lorry—and I think they more or less forgot about me. I faded into a corner, and

looked at books and things. Then out came this tale of Miss
Ardmore's about the cousin who didn't die in Belgium, and
I began to take notice. I'll tell you why, but, of course, the
whole shoot makes you think, doesn't it? I gather there's a
lot of hard cash in the background, and as a writer of crime
stories the general set-up struck a homely chord straight
away."

Mr. Payne flashed his diffident and engaging smile at Mrs.
Tuke, and refreshed himself with coffee.

"It does smack of the novel," Harvey agreed.

"Thinking of making one out of it, Mr. Payne?" Sir
Bruton queried. "You never know. It might be topical."

The novelist gave him a shrewd look. "What a scoop it
would be. On all the bookstalls, just in time for the trial.
It would be jolly thin ice, of course. . . ."

"Who said anything about trials, young man?"

Rockley Payne grinned. Then his ingenuous face sobered.

"One can't use one's friends, I suppose. There's old
Charles. . . . Anyhow, I've been forestalled, in a way. It's
what I came to tell you, Mr. Tuke. You see, I knew something about the family beforehand. Something these cousins
don't know."

"From your contributor, perhaps?"

"Yes, Raymond told me. In the way of business. It had
to do with a story. I nearly let it out at Miss Ardmore's."

Mr. Payne paused to sip his cognac. Mrs. Tuke watched
him with an indulgent smile, and wondered what his wife
was like. Her husband lay back in his chair in his usual extended formation, and Sir Bruton brooded in a pop-eyed
fashion over the peaceful scene.

"I didn't know Raymond Shearsby at all well," Payne
went on. "In fact, we only met three times. When I wanted
to rope him in again for the *Ludgate* he came to see me.
That was eighteen months ago. He dropped in about a year
later, and then I saw him again a few weeks back, in July.
And that's the real point. What he came about, I mean."

"Then you saw him shortly before his death?" Harvey
said.

"Just over a week before. It was the 19th. Well, a couple of months earlier he'd sent a story along. It was a long-short —seven or eight thousand words. It was about a pack of cousins, only there were five, not six, and a lot of money that was going to come to them. And then an uncle who was supposed to have been dead for years turned up. It ended in the style Shearsby was so good at—there were two or three solutions, and you were left wondering which was right. It was quite up to standard, and after a bit—you know what it is now, with your printers trying to claw along with two nonagenarians and a dog—I sent him the proofs. Actually, on the 15th of July. Oh, and by the way, Shearsby called the story *Too Many Cousins*. "

"Almost disquietingly apt," Mr. Tuke commented.

"You may well say so," Rockley Payne agreed, his deceptively youthful face unwontedly serious. "Because this is what happened next. On the 17th Shearsby rang up to make an appointment. I'm only there at odd times, you know —when I'm snaffling a sandwich lunch, or after ministerial hours—so my secretary fixed up a time for the 19th. Shearsby duly rolled up. He said he'd come to withdraw the story. It couldn't be published. He wanted all the proofs scrapped. And then the trouble came out. It was the first I'd heard about his family, but as you've guessed, he'd based the story on them."

Harvey nodded. Sir Bruton's fishlike stare was fixed on the youthful editor.

"You say the story was sent you a couple of months earlier," he rumbled. "That would be some time after one of the bona fide cousins had been killed."

"Yes. The army man called Dresser," Payne said. "But Shearsby said he'd only just heard of that. He'd missed the paragraph in the papers about it, and he hadn't seen Dresser for a couple of years. Anyway, to start with, he roughed out the whole business of his cousins and the money, and explained how it gave him the idea for the story. As he said, he'd covered up the facts so well, and shuffled the personnel about so thoroughly, that nobody would have spotted the connection, or cared two hoots about it if they did. Because all the characters were without stain or blemish—except one. The resurrected uncle. He was the villain of the piece, if there was one. Anyway, he was a bad hat."

"And what had happened to render the story unprintable," Harvey inquired.

Rockley Payne gave him one of the quick acute looks which belied his irresponsible airs.

"I fancy you've spotted the skeleton," he said with a smile. "Yes, a genuine Shearsby uncle had popped up. Or a second cousin, or something. The older generation, anyhow. The fellow was supposed to have died eighteen years ago. And he *had* been a bit of a bad hat. Shearsby never mentioned his name, but I gathered it was from him that he heard of Captain Dresser's death, and I know I got the idea that the bad hat must be Dresser's father. In other words, Cousin Martin of Miss Ardmore's tale. And in the circumstances Shearsby felt it would be a bit injudicious to publish *Too Many Cousins*. Not that he could have had the faintest notion, poor chap," said Rockley Payne, shaking his head, "how devilishly like the story things were going to pan out. All he was worried about was this fellow's feelings, and the general awkwardness of sailing so near the truth."

"He was quite sure about his facts, I suppose?" Harvey asked.

"Oh, lord, yes," Payne replied. "You see, he'd met the man."

PART TWO:

COMBINATIONS AND PERMUTATIONS

CHAPTER X

WHETHER chief constables grind their teeth fast or slowly, the machinery of Scotland Yard, once put in motion, works rapidly and smoothly, even in wartime. The re-opening of the inquiries into the deaths of Raymond Shearsby and Mrs. Porteous was put in hand within half an hour of Harvey Tuke's visit to the Assistant Commissioner on the morning of Monday, August the 21st.

Negotiations by telephone with the chief constables concerned, those of Hertfordshire and Surrey, conducted by Wray with the tact and persuasiveness of long practice, having reached the foregone conclusion that this new investigation would have to be undertaken by the Central Office, Detective-Inspector W. H. Vance was relieved of some dull researches connected with a corpse dredged from the River Lea and instructed to take over the two cases. Mr. Vance was a quick worker. Having made himself familiar with what was known of the fatalities, and of the family background, he decided to deal with the former in chronological order; and that same afternoon, accompanied by a detective sergeant, he went down to Hertfordshire.

At the small town of Cotfold he discussed the death of Raymond Shearsby with the local police. The police doctor repeated the evidence he had given at the inquest. The body having lain all night in the waters of the Cat Ditch, it might have got there at any time between 7.15, when the writer was last seen alive, and midnight. His last meal had been a light one, probably a meat tea. Before death he had sustained a very severe blow on the side of the head, but this could have been caused by a stumble and violent fall against the brickwork of the bridge beneath which he was found. After a week's heavy rain the stream itself was very full.

Inspector Vance then drove to the village of Dry Stocking, near the Cambridgeshire border, the scene of the tragedy; but preliminary inquiries there added nothing of value. Mortimer Shearsby, in his account to Harvey Tuke, seemed in fact to have covered all that was known about his cousin's end. Mr. Vance left a local sergeant, Oake by name, to carry on inquiries in the district, and with his assistant returned to London by a late train, to be met there by the news, just passed on to the Assistant Commissioner by Mr. Tuke, of the resurrection of Martin Dresser.

Leaving this to be dealt with by routine, the inspector and his aide travelled next day, the 22nd, to Guildford. Here there was more to bite on; for the circumstances of Mrs. Porteous's death were, to say the least, peculiar.

Blanche Porteous had lived in a small bungalow on the Leatherhead road, two miles from the centre of Guildford. She had come to this home with her husband, fifteen years before, and here Cyril Porteous had died. Afterward his widow occasionally took in paying guests, but at the time of her own death she was living alone. By the time of the weekend in question, the August Bank Holiday weekend, school holidays had already begun. On the Saturday morning, the 5th of August, she was seen shopping in Guildford, and it was understood by the woman who cleaned the bungalow and cooked certain meals there that her employer was going to London on the Sunday for the whole day. This woman, a Mrs. Steptoe, did not come on Sundays, and she also had the Monday off; and, accordingly, it was not until the morning of Tuesday, the 8th, that the death of Mrs. Porteous became known. Mrs. Steptoe found her lying on the floor of her little kitchen. On the draining-board of the sink were the dirty plates and cutlery from her last meal—cold meat, potatoes, late rhubarb and cheese. The police surgeon, who carried out the autopsy, gave the approximate time of death as Sunday evening, and the cause poisoning by one of the nitrous salts. A Home Office pathologist later identified this as sodium nitrite, and stated that the acid in the rhubarb would quickly decompose the nitrite and form nitrous oxide, a recognized toxic gas. There were traces of sodium nitrite in some potatoes remaining on a plate, and these had turned a blackish colour. Sodium nitrite in appearance closely resembled common salt, but was less strong in taste, and consequently if mistaken for the latter might be used in greater quantity.

In the kitchen were found a metal salt-caster three parts full of sodium nitrite, and there were several ounces of this in a large tin labelled cooking salt. In a small room said to have been used by the late Cyril Porteous as a laboratory for simple chemical experiments in connection with his work as a science master, a glass container, unlabelled, was found to be half full of sodium nitrite.

Mrs. Steptoe was quite unable to account for the presence of this salt in the kitchen utensils. She had last used the caster while preparing a meal for Mrs. Porteous on the previous Friday evening, the 4th. Mrs. Porteous was perfectly well the following morning, a statement confirmed by acquaintances who later met the school teacher shopping in the town. The caster had been refilled from the tin labelled cooking salt several days before. Mrs. Steptoe could not remember the exact date. She had not been in the little laboratory for some weeks. Mrs. Porteous seldom used the room, and it was only cleaned out occasionally. So far as Mrs. Steptoe knew, the chemicals there had neither been added to nor replenished since Mr. Porteous's death in 1938.

From the report of the inquest, which was held two days later, it was apparent to Inspector Vance that everybody concerned started with the preconceived idea that they were dealing with a case of accidental death. This was, perhaps, only to be expected. Blanche Porteous had been well known and well liked in Guildford for fifteen years. There was no mystery about her. It was common knowledge that her nearest living relatives were a brother and some cousins, a fact confirmed by the former, Mortimer Shearsby, at the inquiry. The chemist did not add to this known domestic background any mention of the considerable fortune involved, presumably because he accepted the prevailing theory of misadventure. There was nothing in the evidence to suggest an alternative to this theory, which was indeed fortified by the dead woman's connection with chemicals and the presence of sodium nitrite in her late husband's laboratory. Even the coroner's assumption that this was the first fatality of its kind helped to support the preconceived idea that someone had blundered. The coroner was, of course, mistaken; and Mortimer Shearsby, though still present, did not draw his attention to the similar case at Bedford a year earlier. The inquiry accordingly became an attempt to fix the blame. Mrs. Steptoe's denial that she had meddled with the chemicals could not be shaken. The coroner pointed out that Mrs. Porteous had prepared her own meals on the Saturday and Sunday, and recorded an open verdict.

The bungalow on the Leatherhead road had been left untouched since its mistress's death, her brother having as yet had no time to dispose of her effects. Inspector Vance's visit there, however, had negative results. Leaving an officer of the Surrey Constabulary to continue researches on the spot, Mr. Vance and his colleague again returned to London. Here, the next morning, that of the 23rd, they began work at the other end, on the movements on or about the essential dates of the interested persons so far known to them. Mlle Boulanger and Miss Ardmore were interviewed. Information received, both from these ladies and from Mr. Tuke, having dragged Messrs. Gartside and Mainward into the orbit of the case, the inspector continued to move in official circles, for while Charles Gartside was at the Ministry of Information, Mr. Mainward was in the Foreign Office. And the afternoon found Mr. Vance at Bedford, calling on Mortimer Shearsby at the laboratories of Imperial Sansil (almost another government department), and on Mrs. Shearsby at 'Aylwynstowe'.

All three cousins had shown signs of strain at these inter-views, but this was to be expected, for police inquiries into deaths by which other persons benefit do not inspire the latter, howsoever innocent, with ease and gaiety. Mlle Boulanger was defensive and aggrieved, Miss Ardmore on her dignity and rather snappy, and Mortimer Shearsby alternately twittery and bellicose. Asked why, at the inquest on his sister, he had remained silent about the previous case of sodium nitrite poisoning, the chemist got on his high horse and lectured Inspector Vance about moral sabotage, on the lines of his apologia to Mr. Tuke. If the inspector said, 'Poppycock' to himself, for the time being he left it at that.

As for Lilian Shearsby and the two young men, the lady had been a little hoity-toity, and revealed plainly her animus against Miss Ardmore, though having perhaps taken her husband's warnings to heart, she also left it at that. Mr. Gartside had looked at the inspector as though he were some noxious species of insect, and Guy Mainward appeared to be doing his best to be helpful.

The outcome of routine questions about dates and times and movements was as inconclusive as such preliminary probings commonly are. These questions were put to all six concerned; for while the two civil servants supplied certain alibis for Miss Ardmore and Mlle Boulanger, Charles Gartside had also an established interest in Vivien's finances, and Guy Mainward, to all appearance, as good as one in Cecile's. And Lilian Shearsby was even more directly a beneficiary by the deaths of her cousins by marriage.

Going back to April the 10th, though Cecile might have cause to remember that she was all but run over by a lorry at approximately 9.10 p.m., the inspector hardly hoped that any of the other five would pretend to remember their move-ments on a particular evening four months ago. And so it proved. Miss Ardmore and the civil servants were admittedly in London, and the Mortimer Shearsbys could easily have got there. The last train back to Bedford did not leave St. Pancras

till 9.50. In the interim report on all these proceedings which
Mr. Vance drew up, he noted that Mlle Boulanger's own
story required confirmation.

Coming to the 28th of July, when Raymond Shearsby met
his death, memories began to improve. The chemist said he
was no doubt in his garden—during the summer months he
was seldom out of it in his spare time—from 6.15 until his
wife returned late from a day in Cambridge. Miss Ardmore
spent the whole evening with her fiancé, while Cecile went
to a lecture at the *Institut Français* and then returned to her
lodgings in Pimlico. Lilian Shearsby attended a W.V.S.
conference at Cambridge, where she also shopped and dined,
leaving at 9 o'clock by bus for Hitchen, where she changed
buses, arriving home at 10.45. Charles Gartside was with his
Vivien from 6 o'clock onwards, and Mr. Mainward passed
the evening in his flat, communing, as he put it, with his Muse.
It appeared that he was something of a poet.

Inspector Vance now came to the Bank Holiday weekend,
which provided chunks of evidence of a peculiarly baffling
sort. He provisionally accepted Mrs. Steptoe's story that
the caster in the kitchen of the bungalow contained ordinary
cooking salt as late as the evening of Friday, the 4th of August,
when she prepared a meal there. On the medical evidence
this gave two whole days, the Saturday and Sunday, during
which the substitution of sodium nitrite for the salt must
have been effected. It was not known whether Mrs. Porteous
had used the caster on the Saturday, and she was believed
to have spent most of the Sunday in London, though where
or with whom remained to be discovered. The movements
of the six persons involved required accordingly to be traced
throughout both those days. All six partook at least in part
of the general holiday. Even if the schoolteacher was at
home on the Saturday afternoon (which was in doubt) any
one of them might have called on her; and as for the Bank
Holiday Sunday the whole world could have walked in.
When Blanche Porteous was out she left her clumsy front door
key, after the casual fashion of the country, on a ledge above
the door. To make things a little more difficult, the bungalow

was two hundred yards from the nearest house, and screened by trees and a bend of the road.

Mortimer Shearsby's weekend, by his own account, was spent as to the Saturday alone in his garden, while on Sunday he took his bicycle and some food and rode to Lilly Hoo, above Hitchen. Leaving the bicycle padlocked under a hedge, he walked about the hills until late in the evening. He did not call anywhere, even for a drink. His tone implied that such was not his habit.

Cecile Boulanger was at work or with friends all the Saturday. On Sunday she took a sandwich lunch and went for a long walk in the Hampton and Kingston district, returning home about six in time to spend the evening with Mr. Mainward. Vivien Ardmore could also claim some sort of an alibi for Saturday, when both she and Mr. Gartside had the day to themselves and went together to Kew Gardens and Richmond. On the Sunday she took herself off alone, like her cousin Cecile, and tramped over the country about Windsor, returning to Falcon Mews East at nine o'clock.

Of the three secondary characters, Lilian Shearsby went to London on the Saturday morning, shopped there, saw a film, dined (at a Corner House, with several thousand other people), and caught the 8.5 train home. The Sunday she spent mostly with the gnomes and frogs in the garden of 'Aylwynstowe', while her husband roamed the hills. Charles Gartside's Saturday stood or fell with Miss Ardmore's, but his Sunday was one long alibi, for he was on duty at the Ministry of Information until a late hour. With Mr. Mainward conversely, the Foreign Office in the morning, a friend in the afternoon, and a Home Guard picquet at the F.O. again from 6 p.m. onwards, carried him happily through the first half of the period; but after his picquet was relieved at 6 a.m. on Sunday his later movements actually brought him within a few miles of Guildford. He had lunch and tea with relatives at Godalming, returning to London just in time to meet Mlle Boulanger in the evening.

All this the Metropolitan police and the constabularies of four counties were endeavouring to check. The Ministry

of War Transport and all haulage concerns were asked for
news of a convoy routed down Warwick Way on the night of
the 10th of April; and in London and Guildford and Bedford,
at Cambridge and Stocking, patient inquiries were covering
the 28th of July and the Bank Holiday weekend. There was
only too little corroboration of the six statements, and of this
little much was suspect. With one married couple, one engaged, and a third apparently verging on betrothal, the
possibility of collusion was always in Inspector Vance's
mind.

That mind was a tidy one, which liked tangible facts to
work on; and so far it was dealing with known people, people
who could be interrogated and watched and described. But
during the last two days of this routine it had been nagged
by the thought of the new and nebulous factor injected into
the case. The mystery of Martin Dresser would have to be
solved. If alive, he had the same incentive as the younger
generation to remove a cousin or two. And there was a suggestive shadow on his past from which theirs was free.

Raymond Shearsby's statement to Rockley Payne, a casual
remark to the Vicar of Stocking, and the evidence of the
cancelled story, formed the meagre support for the case of
survival. They were enough, however, to compel respect,
especially the story, since, good feeling apart, the sacrifice of
twenty-five guineas must have been a consideration to an
impoverished writer. Raymond had undoubtedly met someone whom he believed to be his cousin Martin. That meeting,
vide the Vicar of Stocking, took place in London, and not
earlier than the 15th of July, when the proofs of Too Many
Cousins were despatched from the office of The Ludgate Magazine.
Somewhere, then, among London's eight millions, there must
be sought a man of fifty-seven, of whom no recent description
or portrait was extant, who had in all probability changed his
name, and whose occupation was unknown. And the first
two days' work on the trail had produced not one further
whiff of a scent, even of proof that Martin was alive.

It was scarcely credible that Sydney Dresser had not
known of his father's return to England. But he had kept the

secret well, and not only from his cousins. His personal papers, which had been handed to Mlle Boulanger, who said she had not yet looked through them, were searched in vain for any allusion to Martin. Those of Raymond, less manuscripts and printed matter, were collected from 'Aylwynstowe', to prove equally unhelpful, as was the untidy accumulation of documents in the bungalow at Guildford. Letters might have been abstracted, but why? A guilty conscience would have seen the value of this red herring from the past. Another blank was drawn with Captain Dresser's bank books. There were no untraceable payments, and no large sums had been drawn in cash.

The old story of Martin's defalcations, his old friends in Chelmsford, literary coteries where Raymond might have talked (but where he was almost unknown), the latter's literary agent and one or two acquaintances met since his return from France, even Miss Wicksteed, the companion of the second Mrs. Rutland Shearsby, slowly dying in her flat in Chelsea—these were among further avenues explored which proved to be dead ends. *Non est inventus* Martin Dresser remained.

CHAPTER XI

AND not only Martin Dresser. The police, like archaeologists, never know what they may dig up; and though patient spadework had so far unearthed little of apparent value, it had casually cast upon the scene two new and nameless actors. It was doubtful whether their entry had any bearing upon the case, but as a coincidence it called for explanation. Unfortunately, after brief and mysterious posturings, the pair had vanished again into the unknown from which they had emerged.

Inspector Vance inserted in his report some notes on railways, omnibuses, road-mileages and routes. He remarked on the hopelessness (lacking a stroke of luck) of tracing individuals on the numerous and densely crowded trains running between London and Guildford; nor were those on the London–Bedford line much more promising. Country omnibuses were better, and a fairly frequent service of these over the triangle Bedford–Hitchen–Cambridge included some which passed Stocking Corner, two miles north of the village. Finally, two miles south of it, was Whipstead station, on the King's Cross and Cambridge line.

This station stood isolated, half a mile from Whipstead village. Less than a dozen trains stopped there during the day. It was the sort of place the coy criminal would be expected to avoid, but criminals make mistakes and are tied by circumstances; and inquiries were made at Whipstead as a matter of course. They were fruitful only in the unexpected, for they turned up the two *incogniti*.

On the 28th of July, the evening of Raymond Shearsby's death, the 5.10 from Cambridge to London, stopping at Whipstead at 5.31, emitted about a dozen passengers, all, with one exception, local residents well known to the station staff, which consisted of the stationmaster and a youthful porter. The exception was a young man carrying a suitcase. He had a third class return from Cambridge. The stationmaster, retiring to the ticket office, saw no more of him at that time; but the porter watched him take the road to Whipstead village. Both officials were certain that they had never seen this stranger before. They described him as having a fresh colour and a small-featured, boyish face. He was wearing a neat but by no means new suit of blue serge, with a large cloth cap pulled over his eyes.

Between the infrequent trains the station staff usually dispersed—the stationmaster to his house near by, the porter to his home in Whipstead. The next stopping train after the 5.31 was the 6.43 from King's Cross, on its way to Cambridge. The porter returned to the station soon after half-past six, and while wheeling milk-churns down the platform saw a figure leaning on the parapet of the road bridge which crossed the line just beyond the platform ramp. It was the strange young man in the blue serge suit: the porter recognized him by his large cloth cap. From the high bridge one obtained an extensive view northward over the flat country about Stocking, and the stranger was gazing over this landscape. On hearing the rattle of the milk churns he looked down at the platform and withdrew out of sight.

The 6.43 discharged quite a crowd of local people who had been to London for the day. Among them was a second stranger—a tall, greyhaired man of gentlemanlike appearance, dressed in a grey tweed suit and a grey felt hat. He carried an attaché-case. The stationmaster, who took his ticket—a third class single from King's Cross—thought he had a vaguely ecclesiastical air, but could not explain more precisely what he meant. This newcomer seemed to know his way about, for though he made no inquiry he was seen by the stationmaster, from the ticket office window, strolling at the tail of a little procession taking the footpath which cut across the chord of the loop made by the road from Stocking. Except in very miry weather this path was always used by people walking between that village and the station.

There was an interval of just over an hour before the next train pulled in. This was the 7.48 from Cambridge, which set down some more local residents and provided no surprises. It was followed, at 8.5, by the last stopping train of the day. On the down line, it was due in at Cambridge at 8.27.

This train, like the others, was almost on time. It was signalled, and its smoke could be seen, when the young man in the blue suit hurried into the station. The porter, who clipped his return ticket, said he was a little breathless. He was still carrying his suitcase. The train discharged a further body of passengers: pushing his way through them, the young man boarded it and was conveyed from the scene.

The countryman's passionate interest in strangers having supplied not only news, but quite good descriptions, of these two travellers, Sergeant Oake continued, as a matter of routine, to follow up the clues thus provided. He did not really expect them to lead anywhere: the travellers bore no resemblance to any of the *dramatis personae* of whom he had information, and they had no doubt come to Whipstead

station for legitimate reasons, which would soon appear.
But now came the perplexing part of this piece of by-play.
No such reasons were discoverable. The two strangers had
come to this isolated station, from opposite directions, without
any apparent object.

The young man in blue had been seen in the outskirts of
Whipstead, carrying his suitcase, at about half-past five.
He had then gone down a lane which led nowhere in particular, reappearing in the village an hour later on his way
back to the station. In Whipstead he called nowhere and
spoke to nobody, and he was quite unknown in the place.
He was lost to view again between 6.30, when the porter saw
him on the bridge, and his return to the station to catch the
8.5. He had not gone back to Whipstead, nor on to Stocking.
In short, he seemed to have come from Cambridge for the
pleasure of walking about with his luggage for three hours.

As for the tall elderly man in grey, last seen strolling up
the path to Stocking, that village had not glimpsed hide or
hair of him. A quarter of a mile from the station the path
ran beside a loop of the Cat Ditch, here screened by willows
and other shrubs. At this point a second path forked off to
the west, crossing the stream by a plank bridge, and con-
tinuing over the fields came out in the lane in which Raymond
Shearsby's cottage stood, between that cottage and the
bridge beneath which the writer's body was found. The man
in grey must have taken this route, but where he was bound
there was no showing. He should have been near the cottage
before half-past seven. By that time Raymond Shearsby
could have returned from his visit to the inn.

Here, then, after all, were puzzles which must be cleared
up. Sergeant Oake, aided by the constables who lived in the
two villages, began a thorough raking of the countryside for
news of the two strangers. But up to the hour when Inspector
Vance completed his interim report, no such news had come
in.

CHAPTER XII

"THEY'RE all possibles," Wray said.

It was the morning of Thursday, the 24th, and Inspector Vance's summary of the first three days' work on the case was under discussion. The Assistant Commissioner's appointment with Sir Bruton Kames was about other matters, but the Director, pronouncing them damned dull, demanded what he called a bit of jam. He instanced the affair of the cousins, in which he now seemed to take an interest. Mr. Tuke, meeting him in the interim at the Senior Universities, needed no persuasion to give up another hour of his holiday in the same cause.

"Take La Boulanger," Wray continued. "She may have told a cock and bull story. On the other hand, if it's true, three of the others were on the spot here in London. The chemist knocks off at six, so he could have done it, and still caught his last train back to Bedford. So could his wife. Then this place Stocking is only nineteen miles from Bedford, and he could have got there and back on his bike after work before his wife came home. Or she could have caught an earlier bus from Cambridge, hopped off near Stocking, and picked up the later one after she'd done the job. La Boulanger may have been on her way down there when she says she was at the *Institut Français*. The Ardmore girl's alibi depends on Gartside, and his on her. Mainward has none—he can't call Calliope as a witness."

Sir Bruton, who was sliding under his vast table, heaved himself back into a sitting posture, showering cheroot ash about him as he did so.

"This W.V.S. beano," he said. "The women would be wearing their classy green rig-out. Pretty conspicuous."

Wray grinned foxily. "Mrs. Mortimer's Norman Hartnell creation had gone to the cleaners. She went to Cambridge in ordinary clothes." He paused to light a cigarette, and went on through the smoke: "I've looked at the map. There are footpaths all over the place, and a back lane to Shearsby's cottage and the bridge. No need to go through the village to get there. And the country's like a desert. So the fact that we haven't heard of any stranger so far means nothing. The trouble is, we don't know when the fellow was killed. It could have been immediately after he left the pub. Nobody else seems to have used the lane that evening. He may have found one of his cousins sitting on the bridge in the mellow sunset, waiting for him with a half-brick."

"And you wonder I don't like the country," Mr. Tuke murmured. "But when you say no one else used the lane that evening, what about the mysterious gent from the station, believed to have headed that way?"

"I hadn't forgotten him. I was thinking of the locals. We want to find the man, of course. We've no reason to connect him with the case, but if there was any dirty work in that lane about half-past seven, he may have seen something. Or somebody. Vance will have that in hand. Though he doesn't seem to have made up his mind yet if there *is* a case."

"Haven't you a mind of your own, Wray?"

"There are a good many things on it at the moment besides your holiday task," Wray snapped.

"Now, birdies, birdies!" said Sir Bruton, leering at them. But he seemed abstracted, and the leer became a scowl as Wray laced his fingers and cracked them loudly. "I wish to God you wouldn't do that, Wray. It makes me jump."

"Too much uric acid. Or something. Now about Guildford," Wray went on. "These infernal cousins and their friends seem to have gone out of their way to make trouble. Any one of them could have been there. One day or the other they were mooning about by themselves. Damn it, you wouldn't think any bunch of people would spend so much time alone."

"They're intelligent people, Wray," Mr. Tuke said. "Lacking the herd instinct. You wouldn't know. You don't meet the type."

Wray shrugged this off. "I don't think Vance will make much of the Guildford end, anyway. I've told him Stocking's his best bet. It may be a desert, but if a stranger was anywhere near it on the 28th we'll hear about it sooner or later, or I don't know the country."

A curious internal rumbling was proceeding from Sir Bruton. His scowl became malevolent.

"It's a mess!" he bellowed suddenly. "Take it away, Wray. Tidy it up. I have to give opinions, haven't I? I want *cases*, don't I? Not a lot of damned bits and pieces you haven't even begun to put together. Vance is right. It isn't a case—not yet. Wasting my time. I'm a busy man. Take it away. Take Tuke away. Jumping Jeroboam, when a man's on his holiday, he damn' well ought to *be* on his holiday, not cluttering up busy blokes' offices."

"*J'y suis, j'y reste*," said Mr. Tuke, settling himself deeper in his chair. "I'm here by invitation."

"It's cancelled——"

"And you asked for it," Wray pointed out reasonably. "You wanted some jam. And I'm still in two minds about the business myself. I wanted your ideas on it."

"It isn't jam. It's a mess," said Sir Bruton, removing a mangled Trichinopoli from his mouth and spitting tobacco leaf in the direction of his wastepaper basket. "And you can't soft soap *me*. Ideas? I've given 'em. Tidy the thing up before you bring it here again. Make up what you call your mind whether you've got one murderer, or half a dozen, or a pack of exhibitionists leading you up the garden. And find this missing link. Martin Whatever-his-name-is. If he's alive, it upsets the whole applecart. Alive or dead, you won't have a case till you've found out which. I wouldn't pass it, not if the bench of bishops saw one of these confounded cousins clumping another with a battleaxe. The defence would play Old Harry with this Martin Thingamajig. Just the stuff to muddle a jury. Damn' fools. Well, off you go. Take it away. . . ."

A little later, on the stairs, Mr. Tuke turned to Wray.

"The old boy's right, you know."

"About the zombie, who was dead and is alive? Perhaps you can tell us how to put our hands on him," Wray said rather pettishly. Long experience of the Director had not inured him to the latter's contrariness. "The fellow *would* stage his death in Belgium. Things are chaotic there, and whole rooms full of public records went up in smoke in the Palais de Justice. How is anyone going to trace an obscure Englishman who is said to have died nearly twenty years ago?"

"Yes, I had thought of that difficulty."

"And the only two people here who seem to have known the truth, his son and the writer chap, are very definitely dead. If there's anything in the story, the son must have known. He trumped up the whole thing. Even to having a paragraph in the local paper. It's there, all right. Died at Bruges. . . . Damn it, I don't believe it. Can you tell me why any sane man should go through all that hocus pocus, whatever he'd done?"

"Oh, yes, I can understand that," Mr. Tuke said, and Wray looked at him in some surprise. "Talking of the son, how much did he leave? And to whom?"

"He had a few hundreds. Half went to Mlle Boulanger, and half was shared among the remaining cousins."

"Do you know when he drew up his will?"

"1939, I think. Vance has the details."

"Well, it gives you one suggestive pointer, doesn't it?"

"Which one?" Wray asked cautiously.

"If Dresser's father is alive, he is in no need of money, or his son would surely have left him his savings."

"I don't see that that helps us much."

"It is something to know that you are looking for a man who is probably at least comfortably off."

"Perhaps his son had quarrelled with him. And anyway, the son never had helped him, according to his pass books."

"Think it out, Wray. When the father went abroad, the son was still a boy. He wasn't earning enough to have anything to spare. But everything goes to show that he was willing to do a lot for his father, even to telling elaborate lies about his death and to keeping up the hoax for nearly twenty years. Even if they did quarrel later—which is pure speculation—one would still expect him to do something in his will, if the need was there. In the absence of evidence to the contrary, I prefer the simple explanation that the need was not there. Somehow the elder Dresser has made some money. Apparently he had little or nothing when he went abroad eighteen years ago. There is a family story that he had a job as a waiter. He may have made a fortune out of tips—but not, I should say, in Belgium."

They had reached the lobby, and Wray was glancing at his watch.

"What's this leading to?" he asked impatiently.

"To the suggestion that the elder Dresser came back to this country fairly soon, and managed to get some decent job here."

"Damn it, Tuke, you talk about speculation! We don't even know that the man *is* alive!"

"We're pretty sure he is. I am. You are. In any case, as the old man says, you've got to find him, or prove that he's dead, before you can get anywhere with this case. Fun for you. Have you thought that he might be the elderly bag of mystery at Whipstead station?"

"It occurred to me, yes. But it's the merest supposition."

"Going back to wills, did Raymond Shearsby and Mrs. Porteous leave anything worth having?"

"Shearsby had practically nothing. He seems to have lived from story to story. He left no will. Mrs. Porteous had a little put by. It goes to a friend, another schoolmarm. Even with the sale of her furniture and books, it will only amount to a couple of hundred or so. She pointed out in her will that her cousins always knew they would get their shares in great-grandpapa's money, so she wasn't leaving them anything."

"I suppose none of the six had, or have, any other expectations?"

"None that I've heard· of. What's the point of all this?"

"I don't know. I'm merely fishing round." In his abrupt way Mr. Tuke changed the subject. "What does Vance think of Mortimer Shearsby?"

"He can't make up his mind whether the man's a fool, or very much the reverse and putting it on."

"Rather my predicament. He interests me. The scientific mind is a single-track instrument. Sometimes it runs on a very narrow gauge. And of course our B.Sc. is the complete egotist—which," Mr. Tuke added, "may or may not be significant. All murderers, for example, are egotists. One more thing, Wray . . ."

Wray was heading for the door. "Yes?" he said over his shoulder.

"Kames made another shrewd suggestion. He has an uncanny way of hitting an almost invisible nail on the head. He suggested that you were being led up the garden. I have had rather the same feeling myself."

"I can't say I've felt it," Wray said.

"I expect you will. What I feel to-day, you feel to-morrow."

Wray gave his neigh of a laugh. "I like your nerve, Tuke. We can manage this case ourselves, thank you."

"I love you, Wray," Mr. Tuke said with a grin. "I can always get a rise out of you. Well, it's an interesting case," he added, as they went out into the street. "And if there should be a fourth mishap in the Shearsby family, it will be instructive to see how it is brought about."

Wray gave him a rather startled glance. "We don't want any more."

"Then tell Inspector Vance to stop this silly tinkering with the accident idea. He's dealing with murder, and it becomes a habit. And in this case the motive grows stronger with every death. The whole business has an empirical air, too. I should say it began as a try-out, suggested by Captain Dresser's death. The 'prentice hand had a shot at Mlle Boulanger, and bungled it. But it has steadily improved with practice. The two successful attempts were quite efficiently done. You'll have your work cut out with either to send us up a case we'll even look at."

"I think the inspector can be safely left to handle the thing in his own way," Wray said stiffly.

Mr. Tuke grinned even more diabolically. "By the way," he said, "I'm spending the night at Cambridge. Having saved some petrol, I shall take the car. Anything I can do for you?"

"Nothing, thank you."

"I thought of coming home by way of Stocking and Bedford."

Wray gave him a foxy look. "Sticking your nose in again? I can't stop you, unfortunately."

"I am always interested in backgrounds. Well, bye-bye, Wray. I'll see you when I come back."

"Oh, don't bother," said Wray.

PART THREE:

UNDISTRIBUTED FACTORS

CHAPTER XIII

MR. TUKE's engagement in Cambridge was to dine and sleep at the home on the Madingly road of a bachelor friend of his undergraduate days who was now a don. He drove there at his usual high speed by way of Baldock and Royston; but on departing after breakfast the next morning he turned the Delage down Grange Road, past Selwyn and Newnham, to the road to Wimpole. Crossing Ermine Street he began to explore the tortuous lanes about Wendy and Shingay. He remembered this country from his own Cambridge days, and he had been in the neighbourhood again just before the war, when he got himself mixed up with the murder of Norman Sleight. The landscape was flat and marshy; little streams flowed under little bridges, and in wet seasons were apt to ignore these and take short cuts over the roads. It was not wet now, but merely dull: a sort of sunlight filtered through a canopy of cloud of a shapeless and nondescript type. It was, in fact, a typical August day. Presently the ground began to rise gently, and as the black car passed from Cambridgeshire into Herts a line of low hills rose against the grey sky. Somewhere at the foot of these lay Stocking.

There were, correctly, a pair of Stockings—Dry Stocking and Stocking End, but the map showed the latter to consist of no more than a few cottages. The map also showed Stocking Corner, on the road Mr. Tuke was now following, and the Cat Ditch, which was an affluent of one of the streams he had already crossed and therefore of the Cam, or Rhee, as this mutable river is called in these parts. He did not turn at the Corner, but drove on a couple of miles to a lane which would take him to Stocking by a more roundabout route, past Raymond Shearsby's cottage and over the bridge which featured in the story of the writer's death. Almost all pasture land, this stretch of country was little populated. In the two miles he saw only two farms and a dilapidated bungalow. He met a green omnibus, on its way from Hitchin to Cambridge, and overtook one car. Then he came to the lane he was seeking, and, turning down it, seemed to leave the inhabited world altogether.

The lane, in its windings, headed south and then east. Two miles and more along it stood a lonely little cottage of lath and plaster and thatch, which Harvey knew had been Raymond Shearsby's. It was unoccupied, and when he walked up the neglected garden and peered through the windows he found it as empty as a drum. The scenery around, to his prejudiced eye, was infinitely depressing. No other building was in sight; everywhere stretched pasture, peopled only by cattle switching their tails at the flies. Clumps of old trees lifted their heavy foliage to the cloudy sky. Raymond Shearsby's stories were not those of a morbid or anti-social mind, and he must have taken refuge in this backward corner of Hertfordshire because he escaped from France with little in his pocket and the cottage was cheap. And he had never been able to get away. As Wray had put it, he had lived from story to story.

The lane wound on between high ragged hedges towards the village. A few hundred yards beyond the cottage, in the middle of a bend, it humped itself over a small bridge; and Mr. Tuke pulled up again and got out. But there was little to speak of what had happened on that July evening three weeks ago. At the western end of the bridge there was a gap at one side of the lane between the brick parapet and the hedge, which, like its fellow, rose from a grass verge. Beyond the gap was a steep fall of several feet to the Cat Ditch below, a fall too steep for cattle or horses. Anyone with poor sight, blundering on a dark night into the hedge or the parapet, might easily plunge headlong into the stream. This was a bigger volume of water than its local name had led Mr. Tuke to expect. It was much more than a ditch: it was a little river, some ten feet across. It seemed to be several feet deep, and no doubt carried a good deal more water at the end of that wet July. The turbid current flowed steadily northward, and as it whispered past the slimy brick-work it was seen to be swifter and more powerful than it appeared between the wider banks. At its deepest, however, a kick or two should take a man to these shallows. But the young writer had received a blow on the head, it was assumed from a stumble against the parapet. Half stunned when he fell into the water, he was drowned before he could regain full consciousness.

Mr. Tuke surveyed what little of the winding lane was in sight. Vision was limited to twenty yards either way, and the ragged hedges were head-high. If the writer had died by accident, it must have been after dark, which meant, in July with double summer time, not much before eleven o'clock. He must also have been coming *from* his cottage, for there was no gap at the other end of the bridge. But if his death had been no accident, as Harvey himself firmly believed, then it could have taken place as early as half-past seven, when he was returning from the inn. This blind turn of the land was an ideal spot at which to waylay any-body at any time, for even now, at eleven in the morning, for all visual signs of human life there were one might have been in the Gobi Desert. The faint noise of a tractor, the whistle of a train, the rumble of aircraft, the lowing of cattle—these sounds only accentuated the loneliness of the scene. Harvey Tuke had his own dash of imagination, and he saw with his mind's eye a figure sitting waiting on the little bridge. Now it was a shadow in the darkness, now, in the evening light, a sort of composite of all the other cousins and their friends, or the faceless mask of a man long dead. He saw it getting up with a word of welcome as the victim drew near, pointing to something in the stream below, bidding him turn and look. . . .

His satanic face was very grim as he walked back to his car. Driving on, within a few minutes he had come to the end of the lane, where it entered a wider road fifty yards south of the last houses of Dry Stocking. A short way down the village street a projecting sign depicted a barrel with a lath of wood against it. Discovering that W. Twitchell, the licensee of The Bushel and Strike, sold spirits as well as beer, Mr. Tuke got out once more and entered the inn.

Only Mr. Twitchell himself, a large bald man with an impediment in his speech, was in the bar. Scarcely believing his eyes, the traveller saw among a row of bottles on a shelf a sherry of an excellent and now rare brand. Mr. Twitchell poured him a generous glass, and, on invitation, drew himself a mugful of ale.

"Your health, s-s-sir," said Mr. Twitchell.

They discoursed for a time on the weather, and then Harvey introduced the subject of Raymond Shearsby's death.

"I knew him by name," he said. "A bad business."

"Terrible, sir," said Mr. Twitchell, wagging his bald head. "A very p-p-pleasant young gentleman. In here that v-v-very evening, he was. Had his pint, and says 'g-g-good night, all,' and walks out as happy as Higgin-b-b-bottom."

"Excuse my ignorance, but who is Higginbottom?"

"It's a s-s-saying, sir. As happy as Higginbottom, who laughed when his wife hanged h-h-herself."

"It was still daylight then," Harvey remarked. "I suppose Mr. Shearsby came out again after dark."

"He did most of his writing at n-n-night, sir, and he'd often go for a walk after, before he went to b-b-bed."

"I looked in at the window of his cottage. All the furniture seems to have been taken away."

"His cousin, that was, sir. A gentleman from B-b-bedford. He took ch-ch-charge of everything, and he sold the furniture to p-p-pay for the funeral."

"Mr. Raymond not having left much money, I dare say?"

"Only a few p-p-pounds, his cousin said. He never had a lot. But he was always free with his m-m-money, when he had any. Not like s-s-some," Mr. Twitchell added darkly.

"The cousin, for instance?" Harvey queried at a venture.

"No names, no p-p-pack-drill," said Mr. Twitchell cannily. "But furniture f-f-fetches a rare price these days, and the funeral was done cheap enough. Well, it takes all s-s-sorts to make a world. There's some is freehanded gentlemen, like our Mr. Sh-sh-shearsby, and there's others as mean as M-m-morris."

"I don't think I've heard of him either. What did he do?"

"It's another saying, s-s-sir. As mean as Morris, who hopped on one l-l-leg to save shoe-leather."

Mr. Tuke was so pleased with these parables that he offered Mr. Twitchell a Larranaga. When this was lighted, he said:

"Had Mr. Shearsby any particular friends here?"

"Only the V-v-vicar, sir. He's lived abroad, like Mr. Shearsby, and it was a link b-b-between them, as Hopkins said."

"On what occasion did Hopkins say that?"

"He was handcuffed to a b-b-bobby, sir."

"On that evening Mr. Shearsby left here at a quarter-past seven, I'm told," Mr. Tuke said. "A little early, wasn't it?"

"He'd come and go at all t-t-times, sir. It was just on the quarter that night. I remember he l-l-looked at the clock there, and then at his watch, and w-w-went off."

Mr. Tuke changed the subject. "I had a look at your Cat Ditch. It is quite a little river. What is the depth?"

Mr. Twitchell finished his ale, set down his tankard, and wiped his lips with a hand like a ham.

"Three to f-f-four feet now, sir. But there was another three feet more water at the end of l-l-last month."

"As much as that?"

"It had been raining c-c-cats and dogs, sir, and you'd be surprised the amount of water the old D-d-ditch'll bring down when she's in flood. C-c-cattle get drowned in her, and last w-w-winter a little old pig was c-c-carried clean along to the Cam. Most of the streams hereabouts are shallow and slow, like, but the Ditch is d-d-different. Rises out of a spring, she does, up in the hills behind W-w-whipstead. Slap out of a f-f-face of rock."

"I didn't know there was any rock in this part of the world. I thought it was all chalk and gravel and clay."

"Chalk makes clunch, sir, and it's m-m-mighty hard," Mr. Twitchell said. "And it makes w-w-wonderful clear water, and good beer, too. This here ale comes from the C-c-cat Ditch. Marston's B-b-brewery, at Whipstead. We live by the old D-d-ditch, you might say." He waved his immense hand towards the street and the village at large. "Once upon a time there was a t-t-terrible drought. Even the old Ditch near d-d-dried up, and the wells were dry, and th-th-that's how the village got its name. D-d-dry Stocking they called it, ever after. There's a s-s-saying about it. As d-d-dry as Stocking when there was no b-b-beer."

Two labouring men entered the bar, and in the road outside a car could be heard drawing up before the inn. Mr. Tuke prepared to take his departure, and as he bade Mr. Twitchell good morning two more customers were coming in. The leader was a man in a rather loud check jacket, loose in the shoulders but short as to the sleeves, and flannel trousers that also had the air of being adapted to a different figure. The broad peak of his cloth cap almost rested on a large pair of horn-rimmed spectacles, so that little was to be seen of his face beyond a long nose and an ingratiating smile which showed indifferent teeth. Tufts of silvery hair were visible above his ears. His companion, shorter and stouter, with a coarse red face and hands, was dressed in a stained and shiny suit of blue serge and an ancient felt hat. As Harvey passed the pair, the owlish horn-rims and the smile were turned benevolently on him for a moment.

A blue Morris saloon, a good deal older than the war, was drawn up in rear of the Delage. Before Harvey moved off, he looked at his map: then he backed, turned, and headed south, away from the village. As Inspector Vance had mentioned in his report, the road from Dry Stocking to Whipstead Station curved eastward to take in the few

houses which were Stocking End. Then it turned westward
to complete a wide loop; the embankment and telegraph
poles of the railway appeared ahead; and within a minute
the Delage ran into the station yard. The road passed on,
to turn once more due south and cross the line by a high
bridge on its way to Whipstead village, hidden among trees
half a mile away. The little railway station stood isolated,
with only one house, obviously the stationmaster's, near by.

Map in hand, Harvey strolled onto the bridge. From
this eminence, as Mr. Vance had also remarked, a good
view was obtained of the shallow basin in which Dry Stocking
lay. That village and its church were plainly visible, and
the sweep of the road by which Mr. Tuke had come, and
the footpath cutting the chord of the arc, taken by the man
in the grey suit on the evening of Raymond Shearsby's
death. West of this the willows and shrubs lining the Cat
Ditch made a curve in the opposite direction to that of the
road. Near at hand stream and path and road drew together
as they approached the railway; and here the observer
could see the branch path, with its plank footbridge, striking
off towards the lonely cottage in the lane. The cottage
itself, three miles away, could not be detected among the
distant trees. Just beyond the road bridge on which Mr.
Tuke was standing another bridge, of iron girders, carried
the railway over the Cat Ditch. To the south, beyond Whipstead, rose the low hills where the little river had its spring.

After a thoughtful survey of this green landscape, Harvey
walked back to the station. It was deserted, for only certain
morning and evening trains stopped here. Having studied
the time-tables, he returned to his car and drove back to
Stocking.

CHAPTER XIV

THE Vicarage stood beside the church, an ugly house with
its window surrounds painted the repellent chocolate colour
favoured by the Ecclesiastical Commissioners. Mr. Tuke

pulled gingerly at an old-fashioned bell-knob. Its behaviour was true to type. First it appeared to have stuck, and then about a foot of shank came away in his hand and a fearful clanging rang through the house.

The echoes still reverberated as the front door opened. A woman with a shock of untidy grey curls peered up at the visitor.

"It's my husband's fault," she said. "He's been going to oil that bell ever since he was inducted——"

She stopped abruptly, her mouth open, as she took in Mr. Tuke's features. Any clergyman's wife, meeting a personification of the Devil on her doorstep, might well be startled.

"You can warn your husband what to expect," said Harvey, grinning. "Is he at home?"

Rallying, the lady turned and called loudly: "Athanasius! Athanasius!"

A distant voice replied from somewhere above.

"What's the matter?"

"Someone to see you."

"The name is Tuke," said Harvey. "Your husband would not know me. I am making some inquiries about a late neighbour of yours, Raymond Shearsby."

This news having been relayed, the distant voice announced that its owner was coming down. The Vicar's wife opened a door beside her and led the way into a shabby but comfortable drawing-room.

"Our name is Fawkes, by the way," she said. "My husband is always trying to prove that Guy Fawkes was a member of his family. Ah, here he is!"

A round little man burst into the room. The Reverend Athanasius Fawkes had rather the air of bouncing like a ball, which in figure he resembled. His very bright blue eyes stared aggressively from a pink round face, ornamented by tufts of white eyebrow and a bristle of white hair which grew into an unruly cockscomb. His dress was unorthodox —a baggy flannel suit and a grey flannel shirt with an open collar.

"Well, well," he said, looking truculently at the visitor. "Mr. Duke, eh?"

"Tuke," said Harvey.

"My mistake," said the Vicar in his abrupt way, but with a sudden attractive smile. "So you knew Shearsby?"

"No, I only knew his work."

"Clever fellow. Nice fellow, too. I shall miss him. You a Cambridge man?"

"John's."

"Thought so. I was at Caius. Long before your time, though. Well, why not sit down. Have a cigarette. Have we got any cigarettes, Alice?"

"You gave the last to that tramp yesterday," Mrs. Fawkes said. "I haven't been to the shops yet. Perhaps Mr. Tuke smokes a pipe. Or cigars."

Being assured that cigars were permitted in the drawing-room—shag, said Mrs. Fawkes, was often smoked there, and clung terribly to the curtains—Harvey passed his case to the Vicar. The latter, as they all sat down, remained poised on the edge of his chair with an air of impermanence. His head cocked to one side, he was staring with critical interest at the caller.

"Will you be here at Christmas?" he inquired suddenly.

"It is most improbable."

"Pity. I'm thinking of running a small miracle play. We shall want a Devil. You're just the man. Well, about poor Shearsby. What can I do for you?"

"I gathered at the local pub that you saw more of him than anybody else here."

"I saw a good deal of him. He'd lived in France, you know. I was at Grenoble in my student days, and then curate at Cannes. That gave us something to talk about."

"A link between you, as Hopkins said."

The Vicar chuckled. "I believe Twitchell makes up those sayings of his as he goes along. Well, then Shearsby used to talk books. He borrowed most of mine. Hadn't many himself—he got away from France with what he could carry in a haversack, and about twopence farthing. Not a writer yourself, are you? Look more like a lawyer."

"I am a lawyer. In the Department of Public Prosecutions. Hence, in a way, my interest in Shearsby—which, however, is quite unofficial. And I've met what is left of his family."

Mr. Fawkes raised his tufts of eyebrows. "Public Prosecutions, eh? What is there about Shearsby to interest you? Oh, I know the police have raked it all up again. Fellow called Oake, from Cotfold, has been here. But there's no mystery about it. The inquest cleared it up. The poor chap was practically blind at night, and he was always forgetting his torch, or finding his battery had run down."

"It has more to do with his background," Mr. Tuke replied vaguely. "Did he ever talk about his relations?"

"He mentioned some cousins. I've met one of them. Mortimer Shearsby. He came to the inquest, and handled the funeral." The Vicar's round pink face grew a shade pinker. "And a nice way he handled it, too!" he said explosively, bounding in his chair. "Insufferable prig! Typical little provincial snob. And as mean as——"

"M-m-morris?"

"Twitchell again, eh? Yes, I think I've heard that one. Well, he's right. This insupportable bounder kept moaning about being out of pocket over the funeral expenses. Sold every stick of poor Shearsby's stuff to pay for 'em, and then buried him like a pauper. I offered to pay myself. I did pay for an obituary notice in the *Argus*. Waste of money, says this skinflint. Puffed up pomposity!" said Mr. Fawkes, bouncing again. "Some sort of analytical chemist. Full of himself. Work of the greatest national importance. Stuff and nonsense! He's with Imperial Sansil, making sham silk stockings. He cracked some ponderous joke about the name of this village."

"He's not making them now, my dear," Mrs. Fawkes put in. "And even sham silk stockings *would* be work of the greatest national importance. All the same, Mr. Mortimer Shearsby *was* just a little complacent. He talked of his cousin as though writers were rather disreputable. And he lectured me about my garden."

"Did he want you to stick a few stone imps and frogs about?" Harvey inquired.

"He did, Mr. Tuke. So you know him?"

"We have met. I believe both the Mortimer Shearsbys came to see their cousin a month or two ago?"

"They did," said the Vicar. "I didn't see them. He told me. He said he wondered why. He wasn't much interested in his family, and he couldn't stick that inflated ass, anyway."

"Did he ever comment on any of his other cousins?"

"Comment? No. He only mentioned them casually."

"Or refer to some money that was coming to him?"

"Oh, yes, he talked about that. His great-grandmother, wasn't it?" He said he was content to grub along now, because he wouldn't have to wait much longer. Then he'd be able to write the sort of stuff he wanted to write. Poor fellow!"

"A tragic business," Harvey agreed. "Did he happen to speak recently of meeting another relative whom he'd supposed to be dead?"

The Vicar's energetic nod made his white plume dance.

"Yes, he did. Let me see, when was it? A couple of months ago. He'd been to London, and he met this chap there."

"Did he mention the name?"

"No. I think I assumed it was Shearsby too."

"Did he say how they came to meet, or anything about the man?"

Mr. Fawkes shook his head. "No. He merely said that an odd thing had happened—he'd run across some cousin of sorts who was supposed to have died abroad fifteen or twenty years ago. It was just a casual remark. I'd asked if he'd had a good time in London, or something of the kind. He didn't go into details, and he never mentioned it again."

Mr. Tuke's hopes, which had risen, were being dashed again, but he persisted.

"I should be grateful if you would search your memory, Mr. Fawkes, for anything, however trifling, that Shearsby told you about this meeting."

The Vicar's very blue eyes looked inquisitively at the visitor. They narrowed as his bristling white brows contracted in an effort of recollection.

"I told that policeman all I knew, which wasn't much. Shearsby seemed rather amused. He seemed to think his other cousins might be annoyed if they heard the news. But I gathered they were not to hear it. This—er—resurrection was to be very hush-hush, for some reason. He'd promised not to tell the others. And after that he made a remark about his own work. Something to do with a story, and a coincidence. But I'm afraid I didn't catch the connection. I was on all fours in the garden at the time, grubbing up weeds, and I wasn't paying much attention. Shearsby had really come along to return some books. Sorry I can't be more helpful."

"And that was all?"

"Yes, I'm afraid so." Mr. Fawkes ran a hand through his cockscomb of white hair, turning it into an aigrette, and making him look very like a plump bird. Then suddenly he clicked a thumb and finger. "Shearsby did make some other remark. I'd forgotten. But I'm afraid I missed it too. I remember I said, 'What?' and he laughed, and said it reminded him of some poet. And he quoted a couple of lines of verse."

"Do you remember them?"

"Ah, there you have me again. I don't. I know they didn't strike any chord at the time. There was something about *owing* . . ." The Vicar shook his aigrette, smiling apologetically. Suddenly his bright eyes gleamed. He clicked his fingers again. "Wait a minute! Would you believe it? It was on the tip of my tongue then. Extraordinary how things come back. . . ." Frowning ferociously, he began to mutter to himself. "'Owe', 'woe' . . . 'and then I' . . . No, that wasn't it. 'And *while* I . . . and while I . . . tum-tum-tum . . . and feel'. . . . It's coming! 'And while I comprehend' . . . No. '*Understand*'. That's it. I've got it!" He bounced on his chair, his blue eyes twinkling at Mr. Tuke with excitement and pride. "There it was, all the time!

'And while I understand and feel
How much to them I owe . . .'

Remarkable thing, the memory. I paid no attention. . . .
But I must have come across those lines before, after all.
They seem familiar now."

Mr. Tuke, taking from his pocket a notebook and pencil,
was repeating the couplet as he wrote it down.

"'And while I understand and feel How much to them I
owe'. Just those two lines?"

"That was all. I'm sure that was all."

"You still can't remember what led up to them, that made
Shearsby laugh and quote them?"

Mr. Fawkes frowned again. "No," he said, after further
thought. "That's gone completely. I don't think I really
heard it."

"But he was definitely referring to his new-found cousin?"

"Yes, I feel sure of that."

Harvey studied the lines he had copied in his notebook.

"I can't say they convey anything to me," he said. "They
are not even familiar. It is a long time since I read any verse.
Isn't there a smack of Wordsworth about them?—in one of
his pedestrian moods?"

"The 'old, half-witted sheep'?" quoted the Vicar with a
chuckle. "Yes, they suggest him, as you say. Lines of prose
cut up to scan. Well, I have a Wordsworth here. Somewhere."

He looked dubiously at the untidy ranks of books in some
low shelves beside the fireplace. Mrs. Fawkes got up and un-
erringly picked out a fat green volume.

"Wordsworth was a very prolific writer," she remarked
with a smile, weighing the book in her hand.

"And obviously they are not first lines," her husband
added.

Mr. Tuke looked at the volume with apprehension.

"I think this is a piece of research to be deputed," he said.
"I will get someone to spend a day or two with Wordsworth.
A chastening experience. If the lines are not Wordsworth's,
of course, all English verse lies open to us. A life's task."

"You attach some importance to this quotation?" Mr.
Fawkes queried curiously.

"If we knew the context, it might conceivably help us to identify the resurrected cousin. On the other hand, it might not. It is a faint hope. But the fellow is a mere shade at present, without a local habitation or a trade. A name only. By the way," Mr. Tuke added, "the name is Dresser. Did Shearsby ever mention it, in any connection?"

"I have never heard it before, except in connection with the kitchen and the theatre," the Vicar replied.

"Well, I am very grateful to you," Mr. Tuke went on, as he rose to take his leave. "You have confirmed our belief that Mr. Dresser really is extant. It only remains to find him. One could wish that Raymond Shearsby had not been such a solitary young man. Of course he had been out of England. But one would have expected him to have a friend or two—here, apart from yourself, or elsewhere."

"He'd been buried here ever since he left France, you know," the Vicar said. "He was not gregarious, and, if I may say so without conceit, there is no one in our village, bar myself, with whom he had any interests in common."

"He had a friend in Cambridge," Mrs. Fawkes put in in her quiet way.

"Bless me, so he had. I'd forgotten. Yes, Mr. Tuke, as my wife says, Shearsby used to see some fellow at Cambridge occasionally. I speak colloquially. I don't think the man is a don."

"Do you know his name, or anything about him?"

"His name, no. Did Shearsby ever mention it, Alice?"

"If he did, I'm afraid I don't remember it."

"But I believe he wrote. Sorry to be so vague. But Shearsby was extremely vague himself. He would refer to 'that man', or 'that woman', as if you knew intuitively whom he meant. He had no memory for names. He used to say everybody ought to have a mnemonic name, like mine. Anyway," the Vicar went on, as they moved towards the door, "I hope at least you discover your Mr. Dresser. Another mnemonic. I'm afraid I have only been able to provide a very tenuous clue, but perhaps," he quoted with a chuckle, "'a verse may find him who a sermon flies.'"

CHAPTER XV

THE laboratories of Imperial Sansil are situated on the eastern fringe of Bedford, and Mr. Tuke approached them by way of Sandy and Potton and the more mellifluous and attractive Moggerhanger Park. Influenced, perhaps, by the horizontal landscape of the Ouse valley, the laboratories were long flat functional buildings of yellow brick, with a great deal of glass. Finding as he drew near them that it was nearly one o'clock, Harvey slowed down to time his arrival for that hour. It had barely struck when a stream of men and women, mostly on bicycles, began to issue from the only gate in the ring of heavily barbed wire fencing and turned as one into Bedford. In the rear came a few more dignified or less energetic persons who preferred to take their time, and among these appeared the tall drooping figure of Mortimer Shearsby, riding his bicycle in an aloof and superior manner. Information received had suggested that the chemist was not the man to spend money in a canteen when he had a wife and home within reach; and this conjecture being sufficiently confirmed, Harvey allowed the human torrent to ebb out of sight and then followed into the town to seek his own lunch. To use a metaphor in keeping with this theme, enough of Mortimer Shearsby was as good as a feast, and the call in view would be better made later.

A little after two, accordingly, he was driving slowly along Burnside Avenue, looking for 'Aylwynstowe'. On doorways and gates of semi-detached houses in every style of speculative builder's architecture of the 1930's other and more preposterous names went by—Chatsworth, Audley End, Rest-dene, Dormycot, Number Seventeen, even, incredibly, Nid D'Amour. Mr. Tuke wondered what muddled aspirations inspired this nomenclature. Why did Number Seventeen, to say nothing of the rest, stamp its tenant as one quite apart from his fellows who lived in plain 17's in Houndsditch or Knightsbridge? These sort of questions interested him. He was probably far less of a snob than most of the inhabitants of Burnside Avenue; but he was very much of a realist. Such social mysteries mattered. They might even have some bearing on the business in hand. His thoughts turned once more, as he studied Mortimer Shearsby's background, to the latter's marked divergence from the family level. The difference between the chemist and his cousins was unbridgeable and innate. Mortimer was pure Burnside Avenue. He must have been born like that. It was typical of him to speak of his wife as 'Mrs. Shearsby', and no doubt in his lighter moments (if he had any) he referred to her as 'the wife'. Lilian Shearsby for that matter, was out of the same mould. It was all very odd and instructive.

'Aylwynstowe', standing with its other half midway down the Avenue, looked even more smugly pretentious than its neighbours. Its paint seemed fresh; its window curtains were adjusted to an inch. Those in the lower front room were of pink silk, tied with silk bows. Three revolting china animals stood on the window ledge. The strip of front garden was an epitome of Mortimer Shearsby's peculiar ideas of landscape gardening. Little stone figures—an elf, a crane, a rabbit and a penguin—ornamented the corners of the tiny lawn. A sundial rose in the middle, and beneath the window with the pink silk curtains a stone seat bore inevitably but inexcusably the inscription 'A garden is a lovesome thing, God wot'. A path flagged with extremely crazy paving crossed this pleasaunce to the front door.

Slightly nauseated by this godwottery, as it has so happily been termed, Mr. Tuke advanced to a red-brick and timbered porch from which a sham antique lantern was suspended. He pulled cautiously at a sham antique bell-handle. But it worked better than the genuine museum piece at the Vicarage at Dry Stocking. No bit of mechanism was likely to be left unoiled in Mortimer Shearsby's home.

Mr. Tuke had timed his arrival for this hour because he hoped the chemist would by now have returned to his laboratory and his wife would be at home. He was almost too late. When Mrs. Shearsby herself opened the front door, wearing the becoming costume of the W.V.S. (returned from the cleaners), she was also wearing hat and gloves, and her green and mauve uniform bag hung from her shoulder.

Mr. Tuke's cap and her eyebrows were raised together.

"Oh!" she said. Then her rather startled stare, apparent through the pince-nez, gave way to a still slightly flustered air of welcome. "Quite a surprise, Mr. Tuke! Do come in."

"Can you spare me a few minutes, Mrs. Shearsby?"

"Oh, but of course." She was preceding him into the room with the pink silk curtains. It was the drawing-room, and was very much what Burnside Avenue had led him to expect—overfurnished and oppressively tidy. Everything was in its appointed place, and polished till it shone. No daily woman had lavished this care. True to her type, Mrs. Shearsby was house-proud. But to Mr. Tuke, who did not like rooms to look as though they were on show in the Tottenham Court Road, she seemed to carry this virtue to excess.

"I have to be my own maid in the afternoon," she was saying. She had already recovered her poise. "Life is becoming very difficult, isn't it? And I'm due at the W.V.S. head-quarters at half-past two, though of course I'm not really tied to time there." She gave her little giggle. "I'm afraid that sounds so like a voluntary worker. But really I *am* punctual as a rule. I think punctuality is an obligation, don't you? Like princes, you know. I'm sorry you have missed Mr. Shearsby. He has gone back to the laboratory. Is there anything special you want to see him about? Or will I do?"

If there was a touch of archness in her tone, it seemed to be almost automatic. Behind the pince-nez, while she rattled on, her eyes were watchful, even wary. In her mind, no doubt, Mr. Tuke was part of the mysterious machinery of police. It has been pointed out to him that if he sometimes creates this illusion, he has only himself to blame.

Not unaware of it, and having missed Mr. Shearsby by design, he put on what his wife called his party manners.

"I think you will do very well. It is only a small matter, Mrs. Shearsby. About your husband's cousin Raymond."

The pince-nez flashed in their baffling way. "Raymond?" Lilian Shearsby repeated.

"About some of his belongings, to be exact. I believe your husband took charge of his papers."

"He has given them to the police, Mr. Tuke."

"Only letters and so on, I'm told. I am interested in his literary remains, which are not the sort the police concern themselves with."

"Oh, there's still a pile of junk upstairs, if that's what you mean," Mrs. Shearsby said. "Typewritten stories, and scribblings, and old magazines. I tried to read the magazines. I'm a great reader. Give me a good book, and you can't tear me away. Quite the bookworm, Mr. Shearsby calls me. But most of these mags are too dull for words. There's a thing called *The Ludgate* . . ." She giggled again. "Well, I mean, I like romances and love stories, something to take you out of yourself, not queer tales like Raymond's, or articles about dead and gone writers and old buildings and such. I haven't properly looked at the typewritten stuff."

"Perhaps you will let me have it?"

"I shall be glad to get rid of it. It only collects dust. I've been thinking of burning the lot."

"If there happen to be unpublished stories, they are somebody's property," Mr. Tuke pointed out.

But she merely looked puzzled, and saying she would fetch the things, she left the room. Left to his own devices, Harvey examined it more closely. Upon mass-produced furniture the revealing features of long occupation were super-imposed. There were many photographs on the mantelpiece and the occasional tables. A few of cabinet size in silver frames were of opulent-looking ladies in furs or tweeds—the sort of ladies who open bazaars and hold showy positions in charitable organisations. In one, signed dashingly, 'Yours, Maud Winterbourne', Mr. Tuke recognised the features of a Viscountess who paid freely in this coin for services rendered. But most of the photographs showed the chemist and his wife, the former drooping and looking down his nose, the latter, surprisingly, quite often in an athletic role. Equipped for

tennis and badminton, she revealed a good figure and a well
developed forearm. It appeared that she also played golf,
and in a group of people in costume she was discovered in
knee-breeches and a three-cornered hat, and wearing a sword.
Mr. Tuke's limited acquaintance with suburban and provincial life had not prepared him for such versatility. The
camera offered no evidence that Mortimer Shearsby indulged
in similar frivolities, but plenty of his passion for godwottery.
He was posed all over his fussy garden, generally in shirt-
sleeves and grasping fork or hoe, amidst gnomes and frogs
and pergolas and things. Mr. Tuke made a diabolical face
at his absent host, and turned his attention to a small set of
bookshelves. He had it on the chemist's own authority that
the latter had no time for reading, and on his wife's that she
could not be torn away from a good book, and it might
therefore be taken that the volumes in her drawing-room
represented her personal tastes. Regardless of subject, they
were carefully ranked according to size. There were not
many novels; no doubt she got her fiction from a lending
library; but among the authors in this *genre* Mr. Tuke noted
the names—they were no more than names to him—of Berta
Ruck, Denise Robins and Lady Eleanor Smith. Two or
three crime stories, one by Austin Freeman and the others by
writers familiar, perhaps, to Sir Bruton Kames but not to
his legal assistant, rather oddly leavened an array of titles
which suggested the romantic themes the ardent reader
admittedly preferred. Those of the far more numerous
general works were even more revealing. Most of these
appeared to have been bought second-hand. *My Life at the
Court of St. Petersburg, Intimate Memories of the Hapsburgs, Kings,
Queens and Courtiers, Memoirs of a Lady in Waiting, Romances
of the Peerage, Great Love Stories*——here was the true stuff of
Lilian Shearsby's dreams. The investigator, rising from the
stooping posture he had adopted to read these glittering
names, stood gazing sardonically at the neatly ordered shelves.
He thought of the books in Vivien Ardmore's very different
room. He could imagine Miss Ardmore's or the dead
Raymond's comments on this literary pabulum. Its devourer

was not of course a Shearsby, but her husband obviously had a mind of the same order. The pair were well matched. And yet. . . . Mr. Tuke pondered a moment. After all, were they? He recalled Lilian Shearsby's remark about wanting something to take her out of herself. Why should she feel this need? Did life with the egotistical and close-fisted Mortimer fail to satisfy? Her varied activities again suggested that it did, and it was perhaps significant that there were no photographs of her doing anything in the garden, even picking a flower. Could it be that godwottery made no appeal?

An end was put to these reflections by the return of their subject, carrying a large parcel wrapped in brown paper. On an occasional table, cleared of its knick-knacks, Harvey went through Raymond Shearsby's literary remains—a sad jumble of typescripts, manuscripts, notebooks, odd scraps of paper, press-cuttings and other trivia, thrown together anyhow, no doubt by Mortimer Shearsby for removal from the cottage at Dry Stocking. There was nothing here that the chemist could sell, and it was a marvel that he had not made a bonfire of the lot in the cottage garden. A quick inspection for the only item in which Harvey was interested produced the typescript and two proofs of *Too Many Cousins*, and he began to wrap the package up again.

Lilian Shearsby watched him with no more than polite curiosity. As he replaced the objects taken from the table, a photograph led him to glance at the others so thickly scattered about the room.

"You seem to lead an active life, Mrs. Shearsby."

She laughed a little self-consciously. "Have you been looking at our snaps? Oh, one must do something in a place like this. Perhaps you recognised one or two of the other portraits? There's Maud Winterbourne—a great friend of mine. She lives near here, at Weedon Hall. Do you know her?"

"We have met," said Mr. Tuke non-committally, as he picked up his parcel and cap and moved towards the door.

"She is doing such wonderful work. The life and soul of our war effort here, I always say. Though most of us are doing our bit. I'm a very keen tennis player, as you'll have guessed, but I gave it up long ago. The W.V.S. was taking up all my time. The evacuees, you know. And now we're a little less busy, I'm back again with Imperial Sansil. Part time, of course."

"So you were with Imperial Sansil before?"

"Oh, yes." Lilian Shearsby giggled in her rather meaningless way. "There was no *need*, of course, but I think all girls ought to do *some* work, don't you? I'm sure I never thought I'd go back, but they're terribly short of experienced secretarial staff, and we must all put our shoulders to the wheel, as Mr. Shearsby says."

"I'm sure he does."

She stared for a moment, and then her lips twitched. Mr. Tuke had preceded her into the hall, and a belated gleam of sunlight, transmuted by some hideous coloured glass in the front door, gave his features a peculiarly devilish if somewhat mottled appearance as she looked up at him. He could see her pale grey eyes now, through her rimless pince-nez. They narrowed as she suddenly put out her hand.

"Mr. Tuke——" She hesitated, and began again. "Mr. Tuke, what do you think of all this?"

"All what?"

"Oh, you know quite well. These—these deaths, and all the rest of it." Her hands, in their light string gloves, through which her rings glittered, began to twist together. "A few days ago it all seemed so wildly improbable. But things are different now, aren't they? I mean, Martin Dresser turning up like this. Why don't the police find him?"

"They are doing their best. And that is quite good. What do you know about Martin Dresser, by the way, Mrs. Shearsby? Did you ever meet him?"

"No. And all I know about him is that he robbed a bank, and went to prison. It was soon after Mr. Shearsby and I were married, and he was very much upset about it. Well, naturally. He had his position to think of. All sorts of things might have been said. You know what it is in a town like this, full of old cats with nothing to do but spread scandal.

Luckily, I don't think anyone here heard the story. Well, then we heard the wretched man had died abroad."

"Which was a relief to your husband, no doubt?"

"Well, naturally," Lilian Shearsby said again. "It was a relief to both of us. Black sheep, even if they're only first cousins once removed, are no help to anyone." After which artless remark she paused, the blank pince-nez trained on Mr. Tuke's face, before adding meaningly: "And now he's alive after all. Well, all I can say is, it may be a good thing for some people."

"For whom?" Mr. Tuke inquired with unfeigned interest.

A hard expression had come over Lilian Shearsby's rather faded prettiness, carefully made up for voluntary duty.

"If there's something queer about these deaths in Mr. Shearsby's family, well, until Martin Dresser turned up like this there were only Mr. Shearsby himself, and Cecile and Vivien, left to benefit by them. It's ludicrous"—was there the faintest touch of mockery or contempt in her voice?—"it's ludicrous to suspect Mr. Shearsby of doing anything wrong. That leaves Cecile and Vivien. Cecile says someone tried to push her under a lorry Of course, she's more French than English, and somehow, with foreigners. . . . I mean, they're not like us, are they? But I've nothing against Cecile, and if she's telling the truth, well. . . ."

A shrug and a pause allowed Harvey to finish the sentence.

"The argument leaves us with Miss Ardmore."

Lilian Shearsby nodded. "I want to be fair," she said with an air of candour, belied by the ugly line of her mouth. "But I don't like Vivien. And she was here at the time of that other poisoning case."

"The case of the family poisoned by sodium nitrite here in Bedford?"

She nodded again. "Vivien came for the week-end, just after it happened. Naturally we talked about it. She was specially interested because her precious Mr. McIvory, at the Ministry of Supply, handles that sort of thing, and she knows a lot about sodium nitrite. And the Sansil works," added Mrs. Shearsby carefully, "aren't the only place the Ministry gets it from."

Mr. Tuke, theatrically satanic under a blood-red ray from the stained glass, looked at her, his dark brows raised a trifle. She moved restlessly under his gaze, and, as he did not speak, she went on quickly:

"Oh, I know it sounds horrid. But it's all horrid, anyway, isn't it? And Vivien wants money. Lots of money. She says so. She's a snob, and she wants to show off among her smart friends in London, and be able to buy expensive things. And this man she's engaged to hasn't much, except his salary, and what's he going to do when the Ministry of Information comes to an end? Live on Vivien, I suppose." The words were coming fast, and there was malice and envy in Lilian Shearsby's voice, under which its refined accents were breaking down. "I dare say I shouldn't talk like this," she said defiantly. "But I don't care! I know how *she'll* talk! What's the good of mincing matters?"

The shining pince-nez quivered in the particoloured light, and suddenly, beneath her make-up, a flush flooded her cheeks. Her hands were working together again.

"I should try a bit of mincing, all the same," Mr. Tuke said dryly. "It would be wiser, as your husband said." He took out his watch with an air of closing the subject. "Dear me, I shall make you late. Where is your meeting?"

The commonplace question brought her back to earth.

"The meeting? . . . At our headquarters, in the High Street."

"Let me drive you there. It is the least I can do, after imperilling your reputation for punctuality."

Her cheeks still flushed, she was breathing a little fast. Harvey opened the front door, and her glance went past him to the sleek black Delage drawn up at the gate. It was easy to read her thoughts, and she gave the car's owner a smile which he afterwards described to his wife as approaching the arch. Mrs. Tuke retorted that if the poor woman had known him better she would have been rightly suspicious of his unusual politeness. In happy ignorance, Mrs. Shearsby began

to apply a touch of powder in front of a mirror in the hall.
As they left the house she glanced quickly at the neighbouring
windows. Even in wartime, trained observers in Burnside
Avenue were no doubt watching the mistress of 'Aylwynstowe'
depart in style.

CHAPTER XVI

THE attention of Mr. Tuke, as in his unaccustomed role of
the squire of dames he ceremoniously opened the garden
gate, was momentarily elsewhere. A little way down Burnside Avenue another car was drawn up at the kerb. It had
not been there when he arrived. It had a familiar look:
it was uncommonly like the rather battered Morris last seen
outside The Bushel and Strike in Stocking some three hours
ago. It was blue, and he remembered the registration letters.
Through the windscreen he could see two figures in the front
seat.

As the Delage began to move, so did this other car. On
the way to the High Street, while Mrs. Shearsby spent much
of her time scanning the pavements, once or twice waving
to acquaintances, Harvey was watching, in the driving mirror,
the blue Morris following behind. He had no doubt now as
to its identity. It had not followed him to the Vicarage, nor
when he took the road to Stocking Corner and so to Bedford.
It must have come direct, probably some time later. It had
been driven to Burnside Avenue, and these subsequent proceedings implied that the tall man in the check jacket and his
tough-looking companion were interested in the tenants of
'Aylwynstowe'. It was natural to wonder whether their
presence in Stocking, of all places, did not fall into some
pattern. But what pattern? Harvey, to his annoyance, could
make nothing of it.

The Delage, the Morris still in its wake, crossed the graceful
bridge over the Ouse, and Lilian Shearsby indicated the
W.V.S. headquarters in the High Street. The arrival could
not have been more happily timed, for three women in

uniform, unloading bundles from a small van, paused to stare in the most gratifying way. The passenger prolonged the sensation by voluble thanks, until Mr. Tuke, watching in the mirror the Morris in its turn drawing up a hundred yards in rear, felt that the need for good manners was past, and reached across her to open the car door. As Mrs. Shearsby got out she hailed her colleagues, still standing staring among their bundles.

"Hullo, Muriel! Sorry if I'm a little late, Mrs. Blake."

"Here are the men's clothes at last," said the woman called Muriel, looking at Mr. Tuke with frank curiosity. "Though they seem to be mostly youths' again. Help us hump these in, and we'll get the rest out."

"And they must be carefully counted this time," Mrs. Blake said, with the air of asserting herself.

Raising his cap about an inch to Lilian Shearsby's final wave and smile, Harvey let in his clutch and drove slowly down the street. The blue Morris was still at the kerb when he turned round the first corner and again pulled up. He slid out from the driving seat and walked back to the corner. The High Street was crowded and busy, and there were a surprising number of cars, hooting their way up and down or parked in accordance with municipal ordinances. Unaware of the stringency and peculiarity of these, Harvey had fortunately drawn up the Delage on the correct side of the road for that day of the week. Glancing back down the High Street, under cover of a group of women walking past his turning, he found the scene in which he was interested unchanged. Mrs. Mortimer Shearsby and her companions were carrying bundles from the van across the pavement in a mannish and energetic manner, and the Morris car, its occupants still visible in the front seat, remained stationary a hundred yards beyond.

Harvey took further stock of the situation. On the far side of the High Street, in the opposite direction and only twenty yards away, stood a telephone cabinet. As another party of shoppers straggled past his turning he dodged across through the traffic and shut himself in the glass box. As he asked for Whitehall 1212, he could still see the distant Morris through the window.

Coins rattled, the connection was made, Button "A" was pushed, and after a brief passage with intermediaries the high voice of Mr. Hubert St. John Wray came thinly over the line. It sounded rather peevish.

"Well?"

"Tuke here," said Harvey, grinning fiendishly at the instrument.

"So they tell me. Where is 'here'?"

"Bedford."

"So you *have* gone there? Well, what is it?"

"I want you to do something, Wray. Highest priority, please. Ring up the police here and ask them to send an intelligent and inconspicuous plainclothes officer, *at once*, with an inconspicuous car or motor-bike, to the telephone box on the east side of the High Street, a hundred yards north of the W.V.S. headquarters. Got that? The number is 06632. Hurry, there's a good chap."

"What the devil——"

"Don't waste time. I want a car followed, and the men in it know mine."

"I was trying to ask what all this is about."

"I don't know myself, but the plot thickens. You know what plot. Now just get on with it, will you? I want the man at once. He'll find me by the box."

"Really, Tuke——"

"*Hurry!*" said Mr. Tuke, and rang off.

Leaving the cabinet, he took up a position a yard or two away, with the box itself concealing him from the men in the Morris, of which, however, in the intervals of the traffic, he could catch glimpses through the glass. He could also dimly see the W.V.S. ladies still hauling bundles from the van. A haughty young woman entered the cabinet, and he shifted his place slightly to see round her. Having glanced at his watch, he took out a cigar and lit it with his usual care.

The young woman left, to be succeeded by a man in a green baize apron. Harvey smoked placidly. Down the street the proceedings continued. In the meantime, however, the telephone system—in spite of occasional lapses still one of our minor modern miracles—was elsewhere doing its stuff; and he had waited only six minutes by his chronometer when a plain green saloon car drew up a few yards away. A man sitting by the driver got out, eyed Harvey in a speculative manner, and came towards him.

"Mr. Tuke?" he said.

"The same."

"I was instructed to look for you here, sir. I am Detective-Sergeant Webley."

"Did they give you a *portrait parlé*? I'm easily described."

Sergeant Webley smiled. He was a nondescript man of middle age, plainly dressed, who might have passed unnoticed anywhere.

"Perhaps I ought to ask for proofs of identity, all the same, sir."

Mr. Tuke, his eyes still on the blue Morris, produced the necessary papers. "You know what this is about, I take it?" he asked.

The sergeant returned the documents. "Those deaths at Stocking and Guildford? Yes, the Yard explained, sir. I am making some inquiries here for Inspector Vance. I happened to be in the station when the call came through just now."

"Better and better." Indicating the blue Morris, Mr. Tuke gave in a few words his reasons for being interested in it. "The attraction seems to be Mrs. Mortimer Shearsby. Don't ask me why. And if you do ask what the devil I'm doing butting in like this, I can only plead a sort of proprietary role in the case. Some of the parties concerned came to me, and I took the matter up with the A.C. And I was born nosy."

Sergeant Webley, watching the Morris, smiled again.

"We know quite a lot about you, Mr. Tuke. There was that case of a man named Sleight. At Steeple Mardyke. It was outside the county, of course, but near enough for us to be interested." He was frowning a little as he peered at the distant car. It was apparent that he had excellent sight when he went on: "That's a Cambridgeshire registration. Wonder what they're up to? Anyway, it looks like it was a good thing you did butt in, sir. I was beginning to think we'd come to a dead end here."

Down the High Street the ladies of the W.V.S. had carried in their last bundle. All three disappeared inside their headquarters. The van moved off. But the Morris remained.

"Nothing on the Mortimer Shearsbys?" Harvey queried.

Cautionary habits die hard, and for an almost imperceptible instant Sergeant Webley hesitated. Then he said:

"No, sir. We can't find a soul who saw Mr. Shearsby at any of the times we want to know about. Washing out that business in April—it's too long ago to hope for a bit of luck— we've still only his word for what he did on July the 28th and over the Bank Holiday week-end. We've had to go careful. Mr. Shearsby's a man in good position, and Sansil's a big firm. We don't want trouble with them. And anyhow, Mr. Tuke," the sergeant added earnestly, "I don't *see* it. Not his own sister. His cousins, yes—he might do *them* in. But not his sister, when there's a couple of cousins left he'd get just as much money from. No, I can't see him doing it. And if he didn't, it lets him out of the other affair at Stocking. At least, that's how I look at it."

"I agree with you there," Harvey said. "And it's a point about his sister, though not entirely convincing. Have you considered his character?"

"His character, sir?" The sergeant withdrew his gaze from the Morris to give his companion a puzzled look. "There's never been anything against him, and he's lived here ever since he started as a boy with Sansil. What they call a lab. assistant he was then. He pays his way and leads a very quiet life. Always in his garden."

Mr. Tuke shuddered. "So I noticed."

"He's not what you'd call popular," Mr. Webley went on. "At least, not with those under him. A bit of a toady, by accounts, with the heads and so on. Then he doesn't smoke or drink, and he's tight with money. For ever talking about it, too. All Bedford knows he's coming into a fortune one of these days. And now he's shooting his mouth about these deaths, saying how much he'll make by them one minute, and the next dropping hints about needing to take care of himself on dark nights." The sergeant shrugged tolerantly. "It's all just silly talk, to show off. Mr. Shearsby likes to feel important."

"Perhaps I should have used the word temperament instead of character," Mr. Tuke said. "To illustrate what I was getting at, do you remember the Seddon case?"

"I've heard of it, sir. It was before my time in the force."

"Seddon was another very mean man. He was always thinking and talking about money. And he buried his victim as cheaply as it could be done."

This time Sergeant Webley's glance was distinctly startled. Precedents carry weight with any official body of men, and there was a frown on his pleasant, nondescript face as he resumed his watch on the motionless Morris.

"I didn't remember that, sir," he said thoughtfully.

"Oh, you can push comparisons too far. But a mean streak will carry a man pretty far, too. Or a woman." Mr. Tuke had taken out his cigar-case. "Can you smoke on this sort of duty? The less you look like a policeman the better. Talking of women, how do Mrs. Shearsby's alibis work out?"

"She has a good one for the 28th of July, sir." Mr. Webley applied a match to his Larranaga. "We've found a woman here who came all the way back with her from Cambridge. They sat together as far as Hitchin. That means Mrs. Shearsby was in Cambridge as late as nine o'clock, like she said. Then she was seen there, after her W.V.S. meeting, by another member, a Mrs. Darby, at a quarter to five. Well, sir, the next bus after that to pass Stocking Corner left at six-forty. It gets to the Corner at seven-ten. At eight-twenty the last bus the other way passes the Corner That gives an hour and ten minutes for a five-mile walk, to that bridge in the lane and back, and a murder thrown in. And then the murderer would have to go through the village. You know what those places are, sir—they'd never miss a stranger walking through on a summer evening. And nobody saw Mrs. Shearsby, nor anyone else. There *is* another way to the lane, by getting off the bus further on, but that makes six miles to the bridge and back, and cuts the time down to just over the hour. It's an impossibility."

"What about the railway?"

"She couldn't have done it that way, either, sir. She might have caught the 5.10 from Cambridge, getting her to Whipstead at 5.30. But the last train *back* to Cambridge leaves at 8.5, and it was punctual that day. Now Mr. Shearsby, him that was killed, was alive at a quarter-past seven. Then he had to get from the inn to the bridge in the lane, or somewhere about there. Near half a mile— say eight or ten minutes. I can't work it out that he was killed much before half-past seven, at the earliest. My own idea is, it was a good deal later. But take seven-thirty. Then the murderer had to get back to the station by 8.5, and the only way from the lane, unless you go by the village, and that isn't much shorter, is by footpaths, and it's over three miles."

"The way the mysterious semi-clerical gent is supposed to have gone after he left the station?"

Sergeant Webley smiled. "Yes, sir. And I've got some news about him. But I ask you—three miles and a bit in thirty-five minutes. No woman could do it, not if she ran the whole way. And supposing she came by the 5.10 and went on to the bus route by the back lanes, its three miles again, and the last bus goes by about eight-ten. Forty minutes. And she'd still have to fit a murder in. Anyway, Mrs. Shearsby didn't come or go either way. There wasn't any strange woman at the station that evening, nor picked up by the bus. The only strangers were the man and the boy you've heard about."

"It sounds fairly conclusive," Mr. Tuke agreed.

Sergeant Webley gazed thoughtfully at the blue Morris through a cloud of cigar smoke.

"Anyhow, Mr. Tuke," he said, "I never did put much stock in the idea of *her* having done it. It isn't a woman's

crime, to my way of thinking. Poisoning, yes—but not this
bashing people over the head and chucking them in rivers."

"Oh, my dear fellow, don't have illusions about women,"
Harvey said. "Think of Mary Borden and her little hatchet,
and Mrs. Pearcey and hers, and a score of others."

Apparently Sergeant Webley had not heard of either of these
ladies, for he looked puzzled again. How odd it was, Mr. Tuke
reflected, that in police work, alone of the professions, no
attempt seemed to be made to teach the history of the subject.

"Wonder how long we've got to wait?" the sergeant
murmured. "Till Mrs. Shearsby comes out, I suppose, if
it's her they're after. Look, sir, are you in a hurry?"

"Far from it. I'm enjoying myself, I'm on holiday, and
I insist on hearing your news about the semi-clerical gent."

The sergeant chuckled. "It's a good name for him. Well,
why not come and sit in my car, sir, while we wait? More
comfortable than standing here. Come to that, if you're
on holiday, why not stay in the car?"

"Join in the hunt, you mean?"

"If you care to, Mr. Tuke. It's a bit irregular, but you
put us on to this, and you're in the P.P's office, and all that.
It might interest you to find out what that car is up to,
and you could tell them about it in London."

"It would interest me extremely. Sergeant, you're a
trump. But what about my own car?"

Mr. Webley jerked a thumb towards his driver. "The
constable there will drive it to the station, and you can pick
it up when we get back. If those fellows come from Cambridge, they'll be going back there. When we've found
out where they go to, we'll hand over to the Cambridge
police." He paused, stared at the Morris, and added: "I'll
have a closer look at them first, if you'll wait here."

He strolled away among the crowd on the pavement. Mr.
Tuke, effaced behind the telephone cabinet, smoked his
cigar and watched the throng. In a few minutes the sergeant
rejoined him.

"I'll know the driver again. But I daren't draw attention to myself, and what with the other chap's peaked cap

and glasses I couldn't make much of him. Except his nose.
What they call Roman. And he's grey-haired, like you
said, sir. Well, we'll be going along, if you like."
They began to walk towards the police car.

CHAPTER XVII

THE constable driver, concealing his disappointment at being
done out of the fun, departed with the keys of the Delage,
and Mr. Tuke and the sergeant settled themselves in the
driving seat. Through the windscreen they got the usual
intermittent view of the blue Morris, as the traffic flowed
by it, its two occupants dimly visible, waiting also, their
eyes presumably on the door of the W.V.S. headquarters.
As it was headed towards the police car, and was a hundred
yards away, whether it eventually turned or came on there
was no danger of losing it.

Sergeant Webley took out his watch. "Ten to three.
That Morris has been parking too long," he added with a
grin. "But I think we'll let it stay. Now, Mr. Tuke, I'll
tell you what I know about the man at Whipstead. Inspector
Vance was on the phone last night, and he passed the
news. It's quite a story. But no use to us, I'm afraid, except
that it clears some more dead wood away."

"You're a minute slow," said Mr. Tuke, who had con-
sulted his own French timepiece. "Carry on."

"Well, it's like this, sir. It seems that on that evening,
the 28th, there was a Yard man doing a job at King's Cross.
I don't know the details, and they don't matter, but he
was on the look-out for someone, and he was on the main
line platform, that the booking office opens out of. Just
after six he saw a man go by him to the booking office—
a man he knew. This chap was carrying an attaché case.
Now the Yard man was interested in him, but he wasn't
the fellow he was after, and he daren't leave the platform.
What he did was to signal one of the railway police. He

was just passing on the information when back came this fellow, and the railway man trailed him. He saw him get into a 3rd class coach on the 6.15 for Cambridge."

Sergeant Webley drew on his cigar. A uniformed constable came in sight, glanced at the police car, caught the sergeant's eye, and passed on.

"Now this man was a crook," the sergeant continued. "At least, the Yard knows he's one, but he's never even been charged. They call him Holy Joe. His name's Joseph Eady, and he's a sort of con man in a small way who gets himself up to look religious, like a lay preacher or such. He's got the face and the patter, and he wheedles money out of soft-hearted folk for cases of destitution and that. They're real cases, and they get the money—or some of it. But some of it sticks to Joe's fingers, and the Yard thinks there are more who never get a penny. But they've never been able to prove anything. This Eady's in with one or two missions and charitable bodies, small affairs but quite O.K., and they won't hear a word against him. Those sort of people mean well," said the sergeant in parenthesis, with tolerant contempt, "but they're just soft, often enough. Mostly old women . . ." He shrugged. "Anyway, the Yard's been watching Holy Joe for some time, and hoping to catch him out, and they like to keep tabs on him. So this officer I'm talking of, as soon as he heard Eady was on the Cambridge train, got the railway policeman to ring up Cambridge and one or two towns on the way, like Hitchin and Baldock, to ask the locals to have a man at the stations to pick him up and see where he went. Though Cambridge seemed the most likely, being a fair-sized place. It seems this Eady, when he does work outside London, keeps to the bigger towns, where he can lose himself better."

The sergeant paused to peer through the traffic at the Morris. But it had not moved. Mr. Tuke adjusted his long legs, which found the car rather cramping after the roomy Delage.

"Cambridge it was," said the sergeant. He chuckled. "But they never set eyes on him there. He slipped them very neat. Inspector Vance thinks he must have spotted the Yard man at King's Cross—he knows him, all right—and instead of taking a ticket right through, bought one to Whipstead. The station master there hit him off to a T, clerical look, attaché-case, and all. Well, when he went up that footpath from the station he'd turn off and get to the lane where young Mr. Shearsby lived, and then along by more lanes, that I spoke of, to the bus route. Anyhow, he hopped on the last bus to Cambridge at about 8.10, a couple of mile short of Stocking Corner. The conductor remembers him. And he hopped off again in Trumpington Road. And that was the last seen of him."

"A quick-witted and ingenious gentleman," Mr. Tuke commented. "So ingenious that some knowledge of the country is suggested. Or Mr. Eady had studied the map very carefully. Has it struck you, sergeant, that maps may have played quite a part in this case?"

"Maps, sir? No. I don't quite get you."

"Our ordnance survey maps," said Mr. Tuke didactically, "are extremely good and full of fascinating detail. They must be a godsend to the intelligent criminal who operates in rural districts. If I contemplated a crime in the country, and did not wish to be observed reconnoitring the ground, I should buy the 6-inch sheets covering it. One could probably do well enough with the 1-inch. It's surprising, of course, how many educated people can't read a map. But I fancy someone we know of has a well-used one of the Stocking area."

Sergeant Webley was obviously thinking it over. As he sat leaning forward, his eyes on their quarry, he was frowning. His cigar smouldered, forgotten, drooping a little.

Then he said: "I think I see what you mean, sir. But *who* do you mean?"

"Oh, if we knew that, the chase would be half over."

"Mr. Mortimer Shearsby, of course, would use maps a lot, being a keen cyclist."

"So he would." Mr. Tuke shifted his cramped legs again. "By the way," he went on, "though your job has been to run the rule over the Mortimer Shearsbys, I take it you are well up on the case as a whole? You know all about the other surviving members of the family?"

"Yes, sir. Mr. Vance has kept me up-to-date on the London end."

"Including the news of the extra cousin from Belgium?"

The sergeant nodded. "A bit of a teaser *he* is, isn't he? I mean, it seems to me unless something can be pinned on one of the others, he's got to be found."

"He's got to be found, anyway. Well, who has figured in the case so far who might fill the bill?"

The puzzled look returned to Sergeant Webley's face. "No one, sir."

"What about Mr. Joseph Eady?"

The Sergeant turned from his steady watch on the Morris to stare, a little open-mouthed, at his passenger.

"Crumbs!" he said. "I never thought of that!" Then he frowned. "But this Eady's a crook. They know all about him at the Yard." He paused, peering through the windscreen again, his lips pursed in a soundless whistle. "My word, of course this other chap . . ."

"Yes, he was a crook too, when last heard of."

"And he'd know where young Mr. Shearsby lived," the Sergeant said, half to himself. "They'd met. That would account for the ticket to Whipstead. Eady always meant to go there. How do the times fit? . . ." He shook his head as he glanced at Mr. Tuke. "No, it won't work, sir. The train was on time, 6.43. Say Eady left the station a minute later. He had to walk nearly six miles to get that bus at 8.10. He only had a bit over an hour and twenty-five minutes. He must be a fast walker to have done it at all. He'd have no time for any fancy work. And anyway, Mr. Shearsby was in the pub in the village at seven-fifteen, when Eady couldn't even have got to the lane."

"You've run ahead of me," Mr. Tuke said with a smile. "I hadn't got so far as to envisage your Holy Joe as a murderer. That he might be the missing cousin was just an idea that came into my head. It leaves a whole lot unexplained."

"It's worth following up, sir," the sergeant said. "How old would this cousin be?"

"In the late fifties."

"And Eady's grey-haired and sort of venerable looking. And once a crook, always a crook, generally speaking."

"There is also this, for what it's worth," Mr. Tuke remarked, warming to his own theory. "I observed to the A.C. the other day that this Martin Dresser, if he is alive and in England, must have been earning his living somehow since he came back. Because his son never paid any money to him that can be traced. And the son's rather odd reticence about his father might be accounted for if the latter was making a living by some shady means, and the son knew it."

Sergeant Webley seemed scarcely to be listening. His brows met in another frown of concentration as he stared, almost unseeing, at the Morris car down the street.

"Wait a minute! Wait a minute," he muttered. "Do you know if Mr. Raymond Shearsby had a bicycle?"

"I'm afraid I don't."

"I bet he did. Everybody in the country has a bike nowadays. And he never had a car. How about this, Mr. Tuke? Say Mr. Shearsby went to the pub that evening on foot. No one's mentioned a bike. Well, then, while he's gone Eady comes into the lane, about seven-thirty. He goes on to the cottage. He'd have to pass it. Nobody there, but the bike's lying somewhere in view. Eady walks back down the lane and meets Mr. Shearsby on his way home. Perhaps he'd taken his time, and sat on the bridge for a smoke, or something. Well, Eady knocks him out, and shoves him in the stream. Then he runs back to the cottage, nips on the bike, and rides like smoke for the bus route. He leaves the bike under a hedge, and catches the bus easy."

Mr. Tuke was laughing. "It does you credit, Sergeant. I mean it."

"Well, it's possible, sir. And you can't get over Eady being in that lane just about the right time. It makes the murder earlier than I thought, but that's nothing. I don't really know a lot about this Stocking affair. The Herts people are handling it, under Mr. Vance—I've just followed it on the map, so to speak, having an eye on Mr. Mortimer Shearsby and *his* bike, and knowing the country a bit. It's a pity," said the Sergeant, shaking his head, "that Eady's never been charged. They won't have his dabs. They'll have the cousin's, because of that old trouble at the bank."

Mr. Tuke knocked the ash of his cigar out of the car window. "Incidentally," he observed, "you—and I, for that matter—have been talking glibly of murders. But when I last heard of Inspector Vance he seemed to be still hedging."

The sergeant looked surprised. "He don't talk like it," he said. "You have to hedge a bit in reports, sir. He knows better, I'll lay."

Mr. Tuke grinned. "Well, we'll go on hoping for the best. A chapter of accidents is so dull."

"And we've got something to work on," the Sergeant said, rubbing his hands with professional glee. "The more I think of Eady being this Martin Dresser, the more I like it. And his being in that lane just when he was sticks in my gizzard. As for my notion about the bicycle, we'll soon find out if Mr. Raymond Shearsby had one, and what happened to it. Yes, sir, we're getting a move on, what with all that, and now this car——" He stiffened suddenly. His hand went to the brake. "And *that's* getting a move on, too," he added sharply.

In fact, down the High Street, the blue Morris they had seemed to watch for so long was at length leaving the kerb and gliding into the stream of traffic flowing towards them. But at once, taking advantage of a gap, it began to turn. Sergeant Webley got into gear, and the police car took off in pursuit.

The Morris completed its turn and moved slowly south down the High Street. On account of the traffic, and the crowd on the opposite pavement, the pursuers could not at once confirm their supposition that the blue car was also following somebody. Then Mr. Tuke touched the Sergeant's arm and pointed. A figure in W.V.S. uniform was walking smartly along in the same direction.

The slow progress of the two cars provoked angry blasts from the horns of following vehicles. At the narrow bridge over the Ouse the usual congestion slowed everybody down; and Mrs. Shearsby—there was no doubt now as to her identity —forged ahead. Once over the bridge she suddenly crossed the street, dodging actively through the traffic and under the very bonnet of the Morris, and took the road to Cardington and Sandy, which was also the way to Burnside Avenue. The traffic thinned, the Morris fell back a little, and the police car followed suit.

A few minutes later Mrs. Shearsby turned into Burnside Avenue. Sergeant Webley was keeping well behind, for in these quiet roads there were no other cars in sight. Then, as the Morris turned after the green-clad figure, he shot ahead, crossed the Avenue, turned in the side street beyond, and pulled up.

"Perhaps you'll wait here, sir," he said to Mr. Tuke. "I'll have a look from the corner."

CHAPTER XVIII

MR. TUKE looked at his watch. The time was 3.25. The checking of clothing at the W.V.S. headquarters had perhaps been postponed: Lilian Shearsby, at any rate had not stayed there long, for which her late visitor was duly grateful. He had begun to feel the need of a little action.

It was impossible to tell, from Sergeant Webley's back, as he stood at the corner of Burnside Avenue and peered circumspectly down it, what developments were taking place there. Mrs. Shearsby should by now have reached 'Aylwynstowe.' Harvey lighted a fresh cigar, and again noted the time. Ten minutes had passed. A few people had come by, mostly women. They showed no interest in these proceedings. It was warm in the car, and he had sat up late the night before. He began to feel a little sleepy.

He had closed his eyes when the sound of running footsteps roused him. The sergeant climbed into his seat.

"They're off again," he said.

It was ten minutes to four. The sergeant nosed the car to the corner of Burnside Avenue. At the far end of that prim thoroughfare the blue Morris was receding at a smart speed. The police car turned after it.

"Him in the check coat," said Sergeant Webley, "went in right on her heels. He's just come out again."

The Morris had turned out of sight. The sergeant pressed the accelerator, and they shot down the Avenue, past Aylwyn-stowe and Nid D'Amour and Number Seventeen and the rest. There was no sign of the Morris in the cross street at the end, but the Sergeant turned right and then they were in the Cardington road, and an instant's pause showed them their quarry heading for Sandy and Potton and Cambridge. It had a lead of a quarter of a mile. There was some traffic here, but Sergeant Webley kept his distance. The police car, he explained, had a more powerful engine than its apparent rating implied. Unless the Morris was equally deceptive, he could overhaul it whenever he chose.

They were retracing the route by which Mr. Tuke had come that morning. The laboratories of Imperial Sansil flashed by, and then they were passing the Cardington hangars. The two cars had worked up to a steady forty-five. The woods of Moggerhanger went past, and as they came into Sandy the Sergeant closed the gap to a couple of hundred yards. They mounted the abrupt gravelly ridge from which Sandy takes its name, and swept down into Potton. Here the Morris turned right, for Wrestlingworth, and the sergeant nodded.

"Cambridge," he said.

It was at Wrestlingworth that Mr. Tuke had come out into this road from Stocking that morning. An almost straight run through Tadlow brought them to the Huntingdon road, which he had crossed a little lower down: and once over this; they were reversing his route again, by Wimpole to Barton. A pale blink of sunlight was showing, and a squadron of great bombers, heading south, trailed their swift shadows over the flat fields. The pinnacles of Cambridge, the spires of King's and the ugly tower of the new library, rose against the skyline.

Sergeant Webley, who had dropped back, began to overhaul the Morris once more as the road curved beyond Barton into a fringe of new houses.

They passed the final bus stop in Barton road at half-past four. The Morris kept straight on to Fen Causeway. As it approached Trumpington Street the police car closed in, but a covered army truck, racing up, cut in between pursuer and pursued, and the sergeant swore. The three vehicles crossed Trumpington Street nose to tail, into Lensfield Road and Gonville Place. The Sergeant tried to pull out past the truck as they reached the end of Parker's Piece, but oncoming traffic forced him to drop back. He tried again, saw the Morris turning left, and again had to fall behind the truck to follow. When the Morris was in sight once more it was taking a corner to the right, on its brakes, for it was travelling fast. The police car swung after it. They were in a maze of small streets, and the Morris was skidding round yet another corner. Again the sergeant wrenched at the wheel, and as they took the turn the blue car was not fifty yards in front. It was slowing up by the kerb.

Sergeant Webley kept on, passed it as it came to a stop, and swore a second time, and loudly.

"Blast the beggar, he's slipped us!"

In the front seat of the Morris there was only the driver, turning to stare at them as they went by.

Mr. Tuke twisted himself about to peer through the rear window. They were in a street of mean houses, with two or three depressed looking shops. The Morris had drawn up in front of a newsagent and tobacconist's. The driver was now getting out. He walked round to the pavement with his head over his shoulder and his gaze following the police car. As this turned out of the street at the far end, he was standing before a pair of large gates beside the shop.

Sergeant Webley pulled up round the corner, and in his turn got out and walked back. Within a couple of minutes he returned to the car.

"Drove into the yard there," he said as he took his seat once more. "Runs that Morris for hire, I wouldn't wonder.

Name of Thomsett on the shop, if you noticed, sir. The other
chap did us nicely. Must have hopped out while they were
round one of these corners. Slipped in a doorway, I dare
say, while we sailed by. I'd hoped they hadn't spotted we
were after them."

"They may merely be taking precautions on general principles," Mr. Tuke said. "Everything suggests that they are
a pair of artful dodgers. What are you going to do now?"

"Run along to the police here and see what they know
about Thomsett and that Morris. It ought to give us a line
on the other chap in time. I wouldn't mind, though," the
Sergeant added, as he got into gear, "having some notion of
what all this is about."

"I heartily agree. I dislike being mystified. We seem to
have tumbled on an entirely new feature in the case. But it's
all very interesting, don't you think?"

"Puts a bit of life into it," Sergeant Webley concurred.

At the police station in St. Andrew's Street Mr. Tuke
tactfully elected to remain in the car. But he was not left
there long: within ten minutes the sergeant reappeared,
accompanied by no less a personage than a superintendent,
who looked at Harvey with respectful interest, and, after
introductions, invited him in for a cup of tea.

"We'll have some news before long," the Superintendent said.

In his office was an inspector who knew all about the
blue Morris. It was the property of Mr. Thomsett, of the
tobacco shop, whose description tallied with its driver that
day. It was used for hire purposes. Of Mr. Thomsett himself
the Inspector held a poor view. The shop could be used as
an accommodation address, and, it was believed, for other
and less legal purposes. Mr. Thomsett's friends were of the
cheap, raffish type to be found even in university towns,
and some of them had criminal records. The tobacconist
was now suspected of running a new side line in black market
liquor, but so far all efforts to trip him up over this or anything else had failed. He was a nasty piece of goods, said the
Inspector, and as cunning and impudent as a cartload of
monkeys.

Mr. Tuke had drunk his second cup of strong tea when the expected news arrived. Interviewed by an officer despatched on a bicycle with a specious inquiry about misuse of petrol, Mr. Thomsett had declared that he knew nothing whatever about the fare he had driven to Bedford and back that day. The man, a stranger to him, had come into the shop the morning before to buy cigarettes, and had noticed the advertisement of a car for hire. He returned in the afternoon, and arranged to be taken to Bedford the next day. He gave his name as Farley, and paid cash in advance, Mr. Thomsett holding strong views on bilkers. The police officer, rather hurriedly briefed, had not been told of the Morris's call at Stocking on the way out, and this incident was not mentioned by Mr. Thomsett. Unaware to what extent his movements in Bedford were known, he gave a truthful account of these. He had not asked for any explanation of his fare's rather peculiar behaviour there. Something to do with a woman, of course, said Mr. Thomsett with a leer; but fares were fares, and if you started poking and prying into their doings, you could soon whistle for your custom. He could tell some queer tales, and did tell one or two, with gross and impudent chuckles. Prompted about the return journey to Cambridge, he said his fare arranged to be driven back to the shop, which was as handy for him as anywhere else; but at Parker's Piece Mr. Farley had suddenly remembered an appointment, and had asked to be set down. He had jumped hurriedly from the car before it stopped. Conscious, perhaps, that this was a weak point in his tale, Mr. Thomsett here went over to the offensive, demanding to know why he should be picked on. Had the police ever known him to allow his car to be used for a wrongful purpose? As for petrol, he could account legitimately for every gallon issued to him—and a miserable quota it was, too, for a poor working man who had to live.

In the police officer's opinion, his visit was not unexpected. Mr. Thomsett did not seem surprised, and had all his answers pat. At this point the Inspector, with a look at the Superintendent, left the room, and his superior turned to Sergeant Webley.

"That bit about Parker's Piece doesn't fit with your story, Sergeant."

"The other chap never got off there, I'll swear to it, sir," said the Sergeant. "Mr. Tuke will say the same. The car never slowed up. Besides, we'd have seen him—it's all open on the near side, and I was watching the road, trying to pull out."

"Oh, it's clear enough," the Superintendent agreed. "They spotted you, or had their suspicions, anyway. The fellow wasn't running any risks, so he dodged off when they got into the side streets. And Mr. Thomsett knows a whole lot more about him than he let on to. Well, we're putting a man on him, and another to find out if anybody saw his passenger. The trouble is, fly birds like Thomsett know all our chaps. It's no strain on their memory, because when I say 'all', I mean the three men and a boy we've got left. I'd ask for one from Bedford, Sergeant, but you're as short-handed as we are, and if this is part of Inspector Vance's case I don't see why the Yard shouldn't send a man along." He reached for the telephone, adding, as he caught Mr. Tuke's eye: "Oh, I know what *they'll* say, sir. Run off their feet, and do we think they're made of men?"

"Well, don't mention my name," said Mr. Tuke, preparing to rise, for Sergeant Webley was pushing back his chair. "It might queer your pitch. The Assistant Commissioner seems to think I wished this case on him just to be annoying. *I* think it's rather a nice case. It gets one about, and travel does broaden the mind so. And Sergeant Webley, unless I am much mistaken, has another little trip in view."

CHAPTER XIX

"WHAT makes you think, sir, that I've another little trip in view?" the Sergeant asked when they were in the street again.

"If I were you," said Mr. Tuke, "I shouldn't be happy

till I'd found out what that Morris was doing in Stocking this morning."

"Well, it isn't far out of our way, sir, if you can spare the time."

"I'd like to know myself. You could also test your theory about Raymond Shearsby's bicycle."

"I'd got that in mind, too," the Sergeant admitted with a smile.

And accordingly, for the third time that day, Mr. Tuke was conveyed along A 603 to Wimpole, and for the second time by the winding lanes to Dry Stocking. It was a quarter to six when the police car drew up before a neat little new house, with cream-washed walls and green-painted woodwork, which bore the enamelled sign of the Hertfordshire Constabulary. Sergeant Webley was still outside his own district, and the proprieties had to be observed.

When, a few minutes later, he was ushered out of the house by the village policeman, who was minus his tunic, for he had been gardening, the Sergeant was accompanied by another officer in plain clothes, whom he introduced to Mr. Tuke as Sergeant Oake, Inspector Vance's actual deputy in these parts. For the best part of a week Sergeant Oake had been gleaning and sifting the gossip of the neighbourhood, with little to show for his work beyond the results set out in Mr. Vance's own interim report; and by a happy chance he had just called on the local constable for a cup of tea before cycling back to Cotfold, where he was stationed. This being his territory, his fellow sergeant from Bedford had sought his co-operation in the present inquiries in the village, one of which had already advanced a stage, for as the newcomer got into the back of the car, Sergeant Webley, resuming his seat at the wheel, said to Mr. Tuke:

"Mr. Shearsby did have a bicycle, sir. We're just going to find out what became of it."

By Sergeant Oake's direction, they drove a short way down the street and stopped again before a rambling and somewhat dilapidated house which had a yard and barns behind it. The local officer got out and entered the yard.

"The chap here," explained Sergeant Webley, "does a trade in old furniture and such. He bought all Mr. Shearsby's things from his cousin."

Sergeant Oake soon returned. He was a lean, black-avized man, with a melancholy face and a blue chin, which he was now polishing thoughtfully.

"Looks like you may have hit on something," he said to his colleague. "Old Worboys says there was no bicycle with the stuff he bought. And he took everything, and went over it piece by piece at the cottage with the other Mr. Shearsby. He remembers now that Mr. Raymond Shearsby did have a bike, picked up second-hand from some chap here, but he says he didn't think of it at the time. The cousin was in a hurry, and rushed the sale through, though he didn't forget, Worboys says, to haggle like a shrew over it. To hear Worboys talk, you'd think it was an offence to bargain with a dealer.. Not that the chap wasn't tight about money —they all say that, and he skimped the funeral something shocking. Anyhow, he didn't take the bike away with him, that's certain." Sergeant Oake fingered his blue chin and shook his head sadly. "I ought to have thought of it myself," he said.

Sergeant Webley was looking justifiably pleased.

"I congratulate you," Mr. Tuke said. "What is your next step?"

"If Sergeant Oake's agreeable, we'll set the constable here to work hunting for that bike. Somebody *may* have pinched it from the cottage, after Mr. Shearsby's death— bikes are valuable nowadays—or it may have been found tucked away somewhere in a hedge, like I said."

The police car, accordingly, returned to the constable's neat little house, and that officer was instructed to leave his gardening forthwith and begin to scour the village for news of the missing bicycle. The car was then turned once more and headed down the street for The Bushel and Strike.

On the way there Mr. Tuke leaned round to speak to Sergeant Oake, sitting at the back caressing his chin.

"You must be an authority by now, Sergeant, on the railway service to Whipstead. Do all the trains have corridor coaches?"

"Not all, they don't, sir." Sergeant Oake had also heard of Mr. Tuke, Steeple Mardyke being in his county, and he replied without hesitation. "With some you can't tell— they may be corridor, or they may not, or some'll be mixed. The morning and evening trains all have corridor coaches— the 5.31 and 7.48 from Cambridge, for instance, and the 6.43 and 8.5 from King's Cross."

"Just what I wanted to know. One other query. What do you make of the young man with the suitcase, who came, if I remember correctly, by the 5.31 and left again later. By the 8.5, was it?"

Sergeant Oake polished his chin vigorously. "I'd like to know more about him, I'll own," he said. "Just because I can't find out what he was up to hereabouts. But you always come on these loose ends when you're on a case, as *you'll* know, sir. And this fellow couldn't have had no hand in Mr. Shearsby's death, if that's what you're thinking. He couldn't have got to the lane and back in time. He was by the station just before the 6.43 came in, and he was away by the 8.5."

"I suppose the porter couldn't have been mistaken when he says he saw this chap on the bridge?"

"He says he'll swear to it, sir. They mark down strangers in country places like this. I've checked it other ways, too, and nobody was near the bridge at that time."

At The Bushel and Strike, which was not yet open, Mr. Tuke adhered to his role of the interested onlooker, and remained in the car while the two police officers went inside. They were out again within ten minutes, but stood conferring together a little longer before they rejoined him. Sergeant Webley then passed on their news.

The two men from the blue Morris had stayed in the bar for upwards of an hour that morning. Mr. Twitchell did not think he had seen either of them before. The bar filled up while they were there, and presently the talk came round to the death of Raymond Shearsby. The landlord, busy serving, could not say by whom the topic was introduced; but once it was launched the man in the check jacket had shown much interest in the tragedy, though appearing to hear of it for the first time. Before he and his companion left, they knew all the village knew about it. The companion took little part in the general conversation, concentrating on his beer, for which the other paid. The latter was a pleasant fellow, with an easy, gentlemanly manner. When the pair drove away, they were seen to turn up the lane which led to Raymond Shearsby's cottage.

Deferring consideration of this episode, Sergeant Webley glanced round at Sergeant Oake, who leant forward to broach the subject which, it seemed, the two had been discussing outside the inn. Much impressed by his colleague's reasoning about the missing bicycle, and its prompt confirmation up to a point, the Hertfordshire officer was anxious to apply a further test at once. As he put it, if someone stole the bicycle from the cottage on that July evening with the aim of reaching the main road in time to catch the last bus to Cambridge, it would be discarded very near that road. In which event, having every reason by now to know the neighbourhood, Sergeant Oake thought the machine might still be lying where it had been left, even though three weeks had gone by. The instinct of the thief would be to hide it, and this he must do in some field, behind a hedge, for there were no other hiding places. The lane he took was little used, and the fields thereabouts were all pasture, and when cattle or horses were turned into them it was merely a matter of opening a gate, and the animals would amble in, and for that matter out, of their own volition. Countrymen, said Sergeant Oake, never walked a yard further than they could help, and cowmen and horsemen, who stood for hours in a heat-producing mixture of straw and mud, notoriously suffered torments from their feet. In short, the odds were that nobody had entered the fields in question for weeks past, let alone investigated the hedgerows, and these, there being no hedgers and ditchers, were greatly overgrown, so that a weighty object like a bicycle would sink in among the autumn foliage and be invisible at a casual glance.

Mr. Tuke met Sergeant Webley's eye at this point, and reading in it his natural anxiety to follow whither this further spate of reasoning led, grinned encouragingly at him.

"Don't let him steal your thunder," he said. "And count me in. It's your idea, and your car, and I'm on holiday and enjoying myself hugely. We'll all look for the bicycle."

Sergeant Webley smiled gratefully and got into gear, and soon they were driving up the lane towards Raymond Shearsby's cottage. They halted at the bridge over the Cat Ditch, which the officer from Bedford had not seen, and then went on past the lonely cottage and so along the winding, deserted lanes explored by Mr. Tuke in the reverse direction that morning. It seemed ancient history, so much had happened in the interim.

The sun came out again, to gild the general enthusiasm, and beneath scattered clouds and assorted aircraft the police car eventually pulled up a hundred yards short of the main road and bus route. At this corner, on the 28th of July, the clerical looking gentleman had boarded a bus at 8.10 p.m. It remained to be seen whether any evidence of how he got there was yet left in the hedgerows. These were indeed sprouting untidily and luxuriantly, and would have hidden all the bicycles in Hertfordshire. The fields immediately at hand were empty of livestock, and the car had not passed a single human being since it left Dry Stocking.

The two sergeants took one side of the lane, and Mr. Tuke the other. When they entered the fields, the high hedges concealed them. His hands in his pockets, a Larranaga between his lips, Harvey strolled slowly over the tussocky grass, raking the hedge beside him for a gleam of metal. He reflected that a spur of this kind made even the country enjoyable for a time.

Suddenly he pounced. But what he had seen was only one of those rusted bedstead ends with which the English landscape is so liberally and incomprehensibly bestrewn. He sauntered on again, humming to himself:

> "One said it was a hedgehog,
> But another he said, 'Nay' . . ."

He had not, however, been alone for five minutes when an excited bellow reached him from across the lane. Hurrying back to his gate, he found the two sergeants emerging from theirs. And Sergeant Webley was trundling his sheaves before him, in the shape of a bicycle. His pleasant face was bright with triumph, and even Sergeant Oake was grinning.

"Not two hundred yards from the gate," said Sergeant Webley ecstatically. "Shoved in among the brambles. And as good as new—or as good as second-hand—bar a bit of rust."

"I congratulate you again, and heartily," Mr. Tuke said with genuine warmth. "A long shot, Watson, a very long shot, as Sherlock Holmes said on a memorable occasion. And a damned good shot. Really, you know, this *is* a nice case. It improves every hour. I wonder what we shall find next?"

"This Mr. Holy Joe, I hope," said Sergeant Oake grimly. "*He'll* have a bit of explaining to do."

"And the first thing he'll have to explain," added Sergeant Webley, glancing at Mr. Tuke, "is who he is."

CHAPTER XX

MR. TUKE, who had telephoned to his wife from Bedford, where he dined, reached St. Luke's Court soon after nine. Mrs. Tuke, he found, was not alone. Very much at his ease in the largest chair in her drawing-room, sat or rather sprawled the Director of Public Prosecutions.

"Are you here again?" said Mr. Tuke pointedly.

Sir Bruton gave him a pop-eyed stare through the smoke of the Larranaga with which his hostess had provided him.

"Whaddayou mean, again?" he demanded. "Can't a poor lonely old man enjoy a spot of attractive society now and then without you butting in? Thought you were safely out of the way for another hour or two."

The Director was believed to know more interesting people, including a number of criminals, than anybody in

London. And though a bachelor, he lived in great comfort and untidyness in a house in Ashley Gardens, where several pretty nieces, now in the services, came to look after him, as they put it, when on leave. By their uncle's account, he practically ran a hostel for them and their friends.

"Fact is," he went on, "my niece Eleanor's turned up, with a couple of other gals. Can't get any peace in my own house. Regular Y.W.U.A., that's what it is."

"What does 'U' stand for?" Mrs. Tuke inquired.

"Unchristian," said Sir Bruton. "You ought to see the way they sink my liquor. Don't know what gals are coming to. And what have *you* been up to, Tuke? Wray phoned this afternoon. Said you were interfering again, down in Bedfordshire. Filching police from their duties to go on some wild goose chase, and couldn't I keep my own staff in order?"

Mr. Tuke smiled at his wife, and lowered himself into a chair.

"Wray ought to be grateful. At last the case is making progress."

"What case?"

"Come off it. This assumption of detachment deceives nobody. You really came here to steal a march on him."

Sir Bruton abandoned pretence. "Thought you seemed to be having a good time," he said. "Chasing cars, or something. Always like a bit of action in my stories. And this case grows on you," he admitted grudgingly. "If it is a case, of course. Well, come on. Cough it up."

Having joined his guest in a cigar, Harvey began his tale of the day's adventures. His wife lighted a Turkish cigarette and occupied her fingers with sewing for the French navy. Sir Bruton, to all appearance, fell into a doze. At the end, having omitted nothing but drawn no conclusions, Harvey awaited the Director's reactions with some curiosity. The old boy might look like a comatose codfish, but there was little he missed. And so his first words showed.

"First I've heard of this Holy Joe," he said, opening one eye. "Wray didn't mention him. Too busy with your misdemeanours. Well, they ought to be able to lay hands on him.

That may save trouble all round. If you ask me, he sounds uncommonly like the missing cousin."

"Well done," said Mr. Tuke in a patronising way.

"Think I can't see things as quick as you? Bah! Anyway, you could have spent your day worse. Though the bobbies seem to have done all the real work. Smart fellow, this Bedford man."

"A very intelligent officer."

Sir Bruton began to heave himself more upright in his chair, in the process spraying cigar-ash over his waistcoat. Endeavouring to salve some of this, and conveying the meagre results to an ashtray, he scattered a cloud of fine particles in the air.

"Fact is," he said, "we aren't sensibly dressed. Waistcoats ought to have things like bins stuck on 'em. Same as kangaroos. And look at carving. I need a suit of oilskins and a tent when I carve." Addressing this sort of apologia to Mrs. Tuke, he brushed his hands violently, dissipating more ash. "Well," he went on to Harvey, "what about this other bloke? The one you chased. What do you make of him?"

"What do you?"

"*I* think," said Sir Bruton, fixing his assistant with protuberant glare, "*I* think there are altogether too many mysterious blokes in this business. They keep popping up like rabbits. The missing cousin, and this Holy Joe, and now the fellow in the check doodah. Damn it—beg your pardon, ma'am"—the Director, who liked to describe himself as a lawyer of the old school, practised (towards ladies only) certain Victorian courtesies—"what I mean is, we've quite enough with the original bunch, without another three on top of 'em. Redundant, that's what they are. And even if Holy Joe's the cousin, it's one too many for my liking. See what I mean?"

Mr. Tuke clapped his hands softly. "This is pure reasoning. Very impressive. Because when the same idea occurred to me, I had something to go on. The check jacket was obviously bought off the peg for a shorter and broader man. Mr. Thomsett himself, at a guess. The trousers were short, too.

Well, if the sanctimonious Mr. Eady wanted to revisit the
neighbourhood of Stocking, he might think it politic to drop
his semi-clerical impersonation. So he borrows some duds,
and puts on a pair of horn-rims. It was good enough. Only
a few people at the station actually saw him as himself."

Sir Bruton grunted. "Oh, he's Eady all right. Eady went
to Cambridge—sort of hole he *would* go to—and this chap
comes from there. Now, is Eady the Dresser cousin? And
why was he snooping round this Stocking place?" A cunning
if pop-eyed glance preceded the next query. "Because when
he was there before, he saw something, eh?"

Harvey nodded. "It looks like that. And when he heard
of Raymond Shearsby's death, what he'd seen made him
curious. But what did he see? And why wait three weeks?
The news was in some Cambridge paper at the time. The
Vicar saw to that, because Cousin Mortimer thought it a waste
of money."

"Eady may have only just seen the paper. Or heard in
some other way. Don't make difficulties. We're getting on.
What I want to know is, why all this ballyhoo after the
chemist's wife? You say she couldn't have done it?"

"Apparently she couldn't. But on present evidence her
husband could."

"Then why didn't Eady go to see *him*?"

"He may have had his reasons. He'd hardly call on the
chap at the works, anyway. I don't believe they'd let him
in, and you couldn't do a bit of blackmail, if that's what
you're thinking of, out at the gate, with the attendant
listening. Eady *could* have called there, of course, on his
way in, and found Shearsby had gone home to lunch. But
then where was he in the interval? He turned up in the
street *after* I'd got to the house. Was he having his own
lunch, or did he meet Shearsby coming or going?" Mr.
Tuke shook his head. "After all, I can't explain everything."

"You surprise me," said Sir Bruton, grinding out the
stub of his cigar violently and messily. Mrs. Tuke, with true
hospitality, moved the cigar-box towards him. "Thank'y,"
he muttered absently, and there was a good deal of puffing

and scowling while he lighted a fresh Larranaga. He squinted through the smoke at Mr. Tuke. "Y'know, it's what I said before about this case. Oh, all *right!* It *is* a case. But it won't be one you and I can look at till they've cleared up all this hocus pocus of missing cousins and what not. More than ever now. It's a worse mess than before."

"I wouldn't say that. You have just pointed out that if Dresser is Eady it should simplify matters, and that Vance and Co. ought to lay hands on him soon. But wouldn't it be nice," Mr. Tuke added in a reflective tone, "if one could find him first?"

Sir Bruton snorted. "And how do you propose to set about it?"

"We have at least a rather cryptic clue to Dresser."

"That bit of verse, you mean?" Sir Bruton snorted again. "What was it?"

"'And while I understand and feel How much to them I owe.'"

"What's the fellow writing about? His bookies? Sounds like prose to me, anyhow."

"The higher criticism. And how right you are. That is what suggests Wordsworth." Harvey glanced at a delicate satinwood bookcase. "Like the Vicar of Stocking, we have the collected works somewhere."

Sir Bruton no longer seemed to be listening. Fumbling in his pockets, he produced untidy sheafs of papers. He put on his spectacles to sort these out.

"I looked up that place Stocking on the map. Silly name. There are two of 'em."

"So there are. Are you going to make a joke?"

"I'm going to give you some real poetry." The Director proceeded to recite from the back of an envelope:

"The novels of Silas K. Hocking
    Don't mention the village of Stocking.
        When he learnt that there were
        Not one, but a pair,
    He said, 'This nomenclature's shocking.'"

Yvette Tuke laughed, though she missed much of the point, none of Mr. Hocking's hundred novels having come her way. The versifier gobbled and chuckled.

"Wordsworth! Bah!" He unhooked his spectacles and waved them at Mr. Tuke. "Well, if you do dig those lines out, how are they going to help you?"

"I have no idea. Except that what the poet, whoever he may be, was writing about—it would scarcely be his bookies —seems to have a dim bearing on Martin Dresser. As I don't feel like tackling the whole of Wordsworth, we must try the quotation on some of our literary friends."

"There's that nice Mr. Payne," said Mrs. Tuke.

"A good idea. There's something else I want to ask him."

"I think you will be meeting him again tomorrow evening."

Yvette indicated a card that stood on her bureau. Her husband got up to look at this. Neat typewriting announced that Miss Vivien Ardmore was AT HOME on the following day, Saturday, the 26th, from 6 p.m. to 9 p.m. 'Any gay clothes' said the card. At the top Miss Ardmore had written, in a small hand showing more individuality than is commonly the case with any handwriting nowadays, 'Mr. and Mrs. Harvey Tuke', and below, 'Do forgive short notice and come. All the people you met before will be there.'

"Well, well," said Harvey, his dark brows raised. "How they do pursue one. Shall we go?"

"I felt sure you would want to, so I telephoned to Miss Ardmore and said we should be delighted."

Harvey handed the card to Sir Bruton. "Miss Ardmore is a young woman of intelligence, sense of humour and spirit," he remarked. "This, I take it, is a sort of challenge. Come and meet the suspects again. Yes, I shall be glad to do so. All the same, I don't think I'll wait till then to put my couple of questions to Payne, if I can get him now."

He went off to his study, found Rockley Payne's telephone number, and within a minute was talking to that young man, who in his usual eager way expressed his anxiety to help.

"For one thing," said Mr. Tuke, "I'm trying to track down a quotation."

"Verse or prose?"

"It is in verse form, anyway."

The couplet was once more repeated, and Mr. Payne could be heard muttering it over to himself.

"No," he said. "I can't place it. Sorry."

"Could it be Wordsworth?"

"It might be. I'll tell you what I can do, Mr. Tuke. I'll try it on the office tomorrow. Both offices—*The Ludgate* and the M.O.I. The ministry's full of bards, you know."

"It's very good of you. There's really no hurry. It's merely an interesting little pointer."

"Are we," inquired Mr. Payne, "still on the case, by any chance?"

"We are. I'll tell you about it tomorrow—that is, if you are coming to Miss Ardmore's party. My wife and I have been invited."

"Oh, good. Yes, I shall be there, also complete with wife, if mine can claw her way out of *her* ministry in time. She's in Economic Warfare. All God's chillun got ministries."

"One other question," said Harvey. "Raymond Shearsby seems to have had a friend at Cambridge. Did he happen to mention him to you? The man's name, or anything?"

"He did mention some chap there," the editor of *The Ludgate* replied. "A writer on economics. But his name—all I can remember is that it was something like a county. Cheshire, or Sussex, something of the sort. Shearsby met him in France."

"Many thanks. We creep on. I suppose nothing else that is likely to be of any use has come back to you? Remarks by Shearsby about Dresser, or his other cousins?"

"Not a thing, I'm afraid," said Rockley Payne regretfully. "I never heard of his cousins till that last visit of his, as I told you. Then he didn't mention any names. It was news to me that Miss Ardmore was one of them. I'd met her once or twice with Charles Gartside, but Charles only told me who she was that day we met you at her place."

Mr. Tuke thanked him for his co-operation and returned to the drawing-room. There he found his wife looking slightly perplexed, and Sir Bruton, his spectacles on his nose, waving Miss Ardmore's card of invitation.

"I was saying," said the Director, "you can always bring a guest to these informal do's. What about me?"

"I like your nerve," said Mr. Tuke.

"*You* can't talk. Wild horses wouldn't keep you away. And I'm interested in the case, aren't I? My office seems to be running it, don't it? Or you are. Wray says so, and he ought to know. Fact is," said Sir Bruton plaintively to Mrs. Tuke, "I never do see the people in the cases I have to vet. I sit at a thumping great desk all day, saying what's to be done with 'em, but I don't even know what they look like. Blind justice, that's me. Not the Bench. Though God knows it's blind enough sometimes. Anyhow, I call it tough on an old man. Now here's a chance. I'd like to go to this party."

Mrs. Tuke was still looking a little dubious.

"I am sure Miss Ardmore would be pleased——"

"Besides," said Sir Bruton in a wheedling manner, "the poor gal wants her party to go, don't she? Tuke and me are as good as a knock-about turn. We'll make it hum."

Harvey was grinning sardonically. "I think it's a fair tit for tat," he said. "Obviously Miss Ardmore is not entirely disinterested. She's hoping for some pickings."

Mrs. Tuke shrugged. "I will telephone to her again."

"Only thing is," said Sir Bruton, waving the card, "*I* haven't got any gay clothes. What does the gal mean? Fancy dress?"

"Don't worry if it is," Mr. Tuke adjured him. "Just be yourself."

PART FOUR:
RESULT

CHAPTER XXI

A LITTLE before mid-day on the following morning Mr. Tuke turned under the massive granite gateway of New Scotland Yard and made his way to the Assistant Commissioner's room. Wray gave him one of his foxy smiles, and reached for a telephone.

"Ask Inspector Vance to come up." He took a cigarette and turned to his visitor, now extending himself in a chair, cigar-case in hand. "Glad to see you for once, Tuke."

"What have I done to deserve this?"

"That's what I want to know. I've seen a short report on your proceedings yesterday. I want the whole story, please. Vance will be equally interested. He's upset about this bicycle. Feels he ought to have thought of it himself. This Sergeant Webley seems a cut above the ordinary country bobby."

"He is. He ought to be promoted."

"Your spotting that car was a useful piece of work, too. Though pure luck, of course."

"Plus observation. What a pity it is, Wray, that there's such a disparaging streak in you."

"I'm always trying to damp down your conceit."

Upon this mild bickering Inspector Vance entered. He was a man of forty-five, his fair hair thinning and a once athletic form beginning to suggest that amplitude more befitting superintendents. His perfectly wooden face concealed dark suspicions of Mr. Tuke, for while the latter was on excellent terms with many of the senior officers of the C.I.D., to some of their subordinates he was the fiend in human form who rent to tatters, with vitriolic comments, cases upon which they

had lavished all their care and skill for weeks. Sir Bruton
Kames, though he appended his illegible signature to criticisms
with which he entirely agreed, roused none of these feelings.
He was considered a good-hearted old boy, unfortunately clay
in the hands of his legal assistants, particularly Mr. Tuke.
This popular travesty of the facts was well known to the
Director, and afforded him much amusement.

Though Inspector Vance had often seen Harvey in court,
the two had not hitherto met. As the former disapproved
strongly of unprofessional meddlings in police matters, and
regarded it as insult added to injury that a really helpful
day's work should have been initiated by the D.P.P.'s malig-
nant senior assistant, the circumstances for a first meeting
might have been more happy. Harvey was well aware of these
feelings as he told his story. Mr. Vance listened without a
trace of expression. Wray, his Turkish cigarette smouldering
half the time between his bony fingers, kept his eyes on his
desk, scribbled a few notes, and ignored the slight tension in the
atmosphere.

At the end he leaned back, laced his fingers, and cracked
them sharply.

"Reference Mortimer Shearsby," ·he said. "Your self-
imposed researches, Tuke, seem merely to have confirmed
the fact, already known to us, that he is tight with money.
Now this bit of verse . . ." Wray muttered the lines to
himself, while Mr. Tuke watched him sardonically. "It
means nothing to me. I don't see how it's going to be any
help to us."

"You may be right," Mr. Tuke said accommodatingly.

Wray ground out his cigarette and took another. "Next,
the man in the check coat. Why the devil was he chasing
Mrs Shearsby? Whatever happened at Stocking, *she* wasn't
there. Therefore she wasn't at Guildford. You agree,
Inspector?"

Mr. Vance opened his tight lips for the first time.

"I don't believe there are two in it, sir," he said slowly,
passing a hand over his thinning hair. "If these deaths are
murders, and I've no real doubt about it now, then they

were thought out a good way ahead. That means, taking
the Mortimer Shearsbys first, if they were in it together *her*
alibi for the Stocking business was part of the scheme. Her
husband did his cousin in, while she drew attention to herself,
in a way. It's too much of a coincidence, otherwise, her going
to Cambridge that day, and passing so near the place. It
put us on to her, and then a day or two after she pulls an alibi
out of her pocket by remembering this woman in the bus.
But if I know anything about criminals, they'd have played the
same trick at Guildford. There'd have been a nice little alibi
for the one that didn't do it. But there isn't. Neither of them
have a sniff of one, so far, neither for the Saturday or Sunday."

Mr. Vance drew breath, and Wray gave him a quick nod.

"Yes, that's good, inspector. Damn' good. I hadn't
looked at it that way. How about the other couples?"

"It's just the same, sir. If one of a pair has an alibi for
one of the deaths, then neither has one for the other. So I'm
laying they were both singlehanded jobs."

Wray blew a smoke ring and watched it float away. "I
always thought so. Well, eliminating the chemist's wife, we've
now cut our possibles down to four—of the original six."

"Four?" Harvey queried.

"You won't have heard. We've traced Mlle Boulanger's
lorry. M.O.W.T. had a convoy routed down Warwick Way
that night, and one of the drivers reported a woman almost
chucking herself under his wheels. Weighing pros and cons,
that seems to clear the Frenchwoman, though I don't suppose
we shall ever know whether she was pushed or not." Wray
cracked his fingers again in his fidgety way. "Now let's get
back to your man in the Morris. Well, I fancy we know who
he is. Eh, Inspector?"

"Yes, sir. He'll be Holy Joe."

"He must be. We can't have any more unrelated factors
bobbing up. What's the latest about Joe?"

"He left his home on the afternoon of the 28th," the
Inspector said. "Told his wife he'd be away some days. He
gave the Cambridge poste restante as an address. Apparently
there's nothing in that—he's always on his travels, looking

up these precious hard luck cases of his. But he's not been home since. All his wife's had has been a postcard. As for her, I'd say she knows Eady's a wrong 'un, but she isn't giving anything away. As big a humbug as he is, from the look of her," said Mr. Vance sourly. "White hair, and smiles, and a fine show of false teeth, and eyes like gimlets."

Wray turned to Harvey. "This will be Greek to you——"

"I know Greek. And it isn't. I've heard about Mr. Eady. Sergeant Webley brought me up to date."

Wray was frowning. "What was he up to, anyway? Was he going to this Whipstead place, or did he change his mind at King's Cross? Did he see something when he got there? Or did he meet Raymond Shearsby in that lane? Why did he pinch the bicycle—if he did? To save his legs, or because something had delayed him? A hell of a lot of if's and an's and why's. Curse the fellow! What with the grave giving up its dead, we've one complication too many already. Now we've got another."

"Have we?" Mr. Tuke queried.

Wray stared at him. Inspector Vance was staring too. But the quicker wits of his chief were first off the mark.

"By God!" Wray snapped. "It could be. Holy Joe's trump card is his gentlemanly manner. He's about the same age as Martin Dresser. Dresser was a bad hat. Joe *is* one—we're damned sure of that, in spite of all his benevolent friends. Dresser would have a reason for going to Stocking. What do you think of it, Inspector?"

The Inspector was frowning heavily, pondering the idea.

"As you say, sir, it could be," he agreed. Then, for he was an honest man, he glanced at Mr. Tuke as he added: "Yes, I ought to have thought of it. If the man in the Morris is Joe, and Joe's Martin Dresser, it clears the decks and explains a lot."

"Well, we may not know much about Dresser, but we know a good deal about Joe," Wray said. "I wish you knew whether he'd tumbled to it you were after him, Tuke."

"Neither Sergeant Webley nor I are clairvoyant."

Wray's fingers were drumming on his desk. "Well, get

after him, Vance. You'd better go down to Cambridge
yourself. You know the locals have asked for a man to watch
this taxi-driver?"

"Thomsett, sir? Yes, Detective-Constable Pratt went last
night."

"You'll have Sergeant Gowrie with you, I suppose? Take
another man if you want him. We're on to something at last.
You're watching Joe's house?"

"Yes, sir."

"We ought to have his prints. I've a good mind to take a
warrant out and have his place dusted for them. You've got
Dresser's with you?"

"Yes, sir," said the Inspector again.

"Get Mrs. Shearsby's story about Joe's visit. You'd better
handle that yourself. Though this Sergeant Webley seems to
have his wits about him. But whoever sees her will have to
go carefully——" Wray broke off to give Harvey a foxy look.
"What are *you* grinning at, Tuke?"

"All this zeal and action. Most exhilarating. When you've
finished, may I ask a question or two before Inspector Vance
vanishes in a cloud of dust?"

"I have finished. Fire away."

"How is the London end going? Any developments, apart
from the rehabilitation of Mlle Boulanger?"

Wray nodded. "One bit of news. We've got a line on
Mrs. Porteous's doings on Bank Holiday Sunday. Her friends
in Guildford gave us the names of one or two more here in
London. 'Mrs. Porteous called on a Miss Blissett, another
schoolteacher, just before lunch that day. She was very much
annoyed, because she'd come up to keep an appointment
with a cousin. The cousin had telephoned on the Friday, and
they'd arranged to meet at Waterloo at eleven. Mrs. Porteous
waited in the booking hall for an hour, but the cousin didn't
show up. Unfortunately Miss Blissett was just going out to
lunch, and was in a hurry, so she didn't hear the cousin's
name, or sex. Mrs. Porteous said that as she was in London
she'd look at the bomb damage." Wray lighted another
cigarette from the stump of the old one. "The story suggests

that Mrs. Porteous was deliberately got out of the way that Sunday. Not necessarily by a cousin—a voice can be faked over the phone. But it narrows our time factor."

"If it was a London cousin," Mr. Tuke said, "you'd think she'd trot along to have it out with the culprit."

"Perhaps she did. Perhaps she was too cross. They were both out that day, anyhow. So was Mortimer Shearsby."

Mr. Tuke knocked the ash from his cigar and addressed his next question to Inspector Vance.

"Do you know, Inspector, if Raymond Shearsby had a letter or telegram on the day of his death, or beforehand, making an appointment for that evening? I noticed that there is no telephone at the cottage."

Mr. Vance looked at the Assistant Commissioner, who nodded before glancing curiously at Mr. Tuke.

"There was nothing about any appointment, sir, in the letters I took over from his cousin," the inspector said. "I have heard nothing about any post or telegram for him that day. There were some bits of paper in his pocket, but they'd been so long in the water that the writing had run, and they were just pulp. You'll remember, sir," Mr. Vance added in his most wooden manner, "it was thought to be an accident, so the locals didn't pay much attention to letters and such."

"What are you getting at, Tuke?" Wray inquired.

"Leave me my little mystifications. But in my role of *amicus curiae*, may I make a suggestion?"

"You would, anyhow."

"Then I would suggest an inquiry on these lines. There will be a record of telegrams, and as it was, if you'll pardon the pun, a red-letter day in Stocking, the village postman may still remember if he had anything for the cottage."

Wray continued to stare. Then he shrugged.

"Will you be good enough to humour Mr. Tuke, Inspector?"

"Very good, sir," said the inspector, more flatly than ever. "If that's all, I'll be getting off to Cambridge."

Mr. Tuke reached for his hat. Then he paused.

"I've been reading the cancelled story, by the way. 'Too

Many Cousins'. It is uncannily prophetic. Well, at the end you're left in the air, with strong suspicions of the dead uncle who turns out to be alive. But he also has a wife, collected during his absence. Arising out of that, haven't we forgotten something? Or somebody? What about Mrs. Eady?"

Wray stared again. "Well, what about her?"

"What was *she* doing on the dates in question? Because if Eady is Martin Dresser. . . ."

"What revolting ideas you do have," said Wray.

CHAPTER XXII

FROM the open door and windows of No 10 Falcon Mews East came a babel of talk. It was after seven, and the party was evidently in full swing. Mrs. Tuke, in navy blue, an impertinent blue trifle on her dark head, leading a procession of three up the narrow outside stair, found an overflow in the apple-green hall. Miss Ardmore's sitting-room appeared to be packed with people. A thick layer of tobacco smoke hung under the rather low ceiling, and the noise was deafening. Gradually one or two familiar faces materialised out of the throng. Mr. Mainward was holding aloft a tray of glasses: Charles Gartside's horn-rims and disgusted expression rose above a mass of heads in a corner. Mrs. Tuke felt a touch on her arm, and found Cecile Boulanger beside her. Then a sudden swirl of the scrum heeled out Miss Ardmore herself, tall and slender and surprisingly unruffled in green corduroy slacks and a yellow shirt.

"How nice of you to come," she said to Yvette. "For this sort of thing one really needs expanding rooms, like Oxford bookcases. I'll get you some drinks. Mr. Mainward!"

The tray of glasses began to sway towards them. She was now nodding to Mr. Tuke, and gazing at Sir Bruton with some curiosity. But if she caught his name when Mrs. Tuke effected introductions, it apparently conveyed nothing to her at the moment. Harvey thought she seemed a little abstracted.

"How de do," said Sir Bruton, whose pop-eyed stare appeared to indicate approval. "Kind of you to let me come."

He was feeling for his cigar-case, but Mr. Tuke forestalled him.

"Not one of those things. Have a cigar."

Mr. Mainward had fought his way to them. He carefully lowered his tray and bowed with his customary *impressement* to Mrs. Tuke. Then he saw Sir Bruton, and behind his spectacles, with their immense side-pieces, his eyes looked startled.

"What have you got?" Vivien Ardmore was asking, eyeing the contents of the tray. "I'm sorry there's no Pernod," she said to Yvette. Her slightly worried glance went to Mr. Tuke. "An extraordinary thing's happened. I've been burgled."

"Nothing valuable taken, I hope?"

"Only the Pernod and half a lemon."

"A burglar of discrimination," Harvey said lightly.

Mr. Mainward handed drinks. Vivien still looked worried.

"That's all that's gone, so far as I can see. Oh, and a tumbler. And something was spilt in here—the carpet's been scrubbed. I only found it out when I got back after lunch. It must have happened this morning, while I was at the office, because the carpet was still wet. It's damp now."

She pointed across the room, where little of the carpet was to be seen for feet and legs.

"Has anybody besides yourself got a key?" Harvey asked.

"The woman who cleans the place for me. But she only comes three days a week, and never on Saturdays. And she's a Rechabite or something. She disapproves of what I expect she calls my orgies. But we get on very well for all that, and I've had her three years. And if she's suddenly developed a passion for Pernod, she could have taken it at any time in the last month."

"Has anything of this kind ever happened before?"

A wrinkle of perplexity contracted Miss Ardmore's brow.

"Well, I *have* had a suspicion once or twice lately that somebody's been through my things. Letters, and so on.

I'm not very tidy, so I can't swear to it, but letters I thought were in one part of my bureau I've found in another. And things in the drawers weren't as I remembered leaving them. Annie, my char, never touches the inside of the bureau. Of course, she could ransack it if she wanted to—it's never locked—but why should she start now? It's only during the last few months that I've noticed anything—or thought so." Miss Ardmore shrugged. "Well, I needn't bother you with all this. I only mentioned it because of the Pernod—and the lemon, which is almost as rare."

"Is there any other way into this place?" Harvey inquired.

"No. The back windows look into the yards of the houses in Cranborne Gardens. You'd want a ladder to get to them."

Sir Bruton, over a gin and lime, fixed Miss Ardmore with a shrewd if protuberant eye.

"Bins," he said suddenly. "Who was talking about bins?"

"No one," said Mr. Tuke. "What sort of bins? You were talking of the domestic variety last night, with reference to waistcoats."

"Got a bin in your kitchen?" Sir Bruton demanded of Miss Ardmore.

"Yes, I have."

"Looked in it since you came home to-day?"

"I haven't *looked* in it. I shot some rubbish in."

"Have a squint now, there's a good gal. I'll come along."

"The kitchen's frightfully untidy," Vivien Ardmore said. "I've just left everything till I wash up later."

"I'll stay and help," said Sir Bruton handsomely. "Like old times, when I hadn't a brief to my name, and only three shirts and half a one."

"Why half a one?" Mrs. Tuke wanted to know.

The Director chuckled. "I'd thrown the thing away, and used the tails for dusters or something. Not that I did much dusting. Then I wanted a shirt. It looked all right. Sleeves and collar and two front buttons left. Sort of dicky. Wore it for months like that. Come on, Miss Ardmore. Let's peep into this bin of yours."

With a shrug and a lift of her left eyebrow, Vivien gave

Mr. Tuke a comical look and led the way out of the room, Sir Bruton lumbering after her. Mr. Tuke began to move his head from side to side in an endeavour to see the damp stain on the carpet. He was thus found by Rockley Payne, who having greeted Mrs. Tuke caught his eye and held up a sheet of paper.

"I've got what you wanted," said the editor of *The Ludgate*, *sotto voce*. "It's Southey. 'The Scholar.' I ought to have known. It's in most anthologies."

Harvey took the paper, and standing a little to one side with Mr. Payne, studied a typewritten set of verses. There were four stanzas; and the first two were enough to make Harvey frown so diabolically that the youthful editor said afterwards he felt like crossing his fingers.

> My days among the dead are passed;
> Around me I behold,
> Where'er these casual eyes are cast,
> The mighty minds of old:
> My never-failing friends are they,
> With whom I converse day by day.
>
> With them I take delight in weal
> And seek relief in woe;
> And while I understand and feel
> How much to them I owe,
> My cheeks have often been bedewed
> With tears of thoughtful gratitude. . . .

Under Mr. Payne's curious gaze his companion continued to frown blackly as he read the stanzas a second time. Then the frown lifted, and his lips curled in a sardonic smile.

"You see before you, Mr. Payne, the biggest ass in the legal profession."

"Oh, no, no," said Rockley Payne in a shocked murmur. "But it helps, does it?"

"It does indeed. It's a revelation. I stand blasted with excess of light—which isn't Southey, anyway. I am enormously indebted to you. With tears of thoughtful gratitude," said Mr. Tuke, still staring in a fascinated way at the paper in his hand, "I must leave it at that for the moment. This requires some meditation. I'll tell you all I can later on."

"Right you are," said Mr. Payne in his accommodating way. "I'm glad to have been useful. Have you heard about the burglary?"

Mr. Tuke nodded as he thrust the paper in his pocket.

"I was looking for the damp patch on the carpet."

"I'll show you."

They edged their way through the crush. At the end of the room near the bookshelves, beside a low round table, a considerable area of the grey rug had evidently been recently cleaned with a wet cloth.

"Funny little things seem to pursue this family," Mr. Payne remarked, again in an undertone, though in the clamour of talk all round this precaution seemed superfluous.

"As you say," Mr. Tuke agreed, staring at the damp rug.

"All this mob, by the way," the editor continued, "will be pushing off soon. There's another and more splendiferous do on at Bailey's Hotel. The family are staying for a little symposium about their own troubles. That includes Charles and Mainward. Charles asked me to stop. He's out of his depth in crime. Arboriculture's his passion. He's rather like a tree walking himself." Mr. Payne was craning his head to peer about the crowded room. Suddenly he called and waved. "Oy, Audrey!"

A young woman fought her way to join them, and Harvey was introduced to Mrs. Rockley Payne, who was small and neat and dark, with a lively intelligent face. Her large brown eyes regarded him with faint amusement but no surprise. No doubt, like Sergeant Webley, she had been given a *portrait parlé*.

"Let us see what the bin has produced," Harvey said.

The young couple looked puzzled. As they all moved away, the editor with his slight limp, he stooped to pick up some small object from the carpet. It was a splinter of glass.

"I trod on it. A bit of the missing tumbler, perhaps."

Mrs. Tuke having been collected and introduced, the com-
bined party struggled out into the hall, to which Miss Ardmore and Sir Bruton had returned. The Director, cigar in
one hand, spectacles on his nose, was holding up to this in
his handkerchief a fragment of a tumbler, at which he was
sniffing. Vivien Ardmore, looking harassed, was conveying
two other fragments in a duster.

"Been doing a bit of sleuthing," said Sir Bruton, scowling
over his spectacles at Mr. Tuke. "Deductive reasoning,
if you know what that is. Found this in the bin. There's
half a lemon there too—or most of it. Someone's cut off a
slice. It don't fit the other half that wasn't used. The slice
isn't in the bin—we turned the damned thing out. And this
glass has been washed—it's still wet. Not a sniff of Pernod or
anything else."

"Why wash a tumbler after it has been broken?" Harvey
asked.

"Whaddayou mean, *after?*"

Rockley Payne showed the sliver of glass from the carpet.
It was found to fit into one of the larger fragments held by Miss
Ardmore. That young lady's air of uneasiness was now
marked. Her wide-set eyes were dark and troubled, and the
little frown was etched deep in her forehead.

"What does it all *mean?*" she said. "It's so *silly!* I can
understand a thief going off with the Pernod—though I
don't know why he left all the other stuff. But if the tumbler
was broken in there"—she gestured with a capable, long-
fingered hand towards the room where her unsuspecting
guests still chattered and laughed—"why wash the bits afterwards, as Mr. Tuke says? And what's happened to the slice
of lemon? It was a whole lemon this morning, when I went
to the office. It was on the dresser. The other half's there
now. Why on earth throw half into the bin, and take the
slice away? It's nowhere about. We've looked." She made a
little grimace of exasperation. "Oh, the whole thing's crazy!"

"It is indeed," said Mrs. Tuke, giving her a smile of sympathy. "For who in the world takes lemon with Pernod?"

Cecile Boulanger appeared in the doorway of the living-room, the noticeable horn-rims of Mr. Mainward flashing inquisitively over her shoulder. But before she could be enlightened as to the cause of this conference in the hall, a rush of departing guests, en route for Bailey's Hotel, followed after her. Hasty farewells were made, and hats were seized. Miss Ardmore acknowledged the former in an abstracted and perfunctory manner. For a minute or two the noisy crowd clattered down the steps and over the cobbles of the mews. Then comparative peace descended upon No. 10. Mlle Boulanger and Guy Mainward had withdrawn again out of the way: in the room there remained with them only Charles Gartside and four or five more.

During the confusion Sir Bruton had relieved his hostess of the pieces of the tumbler which she was holding, and adding his own fragment had carried this treasure trove in the duster down the hall to the kitchen. Mr. Tuke followed his chief's movements with a speculative eye. Was the old boy on to something? No high degree of deductive reasoning was required to suggest an exploration of the bin; but the Director's test with the halved lemon was ingenious, and its upshot decidedly odd. Why, indeed, should anyone walk away with a slice of lemon?

Mr. Gartside now loomed gloomily in the doorway, apparently seeking his betrothed. He peered at Harvey and then at Mrs. Tuke with the air of wondering whether he ought to know them, but rather hoping that he would not be expected to. Even Vivien Ardmore's harassed expression lightened a little as she watched him, and she smiled faintly.

"Yes, Charles," she said. "You *have* met. On Monday evening, though I don't suppose you caught the names. Mrs. Harvey Tuke. And Mr. Tuke. And this is——" She threw a comically apologetic look at Sir Bruton, who had just rejoined them. "*I* oughtn't to talk. Because I never caught *your* name. When one's throwing a party, one's mind is so full of things—seeing that everyone has a drink, wondering if the glasses will go round——"

"Don't let a little thing like that spoil your sleep," said Sir Bruton graciously, waving his spectacles about. "Kames is the name, ma'am. I'm Tuke's boss, though you'd never think it from his insubordinate manner to me."

Realisation dawned on Miss Ardmore. Her fine eyes widened.

"Oh, I'd no idea. . . . Then you're the Public Prosecutor?"

"Director, ma'am. Director. Sounds more English. Less of Foquier Tinville and the Committee of Public Safety about it. Though I often wish," added the Director wistfully, "I had some of *his* powers. *I'd* make the heads roll. I'd start with the Bench. . . . What are *you* glowering at, Tuke? Got a smut on my nose, or something?"

"I wasn't aware I was looking at you," Mr. Tuke said. "One must look somewhere. Unfortunately. I was thinking."

"Heaven help us!"

Harvey had turned to his hostess.

"I suppose you've been through all your rooms since you discovered these curious thefts?"

"I've been in my bedroom and the kitchen, Mr. Tuke. And the bathroom. There's a spare room, and a little cubby-hole with a skylight I use for boxes and lumber. I haven't been in them. Anyway, nothing else is missing, so far as I can see, if that's what you mean. I've got a few bits of jewellery, and they're all right."

"We might have a look at those two rooms."

Miss Ardmore's eyebrow went up. "If you like. I haven't been in the lumber room for weeks. There's nothing there but trunks and cardboard boxes and an old chair or two."

Sir Bruton's protuberant eyes were on his assistant as he put away his spectacles.

"What's biting you now?" he wanted to know.

"Nothing in particular. It will do no harm to go through the place, on general security principles."

"Nosy Parker," Sir Bruton grunted.

The worried frown had returned to Miss Ardmore's brow.

"I must have a cigarette," she exclaimed irritably. "I shall be expecting horrors in a minute."

Mr. Gartside having given her a cigarette, she glanced into the living-room, where her remaining guests were happily talking all at once and consuming drinks and snacks of food, and then opened a door across the narrow hall.

"This is my bedroom."

Nothing was to be seen in the pleasantly but sparely furnished bedroom, with its window overlooking the mews, but what might have been expected. Vivien Ardmore passed on and threw open a door beyond. Mr. Tuke and Sir Bruton were behind her, and Charles Gartside, with his habitual air of distaste, lounged after them. Yvette Tuke remained with Rockley Payne and his wife in the front of the hall.

"The spare room," said Miss Ardmore.

This was also devoid of special interest. Its window was one of those above the yards of the houses in Cranborne Gardens.

"You know all about the kitchen," Vivien remarked with a faint smile to Sir Bruton as they stood before a door at the end of the hall. "Here's the bath-room." She revealed that rather cramped apartment, which lay at a right angle to the kitchen. Her hand went to the knob of one more door, behind the living-room. "And this is the lumber room."

She flung open the door.

"*Oh!* . . . " she said, in a queer, dry voice.

She backed so abruptly that she trod on Mr. Tuke's foot. He had already seen what she had seen. So had Sir Bruton, who with surprising agility pushed to the front. As Vivien herself, a hand clapped to her lips, her eyes tight shut, her face drained of all colour, felt blindly behind her with her free hand, from which the cigarette had fallen, until Charles Gartside grasped it and drew her away, the Director and Harvey stood together on the threshold and stared into the little room.

It was a narrow slip-room, with a skylight of frosted glass. The rear end was filled with odd pieces of furniture, suitcases, trunks and boxes. In the space towards the door, which just cleared his head, sprawled the body of a man, lying on his back. His upturned face was distorted in a frightful grimace, the eyeballs protruding, the grey lips drawn back in a snarl, the stained teeth clenched. There was dried froth at the

corners of the lips, and unpleasant evidence on his clothing
that he had been violently sick. The whole dreadful face was
livid. It was almost unrecognisable; but a long nose and thick,
silvery hair, a check jacket rucked up under the armpits,
grey flannel trousers, a cloth cap and horn-rims lying on the
floor, placed the man's identity beyond reasonable doubt.
Mr. Thomsett's fare would take only one more ride.

CHAPTER XXIII

Mr. Tuke, emerging from a fit of profound abstraction,
glanced about him at his companions and leaned over to
murmur to his wife:

> "Hans Breitmann gife a barty——
>   Vere ish dot barty now?"

Mrs. Tuke frowned at him and said, "*Tais-toi!*" under her
breath.

It was indeed a glum little company that sat waiting in
Miss Ardmore's pleasant room. Vivien herself, smoking
cigarettes endlessly, her wide mouth a bitter scarlet slash in
her white face, her narrowed eyes staring before her, leaned
against Charles Gartside on the divan, her corduroyed legs
curled under her. Mr. Gartside, his own lank frame extended,
his hands in his pockets, had some reason for looking more
melancholiously disgusted than ever. A much subdued Mr.
Mainward sat with a protective air beside Cecile Boulanger.
From time to time he ran a well-kept hand over his thick
brown hair, and seemed to be wondering uncomfortably
what the Foreign Office would think of all this. Cecile's set
face, clenched hands and stiff, upright attitude told of the
tight control she was keeping over the French half of her.
Only her dark eyes moved restlessly and warily from one to
another of her companions.

Yvette Tuke, her own charming face serious and a little
pale, always met this anxious look with a smile. At her side,

faute de mieux in a straight spade-backed Queen Anne chair,
Harvey (perhaps for this reason) appeared at his grimmest.
Only Sir Bruton, sprawling in the deepest chair in the room,
his chins resting on his chest, seemed to be contentedly
dozing. His lips, turned down in a sour expression, moved
gently and automatically in and out as he drew on a cheroot,
which he had lighted unrebuked. His hands were clasped on
his stomach. Presently a length of ash fell on his waistcoat,
already liberally powdered.

Half empty bottles, glasses with dregs in them, over-flowing
ashtrays, gave the room a rather sordid, after-the-party air.
The door was closed. From outside, in the hall, and the other
rooms, came the tramp of heavy footsteps and a subdued
murmur of voices. A very different sort of party was in progress there. Inspector Vance being believed to be in Cambridge or Bedford or somewhere, on the trail of the man
whose body had lain in the little lumber room but had since
been transferred to the spare bedroom, Mr. Tuke's telephone
call to the Central Office had resulted in another inspector
arriving to take charge of the proceedings. With him had
come a finger-print expert, a photographer, and several other
policemen. Soon after the arrival of this posse, a superintendent from "F" Division had appeared on the scene, and
he had been followed by a police surgeon. It was at the
superintendent's suggestion that Miss Ardmore's remaining
guests, including the Rockley Paynes, had been allowed to
leave. The editor of *The Ludgate*, as a writer of crime stories,
had gone with some reluctance.

The superintendent had also pointed out tactfully that
there really was no need for Sir Bruton and Mr. and Mrs.
Tuke to inconvenience themselves by staying on. Sir Bruton
had replied blandly that he had promised to help Miss Ardmore with her washing-up. Mr. Tuke merely said if he was not
in the way he would like to remain. Mrs. Tuke said nothing:
she had already decided to take Vivien Ardmore home to
St. Luke's Court. If the superintendent and his colleagues
felt that their style was a little cramped by the presence on
the scene of the crime of the Director of Public Prosecutions

and his most notorious assistant, no doubt they also felt there was little they could do about it. They closed the door on these unfortunately influential busybodies and got on with their work. Some of the supernumeraries presently departed; but the superintendent, the inspector, the doctor and a couple of subordinates were still at No. 10.

It was now half-past eight. Double summer time notwithstanding, the cloudy sky had brought a premature dusk. Shadows crept over the living-room. Harvey looked at his watch, got up from his uneasy seat, and collected a couple of plates on which there was still some food. Mr. Mainward sprang to his assistance, and Sir Bruton opened an eye.

"Wondering when someone 'ud have the gumption to think of that."

A faint air of animation, a sort of ghostly echo of the party so ruthlessly cut short, returned to the room. Though Vivien Ardmore at first refused nourishment, Mr. Gartside, revealing dictatorial qualities, ordered her to stop being silly. Cecile was persuaded by Mr. Mainward to eat a sandwich. Drinks went round. Everybody, in fact, realised the mundane truth that they were exhausted and hungry.

Guy Mainward, in his travels, passed the open window.

"The vultures are gathering," he said.

Half the inhabitants of Falcon Mews, East and West, and others attracted by police cars in Brampton Street, were indeed now forming a small crowd outside. A constable was heard adjuring them to move on, please. Other voices becoming audible in the hall, Mr. Tuke, who was tired of being imprisoned, got up suddenly and went out of the room.

The inspector from Scotland Yard was talking to one of his posse.

"No news yet of Inspector Vance?" Mr. Tuke inquired.

' No, sir." The inspector, whose name was Willows, and who was of a more accommodating type than Mr. Vance, looked thoughtfully at the interrupter. After all, the D.P.P.'s office was the D.P.P's office, and he knew more about Mr. Tuke than the local superintendent. "I'm hoping we'll soon hear from him," he said. "I don't know a lot about this case."

"A bright idea of mine," said Mr. Tuke, "has been exploded by a poet who died a century ago. If it is any news to you, the corpse is Mr. Joseph Eady, and no one else."

"Very likely, sir," the inspector replied. "I couldn't say. I've sent for Mrs. Eady, and for a sergeant who knows Eady himself. There's nothing to show who this man is."

In his mood of candour, Mr. Willows went on to explain that the corpse's pockets contained only small change, cigarettes, a handkerchief, and a bunch of keys. Letters and other papers were conspicuous (in these days of national registration) by their absence. The check jacket bore the name of a multiple clothing firm.

Vivien Ardmore, having steeled herself for a second scrutiny of the terrible dead face, declared that she had never seen the man before; and Mlle Boulanger, put through the same ordeal, made the same reply. For the rest, Vivien said she had no idea how he had got into her flat. She had not been in the box-room for some weeks. She had never owned a third key. That morning she left for her office as usual at nine, and the place should have remained locked until her return after lunch at half-past two. On the previous evening, the Friday, she had been at home from seven o'clock onwards, preparing for her party; and as the intruder was in Cambridge as late as a quarter to five, his entry and death at No. 10 could hardly have occurred overnight without her knowledge. The mystery of the Pernod and the lemon had been thrashed out, and the police surgeon had an idea about this.

That official, carrying his black bag, came out of the spare room at this moment. He and Mr. Tuke were old friends.

"Hullo, Tuke," he said. "I heard you were here. You do get about, don't you. And the P.P. too." He turned to Inspector Willows. "The man's been dead six to eight hours. If I hadn't heard something about the case, all I'd say till I've cut him up is that he died of some violent irritant poison, taken internally. But it may interest you to know that the symptoms look very like those in the Guildford business."

"Sodium nitrite again, sir?"

"I only say it could be. And Pernod would disguise the

salt, and lemon tickle up its peculiar qualities. Well, I'm off. You can take him away, and the sooner the better. As I think I know what to look for, I may be home by midnight."

The doctor paused on his way out to exchange sarcastic greetings with the Director, whose protuberant stare and reeking cheroot had appeared in the doorway of the sitting-room. Inspector Willows had now been joined by the divisional superintendent from the spare room; and, as the doctor departed, several persons could be heard coming up the front steps, for the door was still open. And the first to appear, at a hurried trot, was Inspector Vance.

Shadows were filling the narrow hall, and Inspector Willows, at this moment, turned on the light. A powerful bulb blazed out above Mr. Tuke's head; and as the newcomer saw who was there, for once his wooden reserve failed him. His expression became one of acute exasperation. Then his eye fell on Sir Bruton, and Mr. Vance's whole air, casting restraint and subordination to the winds, was that of a much persecuted camel who feels that the last straw has been laid upon it. In his irritation he opened his mouth to speak, but snapped his lips tight just in time. While he stood obviously if inwardly raging, a fresh arrival broke the tension.

A short, plump middle-aged woman in a grey coat and skirt which somehow suggested a uniform came through the door. A gold cross hung from her neck. Her round face, scarcely lined, was as pink as a child's, and her hair, drawn back beneath an unbecoming hat, was almost white. It was easy to believe that in other circumstances she could look a model of benevolence—a diligent church worker, even a deaconess, perhaps. But she did not look benevolent now. Her small mouth was pinched and angry, and her pale eyes, flitting suspiciously from one to another of the strangers in the hall, were as hard and unfeeling as marbles. A plainclothes policeman who came in behind her touched her arm, keeping her in the doorway, as Inspector Willows advanced to greet his colleague.

"Glad you're back," he said. "I didn't expect you so soon. We've been trying to contact you in Cambridge."

"I left a couple of hours ago," Mr. Vance explained. He had himself in hand again, but he ignored Sir Bruton and Mr. Tuke. "When I got there, I found that Eady'd slipped back to town last night. His pals in Cambridge gave him away fast enough when they heard it was a murder case. I went straight to his house, and met Sergeant McPhee there, just bringing Mrs. Eady along."

Inspector Willows looked curiously at the woman in grey.

"I've sent for Adney, too. He knows Eady."

"And *he's* been done in now?"

"Looks like it's him. It's your Cambridge friend, anyway, from his clothes. Nothing on him to identify him. Sodium nitrite again, the doctor thinks. Same symptoms."

"Well, we'd better settle it," Inspector Vance said.

He turned to beckon to the woman. Sir Bruton, pulling violently at his cheroot, put in a word.

"Inspector Vance, eh?"

Mr. Vance turned stiffly. "Yes, sir."

"Know who I am, eh? Justifiably annoyed. Horrible old man butting in. where he isn't wanted. Not my fault, Inspector. Innocent as a babe. So's Mr. Tuke. We came here to a party."

"Yes, sir," repeated the inspector tonelessly. But his eyes did not look placated. Their glance went past the Director to the half open door of the sitting-room, where he could see Vivien Ardmore and Charles Gartside sitting together on the divan, the young woman's strained white face and her betrothed's horn-rims and supercilious features turned anxiously to the doorway.

Mr. Vance looked at Inspector Willows. "Where is he?"

The other nodded towards the spare room, and the two officers began to walk up the hall. Mrs. Joseph Eady and her escort followed. Her beady eyes flickered warily from Sir Bruton to Mr. Tuke as she brushed past them in the narrow space. Her plump face was less pink, and her tongue wetted her lips. At the spare room door Inspector Vance spoke to her in a low voice, and then the whole party disappeared inside.

Sir Bruton uttered a gobbling chuckle. "We aren't popular, lovey."

"Inspector Vance is a stiff-necked ass," said Mr. Tuke. Sir Bruton chuckled again. And then, from the spare room, came a sudden outcry. A voice rose hysterically.

"I tell you I know who did it! He told me. He was coming to meet her. She was a devil, he said, and he wasn't taking any risks. But she got him. Let me get my hands on the——"

Mrs. Eady's language became such as no deaconess would use. Other voices were heard trying to calm her.

"I haven't got it wrong, you bloody fool!" the woman screamed. "Didn't he give me her name, in case? . . . I wrote it down. I've got it here. Didn't he see her——?"

Mrs. Eady reappeared, impelled by Sergeant McPhee towards the kitchen, where he was adjuring her to rest and simmer down. Breathing fast, her mouth an ugly line in her now pallid face, her beady eyes glittering, she looked more venomous than grief-stricken. The two inspectors, following after, came down the hall. Mr. Vance wore a puzzled frown. He seemed to have forgotten the presence of Sir Bruton and Mr. Tuke.

"She's muddled it somehow," he was saying. "Whatever Eady wanted with Mrs. Mortimer Shearsby, she couldn't have done the Stocking murder. It couldn't have been her he saw there. I've been into all that——"

He stopped as he met Mr. Tuke's sardonic gaze.

"The deceased *is* Eady, then, Inspector?" Harvey inquired. Mr. Vance nodded grudgingly. "Yes, sir."

"And his wife has been flinging accusations about?" The inspector stared frostily.

"Don't be childish!" Harvey said sharply. "We couldn't help hearing you. Or her. And I happen to know something about this case. More than you realise, perhaps. For instance, with regard to Mrs. Mortimer Shearsby and the Stocking murder, if you care to listen, Inspector, I think I can show you how she could have done it."

CHAPTER XXIV

Soon after six o'clock on Thursday evening, the last day of August, a month which, in a wider sphere than that of a lawyer's holiday, had not been uneventful, Mr. Tuke paid another visit to the Sheridan Club. Rather more than a fortnight had passed since his fellow member, Parmiter, had there introduced him to the Shearsby case. In the lounge Mr. Tuke noted the obituarist himself, seated with a group of other men. Parmiter looked up and waved. A few minutes later he left his companions and crossed the big room to where Harvey lay extended in a chair with a glass of Amontillado and a cigar.

"Well met," Parmiter said. "I have been wondering when I should see you again."

"Are you feeling like a game, if we can get a table?"

The obituarist hesitated. For once billiards did not seem to appeal to him. He pulled a chair beside Harvey's.

"Shall we try later?" he said. "The fact is, Tuke, I am devoured by curiosity."

"Indeed? What can I do about it?"

"You remember what we talked about the last time we met here?"

"Certainly I do."

"Did you ever do anything about the story I told you?"

There was unusual animation in Parmiter's rather melancholy face, but Mr. Tuke merely raised his black eyebrows with an air of innocent surprise.

"I? I recall remarking at the time that if there was anything behind your story, it was a case for the police."

"Oh, why fence?" Parmiter exclaimed. Then he smiled. "Cautious devil, aren't you? Anyway, if you *have* been on holiday—yes, I know that—I suppose you read the papers?"

"Only *The Times* and *The Law Journal*."

"I'm referring to a report, which did appear in *The Times*, of an inquest opened and adjourned at Kensington the day before yesterday. It was on the body of a man named Joseph Eady. I am not interested in him professionally. He is unknown to my files, and therefore to fame. I shall not write his obituary. But," said Parmiter, leaning forward, his eyes on Mr. Tuke's inscrutable face, "what did interest me was the cause of death. Sodium nitrite. It struck a chord."

"It would, of course," Mr. Tuke agreed.

"Then," Parmiter went on, "there was an announcement in the papers this morning that in connection with the inquiry a woman has been detained. No name was given. But at lunch in Fleet Street to-day I met a reporter I know who is covering the case for his paper. He said it was obvious at the inquest that the police were keeping a lot up their sleeves. The dead man's wife gave evidence of identification, but when she tried to say more she was firmly dealt with by the coroner. The affair was over in ten minutes. But my journalist friend told me another thing. The woman who has been detained is a Mrs. Lilian Shearsby."

Mr. Tuke drew on his cigar and looked politely interested. Parmiter, watching him from under his heavy lids, moved impatiently.

"Oh, come!" he said. "What is happening? I'm sure you know something, Tuke. Your indifference is too studied. And, after all, I drew your attention to the fatalities in this family. Three are dead, and now, in connection with a second case of poisoning by sodium nitrite, a woman bearing the same name has been detained. Do you wonder I'm interested?"

"Not at all," said Mr. Tuke. "You have made up your mind, I see, that you were correct in linking the three fatalities."

Parmiter pulled at his straggling grey moustache.

"I have been rather taking it for granted," he agreed. "What with their names and their ages, there were strong indications that they were cousins. And now this new development—the same uncommon name——"

"Have you made any inquiries on your own account since we met?"

"No, I have made no further inquiries," Parmiter said.

Mr. Tuke looked at him for a moment. Then he glanced

round the lounge, which, as usual at this time in the evening, was almost empty. He turned to the obituarist again.

"Well, I'll tell you a story in return for yours," he said. "The sequel, in fact. For you were quite right, of course, in connecting those three deaths. But understand this, Parmiter—what I am going to tell you is only a story. An assumption, a piece of fiction. At the same time, you must treat it as strictly confidential. No passing it on to your Fleet Street friends. Not a word of it. They couldn't use it, while the case is still *sub judice*, but I want this embargo clearly understood."

"*I* am not a reporter," Parmiter said a trifle stiffly. "I am a specialist. But I give you my word I will not repeat anything you tell me."

Mr. Tuke nodded as if satisfied. "I can begin," he said, "by adding an item of news to the reports you mentioned. Mrs. Lilian Shearsby was charged to-day with the murder of her husband's cousin Raymond."

The obituarist relaxed his intent attitude. He closed his eyes and gave a little sigh.

"Indeed?" was all he said.

Mr. Tuke finished his sherry and recrossed his long legs. Parmiter had sunk back in his seat, and as the deep leather chairs were touching the two could keep their voices low.

"Well, now for my story," Mr. Tuke said. He smiled to himself as he added: "It will be quite appropriate to begin with a phrase made popular, as I now remember, by the poet Southey. Once upon a time . . ."

He was not looking at Parmiter: his eyes narrowed as he arranged his material in orderly sequence while he talked, he stared before him through recurring clouds of cigar smoke. In a few phrases he sketched the annals of the Shearsby family, which had been first related to him by Cecile Boulanger on that Sunday afternoon at St. Luke's Court nearly a fortnight earlier. From the Victorian importer and his three children and his second marriage and the will which had been the cause of so much hardship and ill-feeling, the history progressed to the next generation, all, or all but one, cut off in the shadow of its injustice. Of Martin Dresser, Mr. Tuke only remarked at this point that he was believed to have died abroad. He did not mention the ex-cashier's downfall. So he came to the six cousins with whose affairs he was by now so familiar, and the story was brought up to the time when the war gathered them all together in England again, still waiting for their inheritance.

Mr. Tuke paused to knock the ash from his cigar. Parmiter sunk in his chair, had taken out a pipe, but he made no attempt to fill it. His heavy-lidded eyes were almost closed; and his lined, cynical face reflected in repose some deep inward melancholy. It hardly seemed that he was listening.

Harvey blew a jet of smoke and resumed his tale.

"That was the situation when in March of this year Captain Dresser was killed in a street accident. It may interest you to know that the police have no misgivings about that accident. No one was to blame but the poor fellow himself."

Parmiter was playing idly with his pipe. His fingers tightened as he glanced from under his lids at his companion, who gazed before him and continued with scarcely a pause:

"At this point we enter the realms of supposition—and very slanderous supposition, too. I rely on your promise."

The obituarist nodded absently, but he seemed more alert.

"Of the five surviving cousins of my story," Harvey went on, "Mortimer, the chemist, was married to a dissatisfied wife. She was infected by the snobbery of a provincial town, and by the even worse snobbery of a large commercial concern whose employees were graded socially according to their salaries. She was constantly meeting the wives and daughters of her husband's colleagues who were in better positions than his. They would not allow her to forget it. She must soon have realised that Mortimer himself would never rise far. He was commonplace, pompous and priggish. He was also very mean. Possibly his obsession with money, about which he was always talking, worked on her, too, in time. At any rate, she wanted more money, a better position, display, equality with the well-to-do. It is an instructive point that she fed her mind on court memoirs and romances of the peerage. When the war came, she achieved a modicum of salvation through good works with the W.V.S., where she met the local nobs, and her taste for high life was whetted, and her disillusionment with Burnside Avenue enhanced. And who," added Harvey, "having seen Burnside Avenue, can blame her?"

Parmiter, now listening with keen attention, gave him a curious look at this last remark, but did not comment on it.

"But if it was money she wanted," he observed, "there was her husband's inheritance to look forward to."

"Oh, no doubt at this time she was counting the months till old Mrs. Rutland Shearsby should die. But the inheritance would be divided among six people. In my story Mrs. Shearsby always resented this. She was jealous of her husband's cousins, and even of his sister. Though all of them had to work for their living, they were socially in a class above hers. Very silly of her, but not an uncommon state of mind. In particular, she hated Miss Ardmore, who without effort was everything she herself wanted to be —smart, sophisticated, able to hold her own in any company. Miss Ardmore was well aware of this animus, and did not put herself out to be conciliatory. It infuriated Lilian Shearsby to think that her *bête noire* would inherit equally with her own husband."

Harvey paused, for two members had strolled to the window near by. They turned away, and he resumed his tale.

CHAPTER XXV

"THE turning point in my story," he said, "is Captain Dresser's death by accident. It meant an increase in Mortimer's share of the money to come. It also put some very evil ideas into his wife's head. With her obsession about money and position, and her jealousy of the rest of his family,

once the ideas were there they grew and flourished. She
had not too much time—old Mrs. Shearsby had only a
few more months to live. Anyhow, in April, she had her
first shot at murder."

"In April?" Parmiter exclaimed.

"Yes. On a dark night she tried to push Mlle Boulanger
under a lorry. She was still in the imitative stage. The
attempt failed, and she realised that murder requires study.
Though in view of her hatred of Miss Ardmore I have wondered if that young woman has not had one or two escapes
of which she is happily ignorant. I am sure Lilian Shearsby
always had her in mind. However, there was a way in which
Miss Ardmore might be involved in the general scheme.
Is this boring you?"

"Boring me? Good heavens, no." As though picking his
words, Parmiter added: "But it is one thing to theorise
about the story behind an item or two in the press, and
quite another to find one's theory come to life. I was wondering, if I had not called your attention to these fatalities—"

"You were not the sole instrument of providence," Mr.
Tuke said drily. "And we are still theorising, remember.
Well, we must now go back a little. About this time last
year a family in Bedford was accidentally wiped out by
sodium nitrite poisoning. The man was employed by Imperial
Sansil. Soon after this, Miss Ardmore spent a week-end
with her cousins there, and this tragedy was discussed. And,
according to my story, something else happened. Mrs.
Shearsby went through her guest's handbag. If you ask
why, I can only say I assume on general principles, inspired
by envy and malice. There might be letters. There was,
naturally, a bunch of keys, and, again on general principles,
our Lilian took impressions of one or two which looked
like latchkeys. It is not a recondite art—all one requires
is some moulding wax, or a cake of soap. She may have
learnt the trick from the detective novels which figure,
rather oddly, among her books."

"But you said just now," Parmiter put in, "that it was
Sydney's—Captain Dresser's death that started everything."

"Oh, I don't think Mrs. Shearsby's general principles envisaged murder at this time. But women inspired by jealousy and hatred will do things quite as extraordinary. Her idea was to enter Miss Ardmore's mews flat and go through the letters and so on there, hoping to discover some weapon that would humiliate and hurt. Few of us have not a secret or two which we would prefer to keep concealed from our enemies. At any rate, that she had a key is certain."

Parmiter pulled at his moustache, looked at his empty pipe, and felt in an abstracted way in his pocket for tobacco.

"This is absorbingly interesting to me," he said.

Mr. Tuke smiled politely. "I am glad you find it so. We now carry my story forward to the events of the last few weeks. I will take the death of Mrs. Porteous first, out of order, because though it is fairly clear how it was brought about, there is a sad lack of evidence, and Lilian Shearsby is not being charged on this count. The *modus operandi* will be obvious to you by now."

"I suppose," Parmiter said, stuffing tobacco into his pipe, "this wretched woman got the notion from the Bedford poisonings—which I now recall, by the way. Did she take an impression of another key?"

"That was not necessary. All she had to do was to get her victim out of the way. This she accomplished on the Bank Holiday Sunday, when her husband was also out of her way. The earlier case shows that sodium nitrite is easily obtainable at the Sansil laboratories, where she was doing part-time work. If necessary, she could pretend she wanted some as a fertiliser. Where she displayed her native ingenuity was in leaving in the bungalow, among the chemicals of the late Cyril Porteous, an unlabelled bottle of the stuff. Its presence at once suggested to a coroner predisposed to the theory of misadventure, that a misadventure had occurred. The round trip would only take her a few hours, and when her husband returned after *his* day's outing she was at home again. About this time her sister-in-law, also just home again from a journey to London in response to a bogus telephone call, was preparing a meal including potatoes, which require cooking in salt, and late rhubarb from her garden. The acid in rhubarb seems to be just what is wanted to bring out the latent devilishness in $NaNO_2$. An uncovenanted bit of luck for Lilian."

Parmiter had filled his pipe. His fingers fumbled with the match, and the first one he struck broke in half. Suddenly he clenched a fist and brought it down on his chair.

"Horrible, horrible!" he muttered. "That poor creature! And do you mean to say, Tuke, that this fiend of a woman will get away with it?"

"For getting her hanged," said Mr. Tuke, "one homicide is as good as another. The police evidently think they have enough evidence on the first count in point of time—the murder of Raymond Shearsby. And arising out of that, I fancy she will also be charged with the murder of Joseph Eady."

"Ah, this man Eady. Where does he come in?"

"I will tell you. But before we leave Mrs. Porteous, you will note the advantage of using sodium nitrite in such an atmosphere of chemistry. There was also the point that Miss Ardmore, at the Ministry of Supply, might be supposed to have means of obtaining it. She too might simulate an interest in gardening. If suspicion should be aroused, it could be diverted in her direction. As it was. In fact, Mrs. Shearsby rather overdid it. It was a tactical error."

As Parmiter at last got his pipe alight, he lay back with a little sigh. He seemed to have tired, to have become older and more lined and melancholy in the last half hour. Harvey, who had glanced at his watch, gave him a quizzical look.

"I must hurry," he said. "I have a dinner engagement. To go back now to the 28th of July, we can follow in my story every step of the murder of Raymond Shearsby. As it also had to look like an accident, the procedure had to be different from that employed at Guildford, no doubt already planned." Mr. Tuke shook the ash from his cigar and put his fingertips together. "To take events in order," he went on, "Lilian Shearsby, as a member of the W.V.S., sometimes went to meetings of this admirable body at Cambridge. At one of these she met a Mrs. Darby. Mrs. Darby's husband, a writer on economics, was one of Raymond Shearsby's few friends in this country, a fact which came out in conversation, and proved very helpful to Mrs. Shearsby later on."

"Ralph Darby," said Parmiter. "He's in my files."

Mr. Tuke made a little grimace. "This Recording Angel touch of yours is slightly macabre. This W.V.S. connection," he continued, "had other uses. There was a big regional conference at Cambridge on the 28th of July, and Mrs. Shearsby decided to carry out her plan under cover of this respectable gathering. Her first step was to pilfer a suit of youth's clothing from a consignment to her own branch at Bedford. She is a tall woman, and looks well got up as a man. She then sent her W.V.S. uniform to the cleaners, so that she could go to Cambridge in a less noticeable costume. When she travelled there by bus on the 28th, she took the youth's outfit and some sort of weapon in a suitcase. At Cambridge she immediately telegraphed to Raymond Shearsby, begging him in urgent terms to meet the 7.48 train that evening at Whipstead station, which is two miles from Stocking. She signed the telegram 'Darby'."

"But surely," put in Parmiter, who seemed more alert, "she was taking chances here? Shearsby might have been away. And the telegram, you imply, has been found."

"Not the original," Mr. Tuke said, "though that was a real risk. She herself may have found it in Shearsby's pocket. If not, and if he had kept it, she must have hoped that it would remain unnoticed until her husband, as the nearest relative available, was notified of the death. This, remember, was to pass as an accident. And she knew her Mortimer— he would rush off, in his fussy way, to take charge, or she would see that he did. If the telegram was among the papers he brought home, no doubt she destroyed it. Anyhow, it has not been found. But there is a copy at Cotfold, the nearest place to Stocking with a telegraph office. Wires to the village are brought out from there, and to reach the cottage the messenger would not pass through Stocking itself. It was not known there that Raymond Shearsby had received a telegram that day."

"Do you suppose she knew all this beforehand?"

"Oh, no doubt she did. She would hardly risk sending a bogus telegram direct to the village post office. An inquiry at Bedford, and a look at the map, would show her how it would be taken to the cottage. The telegram itself, by the way," Harvey went on, "began, 'Am away all day, but must see you.' That stopped any query by the recipient. Then the touch of mystery in the message was no doubt a draw. And as for Shearsby being away, it was most unlikely. He seldom left the cottage except to walk to the village, or to go to Cambridge to see Darby himself. The odds, in fact, were in our Lilian's favour, and the trick came off."

Parmiter had let his pipe go out. He drew absently at it, his eyes half closed again, the shadows in their deep sockets enhancing his look of depression and fatigue.

"Raymond Shearsby," Harvey went on, "left his cottage for the station before seven o'clock. He called at the pub in the village on the way. Though he looked at the clock there, he did not mention that he was meeting a train, and as to reach the station he would turn back towards the lane in which his cottage stands, it was assumed that when he left the pub a quarter of an hour later he went straight home. In the meantime, Lilian Shearsby had attended her meeting. At a quarter to five, after it was over, she was talking to Mrs. Darby. She then caught the 5.10 train to Whipstead, and changed into her youth's suiting in a corridor lavatory. The train was crowded, and probably her transformation was not even noticed. If it was, it was nobody's business. At Whipstead she killed time for an hour, and towards seven she was near the station again, just as a train came in from King's Cross— to her undoing, but she could not foresee that. I suppose you don't know that bit of country?"

"No," Parmiter said.

"Evidently Lilian Shearsby did. She had been to the cottage with her husband, though coming by bus they approached it a different way. But there are always maps, and she may have reconnoitred the ground too. There is a short cut from Stocking to the station, a footpath, which Raymond must have taken that evening, and near the line another path branches off, crosses the local stream, the Cat Ditch, and goes on towards his cottage. No doubt Mrs. Shearsby expected him to come that way. After being near the station again at a quarter to seven, she went to the junction of the paths, close to the footbridge and under a screen of trees. The only house near is the stationmaster's, a quarter of a mile away. She waited under the trees till she saw Raymond coming to meet the 7.48—coming, not from his cottage, but from the village. Luckily for her, he was alone on the path. No one else was meeting that train, and the local people seldom travel towards London so late. What sort of trap she laid for him," said Mr. Tuke, examining his diminished cigar, "we can only conjecture. She may tell her story, but I don't think she will. I think she will fight to the end. But one can imagine a dozen ways of inveigling him into the cover of the trees. Again, we may never know whether he had time to recognise her. She hit him over the head with whatever weapon she had brought, taking care to stun but not to kill. She is an experienced tennis player, with a strong forearm, and they tell me that at tennis you learn to judge the force of your blow with great accuracy." Mr. Tuke's shrug expressed his own opinion of tennis. "She then rolled him into the stream. He was unconscious, and the Cat Ditch would do the rest. It was all over in a minute or two. She was back at the station in time to catch the last train back to Cambridge, changing into her own clothes in a lavatory as before. She took the nine o'clock bus home, establishing the fact that she was in it by talking to a fellow passenger. As far as she knew, everything had gone according to plan."

CHAPTER XXVI

TAKING breath, Mr. Tuke discarded his cigar. Parmiter shading his eyes with his hand, shuddered involuntarily.

"Horrible!" he said.

Harvey looked at him. "I am afraid this is harrowing you."

"No, no, I want to hear." Parmiter dropped his hand from his face. "I have too vivid an imagination. But the mechanics of a crime like this are intensely interesting. Surely this dreadful woman's alibi was very imperfect?"

"Ah, there she had a piece of luck. You will remember that the last week of July was very wet. The Cat Ditch is quite a stream, rising from a spring, and by the 28th it had six feet or more of water in it, and was running very strongly. In these conditions it has been known to carry heavy objects a long distance. No doubt Lilian Shearsby counted on the body being swept well away from where it went in. It was actually carried or rolled during the night some two miles, coming to rest against a bridge in the lane where Raymond had his cottage. It was naturally supposed that he had fallen in there. And it was proved that Mrs. Shearsby could not possibly have reached the lane in the time available to her. When she heard what had happened, she must have felt that providence was indeed on her side."

"But evidently it was not?"

"No. A comforting thought. That is where Mr. Joseph Eady comes in." Harvey again looked at his watch. He began to speak more rapidly. "Eady was a shady character who had never been convicted. He went to Cambridge that day on some business so dubious that the sight at King's Cross of a detective who knew him caused him to alter his plans. He took a ticket only as far as Whipstead. He got there at 6.43 just as Lilian Shearsby took up her post among the trees at the junction of the paths. Eady seems also to have known the country, and in his retiring way he was avoiding the village and making for the path which comes out near Raymond Shearsby's cottage. He could reach the bus route to Cambridge that way. What he saw among the trees we don't know. Presumably Mrs. Shearsby in her male impersonation. Perhaps he recognised her as a woman, perhaps her behaviour roused his curiosity. He lived by his eyes and wits. He was certainly delayed by something, because he stole a bicycle in order to catch his bus. But he did not see the murder. He had gone on some time·before that."

"This is as good as a novel," remarked Parmitter, who had once more lost his air of strain.

"It is a novel," Mr. Tuke reminded him. "And now we come to the penultimate chapter. Some time in the next few days, Eady's affairs took him to Bedford. There he met Lilian Shearsby in the street, in her proper garments, and knew her again. He would not have been Joseph Eady if he had not followed up this little mystery. It was easy to find out who she was, and, thanks to Mortimer's bragging, about the family fortune. And a few days later, in an old copy of a Cambridgeshire paper, Eady read the announcement of Raymond Shearsby's death, inserted by the Vicar of Stocking because Mortimer was too mean to pay for it—— Did you speak?"

"It was nothing. Go on."

"I thought you said, 'Just like him'. Of course, I told you he was mean. Well, the two names, and the date, made Mr. Eady think furiously. Again it was simple to gather further information—there was the Hertfordshire paper, for instance, in which you first read of the affair. In short, Mr. Eady, who earned a modest and precarious livelihood, began to think, very mistakenly, that at last he was on velvet."

"I begin to see," said Parmiter.

"Yes," said Mr. Tuke, assuming a more impermanent attitude. "Yes, he tried a bit of blackmail. This was only last Friday. But Lilian Shearsby is a woman whom a blackmailer should handle with extreme care. She is quickwitted and resourceful. And this time she was desperate. She must have thought out her counter-measures in a few minutes. Considering the shock of Eady's appearance out of the blue," said Harvey reflectively, "it was a very creditable effort. Somehow she persuaded him to meet her in London the next day. She must have told some plausible story of being able to raise money there. She could insist, much more plausibly, on the danger of another meeting in Bedford, where she was well known. She probably explained that she had the run of a friend's flat in Kensington. Eady was to call there for his first instalment. He may have pretended it would also be the last. If he did, she would not be deceived. Altogether, that interview at 'Aylwynstowe', which is the regrettable name of the Mortimer Shearsby's home, must have been as good as a play. It was a play. For though Eady now knew he was dealing with a murderess, he seems to have been fooled. He thought he had frightened Lilian Shearsby. He was never more mistaken."

"Then this friend's flat? . . ." said Parmiter.

"Was of course Miss Ardmore's, of which Mrs. Shearsby had a key. Miss Ardmore would be at work on Saturday morning. To use her place for the end in view was a stroke of genius. It would seem to involve her up to the hilt."

"The woman's a devil!" Parmiter exclaimed.

"Not one of our really nice people. But very ingenious," said Harvey. "Very. For when she came to London early next morning she had in her bag a dose of our old friend, and hers, sodium nitrite. This was her first string, so to speak. That she had hopes of inducing a blackmailer, who knew her to be a murderess, to accept a drink, speaks volumes for her self-confidence. Of course she had an alternative weapon. We don't know what this was. She did not have to use it. Mr. Eady seems to have swallowed poison with a light heart."

"How on earth did she make him do it, Tuke?"

"Your guess is as good as mine," Harvey said. "I can only think of one way. In setting her stage, anyhow, she had another little spot of luck. Hunting in Miss Ardmore's cupboards for a drink that would conceal the taste of the salt, she found a bottle of Pernod and a lemon. She may not have known much about Pernod, but obviously a strong concoction of aniseed would be the very thing. Then the lemon, though one does not usually add a *zeste* to Pernod, would rapidly form nitrous oxide, just as the rhubarb did. So she left in the sitting room a used glass, with dregs of Pernod and a slice of lemon in it, and, of course, the Pernod bottle itself, well laced with sodium nitrite, and a jug of water. Then she waited for Mr. Eady."

"Go on," said Parmiter eagerly.

"In my reconstruction Eady arrived to find his victim in a very emotional state. She would be cowed and frightened. Perhaps she contrived a few hysterics. Obviously, in an effort to pull herself together, she had been having a stiff drink. She may even have pretended to be a little drunk. She would drag out the scene a bit, with supplications and tears. . . . A good piece of acting, in fact. It must have been. Then she could not find her bag, with the money in it. She would get more and more distracted, and in the end would rush from the room, to search for it. . . . "

Parmiter was leaning forward now, his deep-set eyes on Mr. Tuke's dark face. Only two other members remained in the big room. Through the tall windows the autumn sunlight streamed in, as it had done on that earlier evening when the fatalities in the Shearsby family were first discussed.

Mr. Tuke's dry voice went on.

"Eady had no doubt come bristling with suspicion. But perhaps his mind was not wholly on the business in hand. He had other worries. At any rate, he must have been completely taken in. He forgot his doubts and his caution. He could do with a drink too. Obviously Mrs. Shearsby had just had a glass of the Pernod. There could be no danger here. Probably he knew little about Pernod—he may not even have added water. He left the lemon in the glass. He listened to his victim rattling about the flat looking for her bag, and then he took a whacking big drink. And that was the end of Mr. Eady."

Mr. Tuke made a gesture of brushing his hands. He rose to his feet. The obituarist rose too, more slowly.

"Are you really going?"

"I'm afraid I must."

"But you haven't finished. How did they—the police—clear this up so quickly?" Parmiter's stare was inquisitive and shrewd. "Did you have anything to do with it, Tuke?"

"Shall we say that you and I have both contributed in our small way?" Mr. Tuke rejoined. "As for how it all came out, Eady's body was found the same evening. No doubt Lilian Shearsby hoped it would lie in the box-room where she dragged it for some days. It might then be impossible to say exactly when death took place, and Miss Ardmore's position would be still more awkward. Then the Cambridge police had got on Eady's tracks, and he came back to London overnight. He was rather shaken by these attentions at this most inconvenient moment. He did not go to his home, in case it was watched, as it was, but he telephoned to his wife. She evaded the watch on her front door by the simple expedient of leaving by the back, and the precious pair met elsewhere. Eady not only told her that he had a big thing in hand, but, his natural caution being uppermost, just in case there should be a snag somewhere, he gave her Lilian Shearsby's name."

Harvey began to walk towards the door of the lounge, Parmiter lounging by his side.

"I have not mentioned," Harvey remarked casually, "that the case was complicated at one point by the reappearance of a member of the family supposed to be dead. Martin Dresser, of the older generation, who was said to have died in Belgium. An unhappy experience sent him abroad. He seems to be a queer fellow, with an unusual and slightly macabre sense of humour. He persuaded his son Sydney to circulate the news of his death. Sydney was even furnished with an obituary notice for the local paper—a touch," said Harvey, with a sardonic glance at the silent obituarist, "that should appeal to you, Parmiter. Later this Martin returned to England, one presumes under another name. He appears to have managed to earn a living in some way. As a young man he is said to have had a bent for newspaper work. But the family never knew he was alive—except his son, of course. His own generation had not behaved too well to him, and I suspect that Sydney had some of his father's sense of humour, and in his quiet way, enjoyed the mystification. He kept the secret to the end, and Martin, like Southey's 'Scholar', has been able to pass his days among the dead. As, in a sense," Mr. Tuke added, "you do, Parmiter."

They had come to the door. Parmiter did not speak.

"Quite recently," Mr. Tuke went on, "Raymond met Martin. Perhaps Martin sought him out. After the death of his son he may have felt an impulse to get in touch with his family again. And talking of that, he must keep an eye on the papers, particularly on the obituary columns. I feel pretty sure it was he who sent Mlle Boulanger a newspaper account of the inquest on Mrs. Porteous. He may have sent one to Bedford. Perhaps he did not know Miss Ardmore's address. One cannot say what was at the back of his mind, but it may have seemed to him desirable to stir up interest in this sequence of deaths. Queerly enough," said Mr. Tuke lightly, "I have felt from the beginning that a bit of stirring was being done. I have even suspected that I myself was being jogged. *A propos*, I did Martin a grave injustice. I actually thought he and the deplorable Eady might be one and the same person. I owe him profound apologies."

He turned to his silent companion and held out his hand —an unusual gesture as between two club acquaintances.

"I must be off," he said. "I had another piece of news this morning, by the way. Old Mrs. Rutland Shearsby died last night. The remaining cousins will now get their reward. Miss Ardmore will marry, and Mlle Boulanger will probably find herself engaged. Even Mortimer's troubles, if I know him, will be a little assuaged. And there will be a hue and cry after the self-effacing Martin. He is one of the beneficiaries, and the longer he hides, the longer the others will have to wait. So let us hope he will make himself known to his cousins. Mortimer is a poor fish, but the two young women are quite nice."

Parmiter had taken Harvey's hand. His face wore an unreadable expression, yet it seemed to have lightened. He only said:

"It was good of you to tell me all this, Tuke."

"Well, keep it to yourself for the present," Mr. Tuke said briskly. "Remember your promise. But I feel that the family is entitled to know the whole story. Good-bye."

A CATALOG OF
SELECTED DOVER BOOKS
IN ALL FIELDS OF INTEREST

A CATALOG OF SELECTED DOVER BOOKS IN ALL FIELDS OF INTEREST

CONCERNING THE SPIRITUAL IN ART, Wassily Kandinsky. Pioneering work by father of abstract art. Thoughts on color theory, nature of art. Analysis of earlier masters. 12 illustrations. 80pp. of text. 5⅜ × 8½. 23411-8 Pa. $2.50

LEONARDO ON THE HUMAN BODY, Leonardo da Vinci. More than 1200 of Leonardo's anatomical drawings on 215 plates. Leonardo's text, which accompanies the drawings, has been translated into English. 506pp. 8⅜ × 11¾. 24483-0 Pa. $10.95

GOBLIN MARKET, Christina Rossetti. Best-known work by poet comparable to Emily Dickinson, Alfred Tennyson. With 46 delightfully grotesque illustrations by Laurence Housman. 64pp. 4 × 6¾. 24516-0 Pa. $2.50

THE HEART OF THOREAU'S JOURNALS, edited by Odell Shepard. Selections from *Journal*, ranging over full gamut of interests. 228pp. 5⅜ × 8½. 20741-2 Pa. $4.50

MR. LINCOLN'S CAMERA MAN: MATHEW B. BRADY, Roy Meredith. Over 300 Brady photos reproduced directly from original negatives, photos. Lively commentary. 368pp. 8⅜ × 11¼. 23021-X Pa. $11.95

PHOTOGRAPHIC VIEWS OF SHERMAN'S CAMPAIGN, George N. Barnard. Reprint of landmark 1866 volume with 61 plates: battlefield of New Hope Church, the Etawah Bridge, the capture of Atlanta, etc. 80pp. 9 × 12. 23445-2 Pa. $6.00

A SHORT HISTORY OF ANATOMY AND PHYSIOLOGY FROM THE GREEKS TO HARVEY, Dr. Charles Singer. Thoroughly engrossing non-technical survey. 270 illustrations. 211pp. 5⅜ × 8½. 20389-1 Pa. $4.50

REDOUTE ROSES IRON-ON TRANSFER PATTERNS, Barbara Christopher. Redouté was botanical painter to the Empress Josephine; transfer his famous roses onto fabric with these 24 transfer patterns. 80pp. 8¼ × 10⅞. 24292-7 Pa. $3.50

THE FIVE BOOKS OF ARCHITECTURE, Sebastiano Serlio. Architectural milestone, first (1611) English translation of Renaissance classic. Unabridged reproduction of original edition includes over 300 woodcut illustrations. 416pp. 9⅜ × 12¼. 24349-4 Pa. $14.95

CARLSON'S GUIDE TO LANDSCAPE PAINTING, John F. Carlson. Authoritative, comprehensive guide covers, every aspect of landscape painting. 34 reproductions of paintings by author; 58 explanatory diagrams. 144pp. 8⅜ × 11. 22927-0 Pa. $4.95

101 PUZZLES IN THOUGHT AND LOGIC, C.R. Wylie, Jr. Solve murders, robberies, see which fishermen are liars—purely by reasoning! 107pp. 5⅜ × 8½. 20367-0 Pa. $2.00

TEST YOUR LOGIC, George J. Summers. 50 more truly new puzzles with new turns of thought, new subtleties of inference. 100pp. 5⅜ × 8½. 22877-0 Pa. $2.25

THE MURDER BOOK OF J.G. REEDER, Edgar Wallace. Eight suspenseful stories by bestselling mystery writer of 20s and 30s. Features the donnish Mr. J.G. Reeder of Public Prosecutor's Office. 128pp. 5⅜ × 8½. (Available in U.S. only)
24374-5 Pa. $3.50

ANNE ORR'S CHARTED DESIGNS, Anne Orr. Best designs by premier needlework designer, all on charts: flowers, borders, birds, children, alphabets, etc. Over 100 charts, 10 in color. Total of 40pp. 8¼ × 11. 23704-4 Pa. $2.25

BASIC CONSTRUCTION TECHNIQUES FOR HOUSES AND SMALL BUILDINGS SIMPLY EXPLAINED, U.S. Bureau of Naval Personnel. Grading, masonry, woodworking, floor and wall framing, roof framing, plastering, tile setting, much more. Over 675 illustrations. 568pp. 6½ × 9¼. 20242-9 Pa. $8.95

MATISSE LINE DRAWINGS AND PRINTS, Henri Matisse. Representative collection of female nudes, faces, still lifes, experimental works, etc., from 1898 to 1948. 50 illustrations. 48pp. 8⅜ × 11¼. 23877-6 Pa. $2.50

HOW TO PLAY THE CHESS OPENINGS, Eugene Znosko-Borovsky. Clear, profound examinations of just what each opening is intended to do and how opponent can counter. Many sample games. 147pp. 5⅜ × 8½. 22795-2 Pa. $2.95

DUPLICATE BRIDGE, Alfred Sheinwold. Clear, thorough, easily followed account: rules, etiquette, scoring, strategy, bidding; Goren's point-count system, Blackwood and Gerber conventions, etc. 158pp. 5⅜ × 8½. 22741-3 Pa. $3.00

SARGENT PORTRAIT DRAWINGS, J.S. Sargent. Collection of 42 portraits reveals technical skill and intuitive eye of noted American portrait painter, John Singer Sargent. 48pp. 8¼ × 11⅛. 24524-1 Pa. $2.95

ENTERTAINING SCIENCE EXPERIMENTS WITH EVERYDAY OBJECTS, Martin Gardner. Over 100 experiments for youngsters. Will amuse, astonish, teach, and entertain. Over 100 illustrations. 127pp. 5⅜ × 8½. 24201-3 Pa. $2.50

TEDDY BEAR PAPER DOLLS IN FULL COLOR: A Family of Four Bears and Their Costumes, Crystal Collins. A family of four Teddy Bear paper dolls and nearly 60 cut-out costumes. Full color, printed one side only. 32pp. 9¼ × 12¼. 24550-0 Pa. $3.50

NEW CALLIGRAPHIC ORNAMENTS AND FLOURISHES, Arthur Baker. Unusual, multi-useable material: arrows, pointing hands, brackets and frames, ovals, swirls, birds, etc. Nearly 700 illustrations. 80pp. 8⅜ × 11¼. 24095-9 Pa. $3.75

DINOSAUR DIORAMAS TO CUT & ASSEMBLE, M. Kalmenoff. Two complete three-dimensional scenes in full color, with 31 cut-out animals and plants. Excellent educational toy for youngsters. Instructions; 2 assembly diagrams. 32pp. 9¼ × 12¼. 24541-1 Pa. $3.95

SILHOUETTES: A PICTORIAL ARCHIVE OF VARIED ILLUSTRATIONS, edited by Carol Belanger Grafton. Over 600 silhouettes from the 18th to 20th centuries. Profiles and full figures of men, women, children, birds, animals, groups and scenes, nature, ships, an alphabet. 144pp. 8⅜ × 11¼. 23781-8 Pa. $4.95

25 KITES THAT FLY, Leslie Hunt. Full, easy-to-follow instructions for kites made from inexpensive materials. Many novelties. 70 illustrations. 110pp. 5⅜ × 8½.
22550-X Pa. $2.25

PIANO TUNING, J. Cree Fischer. Clearest, best book for beginner, amateur. Simple repairs, raising dropped notes, tuning by easy method of flattened fifths. No previous skills needed. 4 illustrations. 201pp. 5⅜ × 8½. 23267-0 Pa. $3.50

EARLY AMERICAN IRON-ON TRANSFER PATTERNS, edited by Rita Weiss. 75 designs, borders, alphabets, from traditional American sources. 48pp. 8¼ × 11.
23162-3 Pa. $1.95

CROCHETING EDGINGS, edited by Rita Weiss. Over 100 of the best designs for these lovely trims for a host of household items. Complete instructions, illustrations. 48pp. 8¼ × 11. 24031-2 Pa. $2.25

FINGER PLAYS FOR NURSERY AND KINDERGARTEN, Emilie Poulsson. 18 finger plays with music (voice and piano); entertaining, instructive. Counting, nature lore, etc. Victorian classic. 53 illustrations. 80pp. 6½ × 9¼. 22588-7 Pa. $1.95

BOSTON THEN AND NOW, Peter Vanderwarker. Here in 59 side-by-side views are photographic documentations of the city's past and present. 119 photographs. Full captions. 122pp. 8¼ × 11. 24312-5 Pa. $6.95

CROCHETING BEDSPREADS, edited by Rita Weiss. 22 patterns, originally published in three instruction books 1939-41. 39 photos, 8 charts. Instructions. 48pp. 8¼ × 11. 23610-2 Pa. $2.00

HAWTHORNE ON PAINTING, Charles W. Hawthorne. Collected from notes taken by students at famous Cape Cod School; hundreds of direct, personal *apercus*, ideas, suggestions. 91pp. 5⅜ × 8½. 20653-X Pa. $2.50

THERMODYNAMICS, Enrico Fermi. A classic of modern science. Clear, organized treatment of systems, first and second laws, entropy, thermodynamic potentials, etc. Calculus required. 160pp. 5⅜ × 8½. 60361-X Pa. $4.00

TEN BOOKS ON ARCHITECTURE, Vitruvius. The most important book ever written on architecture. Early Roman aesthetics, technology, classical orders, site selection, all other aspects. Morgan translation. 331pp. 5⅜ × 8½. 20645-9 Pa. $5.50

THE CORNELL BREAD BOOK, Clive M. McCay and Jeanette B. McCay. Famed high-protein recipe incorporated into breads, rolls, buns, coffee cakes, pizza, pie crusts, more. Nearly 50 illustrations. 48pp. 8¼ × 11. 23995-0 Pa. $2.00

THE CRAFTSMAN'S HANDBOOK, Cennino Cennini. 15th-century handbook, school of Giotto, explains applying gold, silver leaf; gesso; fresco painting, grinding pigments, etc. 142pp. 6⅛ × 9¼. 20054-X Pa. $3.50

FRANK LLOYD WRIGHT'S FALLINGWATER, Donald Hoffmann. Full story of Wright's masterwork at Bear Run, Pa. 100 photographs of site, construction, and details of completed structure. 112pp. 9¼ × 10. 23671-4 Pa. $6.50

OVAL STAINED GLASS PATTERN BOOK, C. Eaton. 60 new designs framed in shape of an oval. Greater complexity, challenge with sinuous cats, birds, mandalas framed in antique shape. 64pp. 8¼ × 11. 24519-5 Pa. $3.50

THE BOOK OF WOOD CARVING, Charles Marshall Sayers. Still finest book for beginning student. Fundamentals, technique; gives 34 designs, over 34 projects for panels, bookends, mirrors, etc. 33 photos. 118pp. 7¾ × 10⅝. 23654-4 Pa. $3.95

CARVING COUNTRY CHARACTERS, Bill Higginbotham. Expert advice for beginning, advanced carvers on materials, techniques for creating 18 projects— mirthful panorama of American characters. 105 illustrations. 80pp. 8⅜ × 11.
24135-1 Pa. $2.50

300 ART NOUVEAU DESIGNS AND MOTIFS IN FULL COLOR, C.B. Grafton. 44 full-page plates display swirling lines and muted colors typical of Art Nouveau. Borders, frames, panels, cartouches, dingbats, etc. 48pp. 9⅜ × 12¼.
24354-0 Pa. $6.00

SELF-WORKING CARD TRICKS, Karl Fulves. Editor of *Pallbearer* offers 72 tricks that work automatically through nature of card deck. No sleight of hand needed. Often spectacular. 42 illustrations. 113pp. 5⅜ × 8½. 23334-0 Pa. $3.50

CUT AND ASSEMBLE A WESTERN FRONTIER TOWN, Edmund V. Gillon, Jr. Ten authentic full-color buildings on heavy cardboard stock in H-O scale. Sheriff's Office and Jail, Saloon, Wells Fargo, Opera House, others. 48pp. 9¼ × 12¼.
23736-2 Pa. $3.95

CUT AND ASSEMBLE AN EARLY NEW ENGLAND VILLAGE, Edmund V. Gillon, Jr. Printed in full color on heavy cardboard stock. 12 authentic buildings in H-O scale: Adams home in Quincy, Mass., Oliver Wight house in Sturbridge, smithy, store, church, others. 48pp. 9¼ × 12¼. 23536-X Pa. $3.95

THE TALE OF TWO BAD MICE, Beatrix Potter. Tom Thumb and Hunca Munca squeeze out of their hole and go exploring. 27 full-color Potter illustrations. 59pp. 4¼ × 5½. (Available in U.S. only) 23065-1 Pa. $1.50

CARVING FIGURE CARICATURES IN THE OZARK STYLE, Harold L. Enlow. Instructions and illustrations for ten delightful projects, plus general carving instructions. 22 drawings and 47 photographs altogether. 39pp. 8⅜ × 11.
23151-8 Pa. $2.50

A TREASURY OF FLOWER DESIGNS FOR ARTISTS, EMBROIDERERS AND CRAFTSMEN, Susan Gaber. 100 garden favorites lushly rendered by artist for artists, craftsmen, needleworkers. Many form frames, borders. 80pp. 8¼ × 11.
24096-7 Pa. $3.50

CUT & ASSEMBLE A TOY THEATER/THE NUTCRACKER BALLET, Tom Tierney. Model of a complete, full-color production of Tchaikovsky's classic. 6 backdrops, dozens of characters, familiar dance sequences. 32pp. 9⅜ × 12¼.
24194-7 Pa. $4.50

ANIMALS: 1,419 COPYRIGHT-FREE ILLUSTRATIONS OF MAMMALS, BIRDS, FISH, INSECTS, ETC., edited by Jim Harter. Clear wood engravings present, in extremely lifelike poses, over 1,000 species of animals. 284pp. 9 × 12.
23766-4 Pa. $9.95

MORE HAND SHADOWS, Henry Bursill. For those at their 'finger ends," 16 more effects—Shakespeare, a hare, a squirrel, Mr. Punch, and twelve more—each explained by a full-page illustration. Considerable period charm. 30pp. 6½ × 9¼.
21384-6 Pa. $1.95

SURREAL STICKERS AND UNREAL STAMPS, William Rowe. 224 haunting, hilarious stamps on gummed, perforated stock, with images of elephants, geisha girls, George Washington, etc. 16pp. one side. 8¼ × 11.   24371-0 Pa. $3.50

GOURMET KITCHEN LABELS, Ed Sibbett, Jr. 112 full-color labels (4 copies each of 28 designs). Fruit, bread, other culinary motifs. Gummed and perforated. 16pp. 8¼ × 11.   24087-8 Pa. $2.95

PATTERNS AND INSTRUCTIONS FOR CARVING AUTHENTIC BIRDS, H.D. Green. Detailed instructions, 27 diagrams, 85 photographs for carving 15 species of birds so life-like, they'll seem ready to fly! 8¼ × 11.   24222-6 Pa. $2.75

FLATLAND, E.A. Abbott. Science-fiction classic explores life of 2-D being in 3-D world. 16 illustrations. 103pp. 5⅜ × 8.   20001-9 Pa. $2.00

DRIED FLOWERS, Sarah Whitlock and Martha Rankin. Concise, clear, practical guide to dehydration, glycerinizing, pressing plant material, and more. Covers use of silica gel. 12 drawings. 32pp. 5⅜ × 8½.   21802-3 Pa. $1.00

EASY-TO-MAKE CANDLES, Gary V. Guy. Learn how easy it is to make all kinds of decorative candles. Step-by-step instructions. 82 illustrations. 48pp. 8¼ × 11.
     23881-4 Pa. $2.50

SUPER STICKERS FOR KIDS, Carolyn Bracken. 128 gummed and perforated full-color stickers: GIRL WANTED, KEEP OUT, BORED OF EDUCATION, X-RATED, COMBAT ZONE, many others. 16pp. 8¼ × 11.   24092-4 Pa. $2.50

CUT AND COLOR PAPER MASKS, Michael Grater. Clowns, animals, funny faces...simply color them in, cut them out, and put them together, and you have 9 paper masks to play with and enjoy. 32pp. 8¼ × 11.   23171-2 Pa. $2.25

A CHRISTMAS CAROL: THE ORIGINAL MANUSCRIPT, Charles Dickens. Clear facsimile of Dickens manuscript, on facing pages with final printed text. 8 illustrations by John Leech, 4 in color on covers. 144pp. 8⅜ × 11¼.
     20980-6 Pa. $5.95

CARVING SHOREBIRDS, Harry V. Shourds & Anthony Hillman. 16 full-size patterns (all double-page spreads) for 19 North American shorebirds with step-by-step instructions. 72pp. 9¼ × 12¼.   24287-0 Pa. $4.95

THE GENTLE ART OF MATHEMATICS, Dan Pedoe. Mathematical games, probability, the question of infinity, topology, how the laws of algebra work, problems of irrational numbers, and more. 42 figures. 143pp. 5⅜ × 8½. (EBE)
     22949-1 Pa. $3.50

READY-TO-USE DOLLHOUSE WALLPAPER, Katzenbach & Warren, Inc. Stripe, 2 floral stripes, 2 allover florals, polka dot; all in full color. 4 sheets (350 sq. in.) of each, enough for average room. 48pp. 8¼ × 11.   23495-9 Pa. $2.95

MINIATURE IRON-ON TRANSFER PATTERNS FOR DOLLHOUSES, DOLLS, AND SMALL PROJECTS, Rita Weiss and Frank Fontana. Over 100 miniature patterns: rugs, bedspreads, quilts, chair seats, etc. In standard dollhouse size. 48pp. 8¼ × 11.   23741-9 Pa. $1.95

THE DINOSAUR COLORING BOOK, Anthony Rao. 45 renderings of dinosaurs, fossil birds, turtles, other creatures of Mesozoic Era. Scientifically accurate. Captions. 48pp. 8¼ × 11.   24022-3 Pa. $2.25

JAPANESE DESIGN MOTIFS, Matsuya Co. Mon, or heraldic designs. Over 4000 typical, beautiful designs: birds, animals, flowers, swords, fans, geometrics; all beautifully stylized. 213pp. 11⅜ × 8¼. 22874-6 Pa. $7.95

THE TALE OF BENJAMIN BUNNY, Beatrix Potter. Peter Rabbit's cousin coaxes him back into Mr. McGregor's garden for a whole new set of adventures. All 27 full-color illustrations. 59pp. 4¼ × 5½. (Available in U.S. only) 21102-9 Pa. $1.50

THE TALE OF PETER RABBIT AND OTHER FAVORITE STORIES BOXED SET, Beatrix Potter. Seven of Beatrix Potter's best-loved tales including Peter Rabbit in a specially designed, durable boxed set. 4¼ × 5½. Total of 447pp. 158 color illustrations. (Available in U.S. only) 23903-9 Pa. $10.80

PRACTICAL MENTAL MAGIC, Theodore Annemann. Nearly 200 astonishing feats of mental magic revealed in step-by-step detail. Complete advice on staging, patter, etc. Illustrated. 320pp. 5⅜ × 8½. 24426-1 Pa. $5.95

CELEBRATED CASES OF JUDGE DEE (DEE GOONG AN), translated by Robert Van Gulik. Authentic 18th-century Chinese detective novel; Dee and associates solve three interlocked cases. Led to van Gulik's own stories with same characters. Extensive introduction. 9 illustrations. 237pp. 5⅜ × 8½. 23337-5 Pa. $4.50

CUT & FOLD EXTRATERRESTRIAL INVADERS THAT FLY, M. Grater. Stage your own lilliputian space battles.By following the step-by-step instructions and explanatory diagrams you can launch 22 full-color fliers into space. 36pp. 8¼ × 11. 24478-4 Pa. $2.95

CUT & ASSEMBLE VICTORIAN HOUSES, Edmund V. Gillon, Jr. Printed in full color on heavy cardboard stock, 4 authentic Victorian houses in H-O scale: Italian-style Villa, Octagon, Second Empire, Stick Style. 48pp. 9¼ × 12¼. 23849-0 Pa. $3.95

BEST SCIENCE FICTION STORIES OF H.G. WELLS, H.G. Wells. Full novel *The Invisible Man*, plus 17 short stories: "The Crystal Egg," "Aepyornis Island," "The Strange Orchid," etc. 303pp. 5⅜ × 8½. (Available in U.S. only) 21531-8 Pa. $4.95

TRADEMARK DESIGNS OF THE WORLD, Yusaku Kamekura. A lavish collection of nearly 700 trademarks, the work of Wright, Loewy, Klee, Binder, hundreds of others. 160pp. 8¾ × 8. (Available in U.S. only) 24191-2 Pa. $5.00

THE ARTIST'S AND CRAFTSMAN'S GUIDE TO REDUCING, ENLARGING AND TRANSFERRING DESIGNS, Rita Weiss. Discover, reduce, enlarge, transfer designs from any objects to any craft project. 12pp. plus 16 sheets special graph paper. 8¼ × 11. 24142-4 Pa. $3.25

TREASURY OF JAPANESE DESIGNS AND MOTIFS FOR ARTISTS AND CRAFTSMEN, edited by Carol Belanger Grafton. Indispensable collection of 360 traditional Japanese designs and motifs redrawn in clean, crisp black-and-white, copyright-free illustrations. 96pp. 8¼ × 11. 24435-0 Pa. $3.95

CHANCERY CURSIVE STROKE BY STROKE, Arthur Baker. Instructions and illustrations for each stroke of each letter (upper and lower case) and numerals. 54 full-page plates. 64pp. 8¼ × 11. 24278-1 Pa. $2.50

THE ENJOYMENT AND USE OF COLOR, Walter Sargent. Color relationships, values, intensities; complementary colors, illumination, similar topics. Color in nature and art. 7 color plates, 29 illustrations. 274pp. 5⅜ × 8½. 20944-X Pa. $4.50

SCULPTURE PRINCIPLES AND PRACTICE, Louis Slobodkin. Step-by-step approach to clay, plaster, metals, stone; classical and modern. 253 drawings, photos. 255pp. 8⅛ × 11. 22960-2 Pa. $7.50

VICTORIAN FASHION PAPER DOLLS FROM HARPER'S BAZAR, 1867-1898, Theodore Menten. Four female dolls with 28 elegant high fashion costumes, printed in full color. 32pp. 9¼ × 12¼. 23453-3 Pa. $3.50

FLOPSY, MOPSY AND COTTONTAIL: A Little Book of Paper Dolls in Full Color, Susan LaBelle. Three dolls and 21 costumes (7 for each doll) show Peter Rabbit's siblings dressed for holidays, gardening, hiking, etc. Charming borders, captions. 48pp. 4¼ × 5½. 24376-1 Pa. $2.25

NATIONAL LEAGUE BASEBALL CARD CLASSICS, Bert Randolph Sugar. 83 big-leaguers from 1909-69 on facsimile cards. Hubbell, Dean, Spahn, Brock plus advertising, info, no duplications. Perforated, detachable. 16pp. 8¼ × 11. 24308-7 Pa. $2.95

THE LOGICAL APPROACH TO CHESS, Dr. Max Euwe, et al. First-rate text of comprehensive strategy, tactics, theory for the amateur. No gambits to memorize, just a clear, logical approach. 224pp. 5⅜ × 8½. 24353-2 Pa. $4.50

MAGICK IN THEORY AND PRACTICE, Aleister Crowley. The summation of the thought and practice of the century's most famous necromancer, long hard to find. Crowley's best book. 436pp. 5⅜ × 8½. (Available in U.S. only) 23295-6 Pa. $6.50

THE HAUNTED HOTEL, Wilkie Collins. Collins' last great tale; doom and destiny in a Venetian palace. Praised by T.S. Eliot. 127pp. 5⅜ × 8½. 24333-8 Pa. $3.00

ART DECO DISPLAY ALPHABETS, Dan X. Solo. Wide variety of bold yet elegant lettering in handsome Art Deco styles. 100 complete fonts, with numerals, punctuation, more. 104pp. 8⅛ × 11. 24372-9 Pa. $4.00

CALLIGRAPHIC ALPHABETS, Arthur Baker. Nearly 150 complete alphabets by outstanding contemporary. Stimulating ideas; useful source for unique effects. 154 plates. 157pp. 8⅜ × 11¼. 21045-6 Pa. $4.95

ARTHUR BAKER'S HISTORIC CALLIGRAPHIC ALPHABETS, Arthur Baker. From monumental capitals of first-century Rome to humanistic cursive of 16th century, 33 alphabets in fresh interpretations. 88 plates. 96pp. 9 × 12. 24054-1 Pa. $4.50

LETTIE LANE PAPER DOLLS, Sheila Young. Genteel turn-of-the-century family very popular then and now. 24 paper dolls. 16 plates in full color. 32pp. 9¼ × 12¼. 24089-4 Pa. $3.50

KEYBOARD WORKS FOR SOLO INSTRUMENTS, G.F. Handel. 35 neglected works from Handel's vast oeuvre, originally jotted down as improvisations. Includes Eight Great Suites, others. New sequence. 174pp. 9⅜ × 12¼.

24338-9 Pa. $7.50

AMERICAN LEAGUE BASEBALL CARD CLASSICS, Bert Randolph Sugar. 82 stars from 1900s to 60s on facsimile cards. Ruth, Cobb, Mantle, Williams, plus advertising, info, no duplications. Perforated, detachable. 16pp. 8¼ × 11.

24286-2 Pa. $2.95

A TREASURY OF CHARTED DESIGNS FOR NEEDLEWORKERS, Georgia Gorham and Jeanne Warth. 141 charted designs: owl, cat with yarn, tulips, piano, spinning wheel, covered bridge, Victorian house and many others. 48pp. 8¼ × 11.

23558-0 Pa. $1.95

DANISH FLORAL CHARTED DESIGNS, Gerda Bengtsson. Exquisite collection of over 40 different florals: anemone, Iceland poppy, wild fruit, pansies, many others. 45 illustrations. 48pp. 8¼ × 11.

23957-8 Pa. $1.75

OLD PHILADELPHIA IN EARLY PHOTOGRAPHS 1839-1914, Robert F. Looney. 215 photographs: panoramas, street scenes, landmarks, President-elect Lincoln's visit, 1876 Centennial Exposition, much more. 230pp. 8⅞ × 11¾.

23345-6 Pa. $9.95

PRELUDE TO MATHEMATICS, W.W. Sawyer. Noted mathematician's lively, stimulating account of non-Euclidean geometry, matrices, determinants, group theory, other topics. Emphasis on novel, striking aspects. 224pp. 5⅜ × 8½.

24401-6 Pa. $4.50

ADVENTURES WITH A MICROSCOPE, Richard Headstrom. 59 adventures with clothing fibers, protozoa, ferns and lichens, roots and leaves, much more. 142 illustrations. 232pp. 5⅜ × 8½.

23471-1 Pa. $3.95

IDENTIFYING ANIMAL TRACKS: MAMMALS, BIRDS, AND OTHER ANIMALS OF THE EASTERN UNITED STATES, Richard Headstrom. For hunters, naturalists, scouts, nature-lovers. Diagrams of tracks, tips on identification. 128pp. 5⅜ × 8.

24442-3 Pa. $3.50

VICTORIAN FASHIONS AND COSTUMES FROM HARPER'S BAZAR, 1867-1898, edited by Stella Blum. Day costumes, evening wear, sports clothes, shoes, hats, other accessories in over 1,000 detailed engravings. 320pp. 9⅜ × 12¼.

22990-4 Pa. $9.95

EVERYDAY FASHIONS OF THE TWENTIES AS PICTURED IN SEARS AND OTHER CATALOGS, edited by Stella Blum. Actual dress of the Roaring Twenties, with text by Stella Blum. Over 750 illustrations, captions. 156pp. 9 × 12.

24134-3 Pa. $8.50

HALL OF FAME BASEBALL CARDS, edited by Bert Randolph Sugar. Cy Young, Ted Williams, Lou Gehrig, and many other Hall of Fame greats on 92 full-color, detachable reprints of early baseball cards. No duplication of cards with *Classic Baseball Cards.* 16pp. 8¼ × 11.

23624-2 Pa. $3.50

THE ART OF HAND LETTERING, Helm Wotzkow. Course in hand lettering, Roman, Gothic, Italic, Block, Script. Tools, proportions, optical aspects, individual variation. Very quality conscious. Hundreds of specimens. 320pp. 5⅜ × 8½.

21797-3 Pa. $4.95

HOW THE OTHER HALF LIVES, Jacob A. Riis. Journalistic record of filth, degradation, upward drive in New York immigrant slums, shops, around 1900. New edition includes 100 original Riis photos, monuments of early photography. 233pp. 10 × 7⅞. 22012-5 Pa. $7.95

CHINA AND ITS PEOPLE IN EARLY PHOTOGRAPHS, John Thomson. In 200 black-and-white photographs of exceptional quality photographic pioneer Thomson captures the mountains, dwellings, monuments and people of 19th-century China. 272pp. 9⅜ × 12¼. 24393-1 Pa. $12.95

GODEY COSTUME PLATES IN COLOR FOR DECOUPAGE AND FRAMING, edited by Eleanor Hasbrouk Rawlings. 24 full-color engravings depicting 19th-century Parisian haute couture. Printed on one side only. 56pp. 8¼ × 11. 23879-2 Pa. $3.95

ART NOUVEAU STAINED GLASS PATTERN BOOK, Ed Sibbett, Jr. 104 projects using well-known themes of Art Nouveau: swirling forms, florals, peacocks, and sensuous women. 60pp. 8¼ × 11. 23577-7 Pa. $3.50

QUICK AND EASY PATCHWORK ON THE SEWING MACHINE: Susan Aylsworth Murwin and Suzzy Payne. Instructions, diagrams show exactly how to machine sew 12 quilts. 48pp. of templates. 50 figures. 80pp. 8¼ × 11. 23770-2 Pa. $3.50

THE STANDARD BOOK OF QUILT MAKING AND COLLECTING, Marguerite Ickis. Full information, full-sized patterns for making 46 traditional quilts, also 150 other patterns. 483 illustrations. 273pp. 6⅞ × 9⅝. 20582-7 Pa. $5.95

LETTERING AND ALPHABETS, J. Albert Cavanagh. 85 complete alphabets lettered in various styles; instructions for spacing, roughs, brushwork. 121pp. 8¾ × 8. 20053-1 Pa. $3.75

LETTER FORMS: 110 COMPLETE ALPHABETS, Frederick Lambert. 110 sets of capital letters; 16 lower case alphabets; 70 sets of numbers and other symbols. 110pp. 8⅛ × 11. 22872-X Pa. $4.50

ORCHIDS AS HOUSE PLANTS, Rebecca Tyson Northen. Grow cattleyas and many other kinds of orchids—in a window, in a case, or under artificial light. 63 illustrations. 148pp. 5⅜ × 8½. 23261-1 Pa. $2.95

THE MUSHROOM HANDBOOK, Louis C.C. Krieger. Still the best popular handbook. Full descriptions of 259 species, extremely thorough text, poisons, folklore, etc. 32 color plates; 126 other illustrations. 560pp. 5⅜ × 8½. 21861-9 Pa. $8.50

THE DORÉ BIBLE ILLUSTRATIONS, Gustave Doré. All wonderful, detailed plates: Adam and Eve, Flood, Babylon, life of Jesus, etc. Brief King James text with each plate. 241 plates. 241pp. 9 × 12. 23004-X Pa. $8.95

THE BOOK OF KELLS: Selected Plates in Full Color, edited by Blanche Cirker. 32 full-page plates from greatest manuscript-icon of early Middle Ages. Fantastic, mysterious. Publisher's Note. Captions. 32pp. 9¾ × 12¼. 24345-1 Pa. $4.50

THE PERFECT WAGNERITE, George Bernard Shaw. Brilliant criticism of the Ring Cycle, with provocative interpretation of politics, economic theories behind the Ring. 136pp. 5⅜ × 8½. (Available in U.S. only) 21707-8 Pa. $3.00

CATALOG OF DOVER BOOKS

THE RIME OF THE ANCIENT MARINER, Gustave Doré, S.T. Coleridge. Doré's finest work, 34 plates capture moods, subtleties of poem. Full text. 77pp. 9¼ × 12. 22305-1 Pa. $4.95

SONGS OF INNOCENCE, William Blake. The first and most popular of Blake's famous "Illuminated Books," in a facsimile edition reproducing all 31 brightly colored plates. Additional printed text of each poem. 64pp. 5¼ × 7. 22764-2 Pa. $3.00

AN INTRODUCTION TO INFORMATION THEORY, J.R. Pierce. Second (1980) edition of most impressive non-technical account available. Encoding, entropy, noisy channel, related areas, etc. 320pp. 5⅜ × 8½. 24061-4 Pa. $4.95

THE DIVINE PROPORTION: A STUDY IN MATHEMATICAL BEAUTY, H.E. Huntley. "Divine proportion" or "golden ratio" in poetry, Pascal's triangle, philosophy, psychology, music, mathematical figures, etc. Excellent bridge between science and art. 58 figures. 185pp. 5⅜ × 8½. 22254-3 Pa. $3.95

THE DOVER NEW YORK WALKING GUIDE: From the Battery to Wall Street, Mary J. Shapiro. Superb inexpensive guide to historic buildings and locales in lower Manhattan: Trinity Church, Bowling Green, more. Complete Text; maps. 36 illustrations. 48pp. 3⅞ × 9¼. 24225-0 Pa. $2.50

NEW YORK THEN AND NOW, Edward B. Watson, Edmund V. Gillon, Jr. 83 important Manhattan sites: on facing pages early photographs (1875-1925) and 1976 photos by Gillon. 172 illustrations. 171pp. 9¼ × 10. 23361-8 Pa. $7.95

HISTORIC COSTUME IN PICTURES, Braun & Schneider. Over 1450 costumed figures from dawn of civilization to end of 19th century. English captions. 125 plates. 256pp. 8⅜ × 11¼. 23150-X Pa. $7.50

VICTORIAN AND EDWARDIAN FASHION: A Photographic Survey, Alison Gernsheim. First fashion history completely illustrated by contemporary photographs. Full text plus 235 photos, 1840-1914, in which many celebrities appear. 240pp. 6½ × 9¼. 24205-6 Pa. $6.00

CHARTED CHRISTMAS DESIGNS FOR COUNTED CROSS-STITCH AND OTHER NEEDLECRAFTS, Lindberg Press. Charted designs for 45 beautiful needlecraft projects with many yuletide and wintertime motifs. 48pp. 8¼ × 11. 24356-7 Pa. $1.95

101 FOLK DESIGNS FOR COUNTED CROSS-STITCH AND OTHER NEEDLE-CRAFTS, Carter Houck. 101 authentic charted folk designs in a wide array of lovely representations with many suggestions for effective use. 48pp. 8¼ × 11. 24369-9 Pa. $2.25

FIVE ACRES AND INDEPENDENCE, Maurice G. Kains. Great back-to-the-land classic explains basics of self-sufficient farming. The one book to get. 95 illustrations. 397pp. 5⅜ × 8½. 20974-1 Pa. $4.95

A MODERN HERBAL, Margaret Grieve. Much the fullest, most exact, most useful compilation of herbal material. Gigantic alphabetical encyclopedia, from aconite to zedoary, gives botanical information, medical properties, folklore, economic uses, and much else. Indispensable to serious reader. 161 illustrations. 888pp. 6½ × 9¼. (Available in U.S. only) 22798-7, 22799-5 Pa., Two-vol. set $16.45

DECORATIVE NAPKIN FOLDING FOR BEGINNERS, Lillian Oppenheimer and Natalie Epstein. 22 different napkin folds in the shape of a heart, clown's hat, love knot, etc. 63 drawings. 48pp. 8¼ × 11. 23797-4 Pa. $1.95

DECORATIVE LABELS FOR HOME CANNING, PRESERVING, AND OTHER HOUSEHOLD AND GIFT USES, Theodore Menten. 128 gummed, perforated labels, beautifully printed in 2 colors. 12 versions. Adhere to metal, glass, wood, ceramics. 24pp. 8¼ × 11. 23219-0 Pa. $2.95

EARLY AMERICAN STENCILS ON WALLS AND FURNITURE, Janet Waring. Thorough coverage of 19th-century folk art: techniques, artifacts, surviving specimens. 166 illustrations, 7 in color. 147pp. of text. 7⅞ × 10¾. 21906-2 Pa. $9.95

AMERICAN ANTIQUE WEATHERVANES, A.B. & W.T. Westervelt. Extensively illustrated 1883 catalog exhibiting over 550 copper weathervanes and finials. Excellent primary source by one of the principal manufacturers. 104pp. 6⅛ × 9¼. 24396-6 Pa. $3.95

ART STUDENTS' ANATOMY, Edmond J. Farris. Long favorite in art schools. Basic elements, common positions, actions. Full text, 158 illustrations. 159pp. 5⅜ × 8½. 20744-7 Pa. $3.95

BRIDGMAN'S LIFE DRAWING, George B. Bridgman. More than 500 drawings and text teach you to abstract the body into its major masses. Also specific areas of anatomy. 192pp. 6½ × 9¼. (EA) 22710-3 Pa. $4.50

COMPLETE PRELUDES AND ETUDES FOR SOLO PIANO, Frederic Chopin. All 26 Preludes, all 27 Etudes by greatest composer of piano music. Authoritative Paderewski edition. 224pp. 9 × 12. (Available in U.S. only) 24052-5 Pa. $7.50

PIANO MUSIC 1888-1905, Claude Debussy. Deux Arabesques, Suite Bergamesque, Masques, 1st series of Images, etc. 9 others, in corrected editions. 175pp. 9⅜ × 12¼. (ECE) 22771-5 Pa. $5.95

TEDDY BEAR IRON-ON TRANSFER PATTERNS, Ted Menten. 80 iron-on transfer patterns of male and female Teddys in a wide variety of activities, poses, sizes. 48pp. 8¼ × 11. 24596-9 Pa. $2.25

A PICTURE HISTORY OF THE BROOKLYN BRIDGE, M.J. Shapiro. Profusely illustrated account of greatest engineering achievement of 19th century. 167 rare photos & engravings recall construction, human drama. Extensive, detailed text. 122pp. 8¼ × 11. 24403-2 Pa. $7.95

NEW YORK IN THE THIRTIES, Berenice Abbott. Noted photographer's fascinating study shows new buildings that have become famous and old sights that have disappeared forever. 97 photographs. 97pp. 11⅜ × 10. 22967-X Pa. $6.50

MATHEMATICAL TABLES AND FORMULAS, Robert D. Carmichael and Edwin R. Smith. Logarithms, sines, tangents, trig functions, powers, roots, reciprocals, exponential and hyperbolic functions, formulas and theorems. 269pp. 5⅜ × 8½. 60111-0 Pa. $3.75

HANDBOOK OF MATHEMATICAL FUNCTIONS WITH FORMULAS, GRAPHS, AND MATHEMATICAL TABLES, edited by Milton Abramowitz and Irene A. Stegun. Vast compendium: 29 sets of tables, some to as high as 20 places. 1,046pp. 8 × 10½. 61272-4 Pa. $19.95

REASON IN ART, George Santayana. Renowned philosopher's provocative, seminal treatment of basis of art in instinct and experience. Volume Four of *The Life of Reason*. 230pp. 5⅜ × 8.   24358-3 Pa. $4.50

LANGUAGE, TRUTH AND LOGIC, Alfred J. Ayer. Famous, clear introduction to Vienna, Cambridge schools of Logical Positivism. Role of philosophy, elimination of metaphysics, nature of analysis, etc. 160pp. 5⅜ × 8½. (USCO)
20010-8 Pa. $2.75

BASIC ELECTRONICS, U.S. Bureau of Naval Personnel. Electron tubes, circuits, antennas, AM, FM, and CW transmission and receiving, etc. 560 illustrations. 567pp. 6½ × 9¼.   21076-6 Pa. $8.95

THE ART DECO STYLE, edited by Theodore Menten. Furniture, jewelry, metalwork, ceramics, fabrics, lighting fixtures, interior decors, exteriors, graphics from pure French sources. Over 400 photographs. 183pp. 8⅜ × 11¼.
22824-X Pa. $6.95

THE FOUR BOOKS OF ARCHITECTURE, Andrea Palladio. 16th-century classic covers classical architectural remains, Renaissance revivals, classical orders, etc. 1738 Ware English edition. 216 plates. 110pp. of text. 9½ × 12¾.
21308-0 Pa. $11.50

THE WIT AND HUMOR OF OSCAR WILDE, edited by Alvin Redman. More than 1000 ripostes, paradoxes, wisecracks: Work is the curse of the drinking classes, I can resist everything except temptations, etc. 258pp. 5⅜ × 8½. (USCO)
20602-5 Pa. $3.50

THE DEVIL'S DICTIONARY, Ambrose Bierce. Barbed, bitter, brilliant witticisms in the form of a dictionary. Best, most ferocious satire America has produced. 145pp. 5⅜ × 8½.   20487-1 Pa. $2.50

ERTÉ'S FASHION DESIGNS, Erté. 210 black-and-white inventions from *Harper's Bazar*, 1918-32, plus 8pp. full-color covers. Captions. 88pp. 9 × 12.
24203-X Pa. $6.50

ERTÉ GRAPHICS, Erté. Collection of striking color graphics: *Seasons, Alphabet, Numerals, Aces* and *Precious Stones*. 50 plates, including 4 on covers. 48pp. 9⅜ × 12¼.   23580-7 Pa. $6.95

PAPER FOLDING FOR BEGINNERS, William D. Murray and Francis J. Rigney. Clearest book for making origami sail boats, roosters, frogs that move legs, etc. 40 projects. More than 275 illustrations. 94pp. 5⅜ × 8½.   20713-7 Pa. $2.25

ORIGAMI FOR THE ENTHUSIAST, John Montroll. Fish, ostrich, peacock, squirrel, rhinoceros, Pegasus, 19 other intricate subjects. Instructions. Diagrams. 128pp. 9 × 12.   23799-0 Pa. $4.95

CROCHETING NOVELTY POT HOLDERS, edited by Linda Macho. 64 useful, whimsical pot holders feature kitchen themes, animals, flowers, other novelties. Surprisingly easy to crochet. Complete instructions. 48pp. 8¼ × 11.
24296-X Pa. $1.95

CROCHETING DOILIES, edited by Rita Weiss. Irish Crochet, Jewel, Star Wheel, Vanity Fair and more. Also luncheon and console sets, runners and centerpieces. 51 illustrations. 48pp. 8¼ × 11.   23424-X Pa. $2.00

YUCATAN BEFORE AND AFTER THE CONQUEST, Diego de Landa. Only significant account of Yucatan written in the early post-Conquest era. Translated by William Gates. Over 120 illustrations. 162pp. 5⅜ × 8½.   23622-6 Pa. $3.50

ORNATE PICTORIAL CALLIGRAPHY, E.A. Lupfer. Complete instructions, over 150 examples help you create magnificent "flourishes" from which beautiful animals and objects gracefully emerge. 8⅛ × 11.   21957-7 Pa. $2.95

DOLLY DINGLE PAPER DOLLS, Grace Drayton. Cute chubby children by same artist who did Campbell Kids. Rare plates from 1910s. 30 paper dolls and over 100 outfits reproduced in full color. 32pp. 9¼ × 12¼.   23711-7 Pa. $3.50

CURIOUS GEORGE PAPER DOLLS IN FULL COLOR, H. A. Rey, Kathy Allert. Naughty little monkey-hero of children's books in two doll figures, plus 48 full-color costumes: pirate, Indian chief, fireman, more. 32pp. 9¼ × 12¼.
          24386-9 Pa. $3.50

GERMAN: HOW TO SPEAK AND WRITE IT, Joseph Rosenberg. Like *French, How to Speak and Write It.* Very rich modern course, with a wealth of pictorial material. 330 illustrations. 384pp. 5⅜ × 8½. (USUKO)   20271-2 Pa. $4.75

CATS AND KITTENS: 24 Ready-to-Mail Color Photo Postcards, D. Holby. Handsome collection; feline in a variety of adorable poses. Identifications. 12pp. on postcard stock. 8¼ × 11.   24469-5 Pa. $2.95

MARILYN MONROE PAPER DOLLS, Tom Tierney. 31 full-color designs on heavy stock, from *The Asphalt Jungle,Gentlemen Prefer Blondes,* 22 others.1 doll. 16 plates. 32pp. 9⅜ × 12¼.   23769-9 Pa. $3.50

FUNDAMENTALS OF LAYOUT, F.H. Wills. All phases of layout design discussed and illustrated in 121 illustrations. Indispensable as student's text or handbook for professional. 124pp. 8⅛.× 11.   21279-3 Pa. $4.50

FANTASTIC SUPER STICKERS, Ed Sibbett, Jr. 75 colorful pressure-sensitive stickers. Peel off and place for a touch of pizzazz: clowns, penguins, teddy bears, etc. Full color. 16pp. 8¼ × 11.   24471-7 Pa. $2.95

LABELS FOR ALL OCCASIONS, Ed Sibbett, Jr. 6 labels each of 16 different designs—baroque, art nouveau, art deco, Pennsylvania Dutch, etc.—in full color. 24pp. 8¼ × 11.   23688-9 Pa. $2.95

HOW TO CALCULATE QUICKLY: RAPID METHODS IN BASIC MATHE-MATICS, Henry Sticker. Addition, subtraction, multiplication, division, checks, etc. More than 8000 problems, solutions. 185pp. 5 × 7¼.   20295-X Pa. $2.95

THE CAT COLORING BOOK, Karen Baldauski. Handsome, realistic renderings of 40 splendid felines, from American shorthair to exotic types. 44 plates. Captions. 48pp. 8¼ × 11.   24011-8 Pa. $2.25

THE TALE OF PETER RABBIT, Beatrix Potter. The inimitable Peter's terrifying adventure in Mr. McGregor's garden, with all 27 wonderful, full-color Potter illustrations. 55pp. 4¼ × 5½. (Available in U.S. only)   22827-4 Pa. $1.60

BASIC ELECTRICITY, U.S. Bureau of Naval Personnel. Batteries, circuits, conductors, AC and DC, inductance and capacitance, generators, motors, trans-formers, amplifiers, etc. 349 illustrations. 448pp. 6½ × 9¼.   20973-3 Pa. $7.95

SOURCE BOOK OF MEDICAL HISTORY, edited by Logan Clendening, M.D. Original accounts ranging from Ancient Egypt and Greece to discovery of X-rays: Galen, Pasteur, Lavoisier, Harvey, Parkinson, others. 685pp. 5⅜ × 8½.
20621-1 Pa. $10.95

THE ROSE AND THE KEY, J.S. Lefanu. Superb mystery novel from Irish master. Dark doings among an ancient and aristocratic English family. Well-drawn characters; capital suspense. Introduction by N. Donaldson. 448pp. 5⅜ × 8½.
24377-X Pa. $6.95

SOUTH WIND, Norman Douglas. Witty, elegant novel of ideas set on languorous Meditterranean island of Nepenthe. Elegant prose, glittering epigrams, mordant satire. 1917 masterpiece. 416pp. 5⅜ × 8½. (Available in U.S. only)
24361-3 Pa. $5.95

RUSSELL'S CIVIL WAR PHOTOGRAPHS, Capt. A.J. Russell. 116 rare Civil War Photos: Bull Run, Virginia campaigns, bridges, railroads, Richmond, Lincoln's funeral car. Many never seen before. Captions. 128pp. 9⅜ × 12¼.
24283-8 Pa. $6.95

PHOTOGRAPHS BY MAN RAY: 105 Works, 1920-1934. Nudes, still lifes, landscapes, women's faces, celebrity portraits (Dali, Matisse, Picasso, others), rayographs. Reprinted from rare gravure edition. 128pp. 9⅜ × 12¼. (Available in U.S. only) 23842-3 Pa. $6.95

STAR NAMES: THEIR LORE AND MEANING, Richard H. Allen. Star names, the zodiac, constellations: folklore and literature associated with heavens. The basic book of its field, fascinating reading. 563pp. 5⅜ × 8½. 21079-0 Pa. $7.95

BURNHAM'S CELESTIAL HANDBOOK, Robert Burnham, Jr. Thorough guide to the stars beyond our solar system. Exhaustive treatment. Alphabetical by constellation: Andromeda to Cetus in Vol. 1; Chamaeleon to Orion in Vol. 2; and Pavo to Vulpecula in Vol. 3. Hundreds of illustrations. Index in Vol. 3. 2000pp. 6⅛ × 9¼. 23567-X, 23568-8, 23673-0 Pa. Three-vol. set $36.85

THE ART NOUVEAU STYLE BOOK OF ALPHONSE MUCHA, Alphonse Mucha. All 72 plates from *Documents Decoratifs* in original color. Stunning, essential work of Art Nouveau. 80pp. 9⅜ × 12¼. 24044-4 Pa. $7.95

DESIGNS BY ERTE; FASHION DRAWINGS AND ILLUSTRATIONS FROM "HARPER'S BAZAR," Erte. 310 fabulous line drawings and 14 *Harper's Bazar* covers, 8 in full color. Erte's exotic temptresses with tassels, fur muffs, long trains, coifs, more. 129pp. 9⅜ × 12¼. 23397-9 Pa. $6.95

HISTORY OF STRENGTH OF MATERIALS, Stephen P. Timoshenko. Excellent historical survey of the strength of materials with many references to the theories of elasticity and structure. 245 figures. 452pp. 5⅜ × 8½. 61187-6 Pa. $8.95

Prices subject to change without notice.

Available at your book dealer or write for free catalog to Dept. GI, Dover Publications, Inc., 31 East 2nd St. Mineola, N.Y. 11501. Dover publishes more than 175 books each year on science, elementary and advanced mathematics, biology, music, art, literary history, social sciences and other areas.